A
FURTHER
EDUCATION

Evelyn Culber

This book is a work of fiction.
In real life, make sure you practise safe sex.

First published in 1996 by
Nexus
332 Ladbroke Grove
London W10 5AH

Copyright © Evelyn Culber 1996

Typeset by TW Typesetting, Plymouth, Devon

Printed and bound by
BPC Paperbacks Ltd, Aylesbury, Bucks

ISBN 0 352 33096 1

The right of Evelyn Culber to be identified as the Author of this Work has been asserted by her in accordance with the Copyright Designs and Patents Act 1988.

All characters in this publication are fictitious and any resemblance to real persons, living or dead, is purely coincidental.

This book is sold subject to the condition that it shall not, by way of trade or otherwise, be lent, resold, hired out or otherwise circulated without the publisher's prior written consent in any form of binding or cover other than that in which it is published and without a similar condition including this condition being imposed on the subsequent purchaser.

One

I stood at the gate waving at the back of Phillip's carriage as, in a cloud of dust, it bore him away on the start of his latest European tour. When it had disappeared from sight, I shut the gate and walked slowly back to our dear little farmhouse, pausing by the yard with thoughts and emotions fluttering through my tired mind like autumn leaves whisked into flight by a gust of wind.

The house was more than just a shelter to me, even though it had already been in Phillip's possession when we married, so I had not been involved in the purchase and had made few alterations to its furnishing and decoration. We were blissfully happy within its thick walls. The bricks had been faded by time and weather to a glorious russet shade and the uneven, moss-covered tiles of the roof added further to its character, while also giving comforting security. Despite a singularly wet winter, not a drop of rain had penetrated their defences.

I gazed at the solid oak front door. My glance lingered on the freshly painted windows, imagining the familiar rooms behind them. The sun room; the main drawing room, with the massive fireplace in front of which only last evening Phillip had bared my quivering bottom, placed me gently across his thighs and spanked me scarlet, before undressing and loving me. My cunny wept a little at the memory.

Our bedroom. He had poked me again before we fell into a troubled sleep. I loved that room. The largest by far of the five bedrooms, it overlooked the lovely, rolling

South Downs in the distance. My other favourite rooms were on the far side of the house. Most secret, and perhaps with the most exciting memories, was my special punishment chamber. I recalled the many sessions with dear little Bertha, in which I had tried to give her the rudiments of an education. Although she had proved to be an adept and willing pupil, who could now read and write with some fluency, I had always managed to invent a reason to bare her chubby little bottom and redden it with some suitable implement. It seemed an age since our last lesson and it occurred to me that we would both derive considerable benefit from a continuation of her scholastic endeavours!

I imagined her with my other servant, Mavis, busily restoring the house to its normal order after the disruptions caused by my beloved husband's chaotic preparations for his long journey. How were they feeling about the absence of the master of the household? The last time he had absented himself for such a period, the three of us had grown very close, with Mavis's natural interest in the female body flowering under my patient tutelage – and, of course, with the example of Bertha's happy embrace of sensual pleasures to inspire her further. I wondered if they were anticipating a renewal of those activities. I was reasonably confident that naughty Bertha could hardly wait to expose her charms and was almost equally impatient to feast her eyes and hands on ours.

Realising that I needed peace and solitude to collect my thoughts, I decided to leave them to their labours and drift quietly round my garden. I ambled past the front of the house towards what had become our favourite hide-away. It was sheltered by a large oak tree, well hidden from all but the most determined Peeping Tom. Many a summer day last year had been enlivened by an *alfresco* picnic, with the three of us donning Eve's costume and revelling in the sense of complete freedom.

It was the perfect spot for deliberation and I sank gratefully down on the grass, pulled my bonnet down over my face and sprawled inelegantly on my back, the early spring sun just sufficient to warm the air comfortably without the risk of burning my skin.

If Phillip was to spend more time away, I needed to reach a decision on the direction my life should take. I concentrated my thoughts on myself, hoping that if I could see myself more clearly, I could more easily decide how to satisfy my desires.

As I had posed – both nude and clothed – on numerous occasions, I had a clearer image of my physical attractions than most. My husband was a most talented artist and had communicated his love for me on to his canvases. He had also taken great pains to discuss the finished paintings with me, lucidly pointing out how he had successfully captured the essence of my features. Apart from knowledge gained in that manner, I derived no little pleasure from arranging looking glasses and studying my body from every angle. I therefore knew that I was of medium height, with a fine bosom, a slender waist, shapely limbs and hair the colour of ripening corn. Add full lips, white, even teeth, a broad smile and bright blue eyes, together with flawless skin – which I knew both from appreciative comments from my lovers and my own caresses to be as smooth as satin to the touch – and the benefits which a kindly nature had bestowed upon me were evident.

I was fully aware that my bottom was especially attractive. I described in the first volume of my memories how a stroke of fortune had brought me into the custody of my benefactors, whom I call my Aunt Grace and Uncle George, her husband. They had run a special house in Richmond, just outside London, where favoured guests were treated to elaborate entertainments, all of which featured spanking and whipping. From the outset, Aunt Grace had adored the form and texture of my posterior and had guessed from my reaction to her first inspection of it that I had a special sensitivity in this part of my burgeoning anatomy. She had been quite correct, and in no time I was willingly proffering it to the attentions of all who desired it.

By the time Phillip had taken me to be his wife, I had fulfilled all Aunt Grace's hopes and become a passionate devotee of most activities involving the human bottom. I learned first to accept chastisement without demur, then to derive sensual pleasure from the unique pain of a sore posterior. I soon welcomed any intimate contact with men or women and my taste for administering a spanking or a whipping had developed in tune with my desires for being on the receiving end.

With Phillip I learned all the pleasures of loving a man. My virgin cunny welcomed his manhood with even more delight than my bottom-hole had opened up to Uncle George's initial intrusion, and soon his penetration of either orifice afforded me intense pleasure. I grew to enjoy being mistress of his household and his work as an artist allowed ample scope for other unusual activities. He used my naked body as a model whenever one of his patrons required a work which featured the female nude. His cousin, the lovely Arabella, happily shed her clothing to join me, and later – when Phillip had been commissioned by a French publisher to produce a series of drawings on corporal punishment – Bertha and Mavis often acted as models and even allowed us to redden their bare bottoms for greater realism!

With two female derrières to spank and my own passive desires catered for with admirable enthusiasm by Phillip, my life as a married woman left little to be desired!

What exercised my mind that morning was how to achieve similar degrees of satisfaction in his absence. I could have let my sensuality lie fallow for six months and devoted myself to my house, garden and other feminine pursuits, such as needlework and painting, with the occasional social diversion. On the other hand, although Phillip's aristocratic lineage gave him an entrée into local society, my yeoman background was insufficient for me to be invited to much on my own account, and as a grass widow, I would often be more of an embarrassment than an asset.

Besides that consideration, our Bohemian way of life had rather isolated us, so my social activities would have been limited to taking tea with ladies more interested in Phillip's connections than my company.

The exception was my friend, Lady Elizabeth A******. She and I had met in the peculiar circumstances I related in the second part of my memories. As she had admitted to me later, it was my beauty which had moved her to arrange for me to be kidnapped in the first place. She had planned simply to incarcerate me for a night, whip me and send me home, but had then been captivated by my bottom and by the way I had responded to the several imaginative beatings she had administered. Later, I had become a member of The Society, a small group of eight women all sharing a great enthusiasm for the rod, and our occasional meetings had lit up my life during Phillip's last tour.

As I lay on the cool grass, memories of the various meetings flitted through my mind: the eight of us in our very best gowns and jewellery, sipping champagne and talking animatedly as we casually fondled the naked servants who attended to our smallest needs; the postprandial activities, all revolving round the basic theme of naked bottoms and punishment; the usual climax, with my bare bottom carefully positioned to delight both my punisher and the avid spectators; my exposed flesh crawling in anticipation of the biting smart which would render me near senseless with ecstasy. If my bottom had been sore for some time afterwards, the song in my heart had lasted far longer than the ache in my flesh.

Then I heard the call of the first cuckoo of spring and it was as though it was sending me a sign: 'This is the season of renaissance. All is new and fresh. Spread your wings.'

I sat up and the blood coursed through my veins, sending little tingles to a number of exciting places. Then I cast all lascivious thoughts from my mind. The main reason for my troubled mind needed my full attention.

Three weeks before, Aunt Grace had passed away after a short illness. That alone was enough to disturb me greatly but, even more thought-provoking, she had left me her house and a small fortune. I was now a woman of independent means, because even though Phillip as my husband had a natural right to my inheritance, Aunt Grace's will had specifically requested that all should be in my name. Phillip, to his eternal credit, had simply congratulated me on my good fortune (while at the same time being in complete sympathy with my sense of loss) and had said that he was quite rich enough for his own good anyway. Apart from which, his various commissions as an artist were proving increasingly rewarding and he, in addition, made a great deal of money from the sales of his spanking drawings.

The overriding problem was what I should do with her house. At that moment, Cook and the maids were still in residence and were laying on the occasional Entertainment, so there were no immediate concerns. I did not, however, see myself as a replacement for Aunt Grace. Neither could I face the prospect of selling and letting that happy establishment fall into the hands of some drearily respectable merchant. Still, knowing the laborious way in which lawyers proceed with their complex rituals, I had time for inspiration to strike! In the meantime, I could fill my lungs with fresh Sussex air and doze in peace, secure in the knowledge that my servants would respect my privacy.

* * *

A week later, I had returned to the best of spirits and a day of typical April showers had done nothing to depress me. In fact, I had taken advantage of the weather to take Bertha up to my 'schoolroom' and further her education. Whether she was being deliberately obtuse, or whether the long interval had caused most of what I had taught her to slip from her mind, I neither knew nor cared. The result was that no more than five minutes had elapsed before I was sighing deeply.

'Bertha, that is *not* how you spell "apple", as you know,' I announced with some severity. 'Now try again, and this time get it right.'

A little smile curled her lips as she frowned at her slate, then she picked up her chalk. Her trembling hand slowly and untidily turned thoughts into letters. APEL. She cocked her head to one side and studied the result of her labours with apparent satisfaction.

'There, ma'am. Apple,' she said softly, then turned to face me. I could read the longings on her pretty little face as clearly as if she had spoken them out loud.

And there was no denying that her desire for a sound spanking was no less intense than mine to administer one. It seemed an age since I had last seen her delectable bottom properly turned up, but some instinct stayed my hand. I was beginning to enjoy the sensation of being in control. Of being a real teacher, rather than play-acting.

'Come on, Bertha, you know better than that,' I chided.

She looked up at me. Then the first glimmer of understanding brought a little smile to her pretty face and she painstakingly corrected her error. Gently I led her through an increasingly demanding set of exercises and with furrowed brow she bent to her slate, her concentration obvious. At last, I knew that the time was right, and with warmth in my voice, I reminded her of all her mistakes, ensuring that she knew where she had erred.

'We shall be revising these subjects tomorrow, Bertha,' I told her. 'I do not want you to make the same mistakes again.'

'No, ma'am, I understand,' she replied seriously. Then she sat back, frowning. 'Please, ma'am, could you remind me again of what a verb is? It ain't quite clear in my mind.'

'Yes, of course, Bertha. Oh, and "is not", not "ain't". Now, every sentence must contain . . .' I made quite sure that she understood, then sat back and looked at her. She returned my stare and a charming blush suffused her face. Her plump little bosoms heaved under her blouse as her breathing grew suddenly unsteady. I continued. 'I am quite impressed with your attitude to learning, Bertha, but only quite. I shall enjoy furthering your education and am determined that we shall both work as hard and as long as possible to that end. However, as you well know, I am a hard task mistress and shall not hesitate to punish you in the traditional and appropriate manner whenever I deem it necessary. You understand me?'

'Yes, ma'am,' she replied quietly. 'You mean that you will smack my bare bottom when I need it.'

I reached across and clasped her trembling little hand in mine. 'That is right, Bertha. But I shall not smack it when you do not need it. Not in this room, in any case.'

It took several moments before the import of my statement was clear to her; namely, that what had in the past been an instructive excuse for turning up her bottom was now an activity to be taken seriously. At the same time, I had clearly intimated that the sensual spankings that we both loved so dearly were not excluded from her life. Only from the schoolroom.

Her expression lightened. 'I see, ma'am,' she said thoughtfully. 'Are you going to spank me now, ma'am?'

'No Bertha,' I replied. 'You were not aware of my new intentions when we started this lesson, so to punish you would not be just. I am quite sure that I shall be able to find ample reasons for spanking you before the next lesson. That is, of course, if I wish to! Now off you trot and help Mavis with the luncheon. I am famished.'

I had long ago decided that it was ridiculous to insist on formality when there were only the three of us in the house, so we reverted to sharing the kitchen table for a simple but satisfying repast. There was a slightly awkward silence at first, but not for long. Then Mavis, stuttering nervously, broke it.

'Madam, Bertha has been telling me that you and her are going to be studying hard, and –' She stopped, blushing.

'Go on, Mavis,' I encouraged.

'Well, madam, my learning is not good. I can read and write a bit, but I find lots of things hard. Adding up the grocer's accounts; making out shopping lists. Ordinary things.'

'I see.' I paused. 'You would like to join the class?'

'Yes, madam,' she replied eagerly.

'I would be delighted to help you, my dear. But I should make it clear to you, as I have to Bertha, that I shall be very strict. Time is precious and I will not tolerate any slackness whatsoever. If you do not work hard at your lessons, I shall punish you quite severely. Is that clear?'

'Yes, madam.'

'Good.'

And we gradually settled into the easy companionship which had so characterised the atmosphere during Phillip's last absence, ending the meal with a slice of Mavis's best fruit cake before happily devoting ourselves to our various tasks.

Two days later, a rainy day provided ideal circumstances for the first proper lesson, and I told Bertha and Mavis to be waiting for me in the schoolroom at eleven o'clock. As the hall clock struck the hour, I swept up the stairs and into the small, intimate room, pleased to see that they had arranged the furniture so that they both had improvised desks on which they could work efficiently, facing the tall chair obviously designated for my use. I was even more pleased that they both stood respectfully to greet me. They were most suitably dressed in neat white blouses and loose working skirts and, delighted with this excellent start, I began.

It proved to be an intensely enjoyable hour. I found the act of passing on my knowledge most satisfying and felt a proper sense of achievement when comprehension dawned. I cajoled rather than reprimanded, I encouraged whenever possible, and I was generally the personification of patience with them. The atmosphere soon became typical of a proper schoolroom, except that both pupils were genuinely keen to learn and concentrated wonderfully. I had to devote most of my attention to Mavis for, as she had confessed, she had little learning, whereas Bertha had been to the village school and had already benefited from my previous efforts. It was, therefore, inevitable that Mavis should be the first to displease me.

'Mavis, that was very careless of you. We have been over that several times and you certainly should have known better. I think that your concentration is slipping and a sharp little spanking is called for. Stand up and come here.'

'Yes, madam. On my bare bottom?'

'Yes please. Raise your skirts at the back and lower your drawers.'

She obeyed swiftly before shuffling awkwardly round to my right side, and as she settled over my lap, I mused on her question. Neither she nor Bertha had ever been spanked – by me anyway – on anything other than their bare bottoms. I could only assume that she had asked because she understood that the purpose of her punishment was to increase the effectiveness of the lesson, not for pleasure.

So I spanked her in the appropriate manner. All the thrilling elements of spanking a plump and naked bottom were in the background of my awareness as my stiffened palm flew up and down. I gave her a round dozen on each buttock, then repeated the question which had flummoxed her and delivered a further dozen when she again failed to answer correctly. As I had long suspected, a sore posterior is an ideal aid to mental effort and she finally remembered the correct response, whereupon I immediately told her to rise, pull up her drawers and resume her seat.

Ten minutes later, Bertha got similar treatment, except that she was further advanced than her friend and so received the back of a wooden hairbrush on her bare bottom, making it bounce and wobble like a blancmange, bringing tears to her eyes.

At the very end of the appointed hour, Mavis annoyed me once again, though only slightly, and I gave her another spanking, but this time over the seat of her drawers, which were not of the traditional split kind and so covered her entirely.

All in all, it had been a most stimulating morning and, to the credit of them both, we ate our luncheon in the happiest of moods with conversation roaming freely over subjects of mutual interest. It is fair to say that, if neither could be described as an educated person, both were naturally intelligent and had a keen if salacious sense of humour. I enjoyed their company as much as I had ever done and the cold cuts of beef were even more palatable than usual!

They were also innately sensual and, with the lack of inhibition which is part and parcel of people born and raised in the country, we could be pleasingly open on subjects which would make members of traditional society swoon in shock! Bertha was even less inhibited than her senior colleague and so I was not surprised when she brought the conversation round to the spankings they had just received.

'That last spanking you gave Mavis, ma'am – why didn't you do it on the bare? It wasn't nearly as much fun watching her get it on those drawers.'

Smiling shyly, Mavis then spoke. 'Actually, madam, it didn't feel quite right somehow. I know that it was only a little smacking because I had only been a bit careless, but even so, I think it would be better if I always get it with my drawers down. As long as Bertha gets treated the same, that is,' she added hastily.

'Of course I should be!' she interjected before I had even had time to collect my thoughts. 'Ma'am, I know that when you spank us for fun it's always on the bare and that when we're being taught it isn't for fun. You wallop us to make us learn better and that's the way it should be. But I know that when I've been stupid, I need to be smacked properly. On the bare skin, so I can really feel it. Even if it is only a little punishment like Mavis had. And it must be nicer for you to see and feel our bottoms all bare – and, as I said, it makes watching much more fun.'

Perhaps I should have felt some irritation at having my methods criticised, but I did not. I was, however, glad that they had both absorbed the different nature of the schoolroom punishments so readily, and as I stared into the distance, collecting my thoughts, I suddenly felt that old, insistent and delightful tingle in my love-nest. Not the same tingle produced when Phillip was advancing with *that* look in his eyes – that one was deeper, starting in the convoluted depths of my cunny, anticipating the plunging fulfilment of his mighty pego. This one was centred on the button, and immediately all my senses craved intimacy with others of my own sex. I did not even try to understand the reasons for this sudden change of mood.

'I am delighted that you both understand the nature of the spankings I have just awarded you and this gives me great confidence in the future of your education, my dears.' I paused for a moment. 'I shall always fit the punishment to the crime and so may not always take your drawers down in the schoolroom. I shall, however, inevitably do so outside it. As I am tempted to demonstrate this very minute.'

They both grinned broadly and clapped their hands in their enthusiasm.

'Can I be first?' cried Bertha.

I slid my chair away from the table, the legs rasping against the stone floor. 'Yes, you may, Bertha. I am quite sure that you have been exceedingly naughty in a great many ways without me knowing, so come on, lay yourself across my knee and I shall redden your impudent little bottom. Bare, of course!'

With a squeal of pleasure, the dear girl prostrated herself, cocking her hips well up so that I had no difficulty in pulling up her skirt and petticoat. Then my trembling hands reached for the tapes at the waistband of her drawers, undid the neat bow, and eased them over the swelling mounds until they rested in limp disorder by her dimpled knees. Her chemise was now the only garment preserving her modesty. It was one that she would normally have kept for Sunday best because it was less coarse than usual and I could clearly see the thin dark line bisecting her derrière. I quickly took a firm grip of the hem and began the delightful process of laying her bare.

I could not even guess how many spankings I have administered in what has been a long and rewarding life. Even all those years ago – it was 1893, when I was just 22 years of age – I was not without experience in this exciting art. None the less – perhaps because it had been some time since I had been able to indulge myself, or maybe the businesslike approach I had adopted earlier had whetted my appetite more than I had realised – the thrill of baring Bertha's bottom on that occasion is still etched clearly on my mind.

I inched the hem of her chemise up her thighs, pausing from time to time to stroke the area of naked skin most recently uncovered, beginning with the backs of her knees. When, eventually, the lowest portion of her bottom was smiling up at me, I tucked the loose folds securely underneath her, freeing both hands to roam up and down her thighs, my eyes greedily following their movements as they stroked and squeezed the satiny skin and firmly yielding flesh. I then moved my gaze up to that small, uncovered area of her bottom, thrilled by the sight of the folds at the tops of her thighs and the inch or so of cleft leading up from the diamond-shaped gap at the conjunction of her legs and buttocks.

My extended forefinger ran softly along the fold at the base of her left cheek, then prodded the fleshy bulge immediately above before slipping into the warmth at the very end of her cleft, stopping only when it encountered the first hint of crisp hair. She moaned softly and clenched her thighs and buttocks, trapping my finger. I pulled it free and trickled it across the other fold, travelling back and forth from one to the other, smiling inwardly at the little sighs of pleasure coming from my left.

As I moved my attentions to the base of the deep cleft separating her fat little buttocks, the glow of contentment within me intensified. The pangs caused by bereavement and the absence of my husband faded away as I gazed down.

Bertha was an exceptionally pretty girl, with a posterior especially favoured by a generous Mother Nature. Even more alluring was the fact that she derived enormous pleasure from any attention to it; quite possibly even more than I. We were of that rare and fortunate minority for whom a sore bottom is usually a source of sensual pleasure and, if the circumstances are right, can even achieve a climax at the conclusion of a good whipping. So, as I stared hungrily at her near-naked charms, on the verge of exposing them entirely, my dormant lusts for feminine flesh burst into renewed life. Abandoning the sensuously slow approach, I suddenly whisked the rumpled chemise right up. Bertha's trembling bare bottom swam before my fevered gaze. I had, of course, just seen it in the schoolroom, but had not studied it in the way such a lovely sight deserves to be studied.

Of all the girls' bottoms I have seen over the years, Bertha's was always among my favourites. As round and firm as an apple, with the clear, pink-shaded skin so typical of those with red hair, and with an especially tight cleft. It was a delight to the most discerning eye and palm. Her skin was flawless and satiny; her cheeks fleshy enough to quiver and wobble most satisfactorily, yet with no trace of flabbiness to her. Best of all, the results of a well-delivered spank were immediately apparent in the flush which suffused the point of impact almost instantaneously, so that even a moderate punishment left her dramatically red.

It is, therefore, not surprising that I studied this very personal expanse of naked femininity with burgeoning desire. I quite deliberately kept the dear girl in further suspense by stroking, pinching, patting and paddling her buttocks before beginning the chastisement we were both longing for. I announced my intentions by rolling up my sleeves, resting my forearm on her naked loins and taking a firm grip on her right hipbone, pressing down to lift her middle portions a fraction. One further manual examination seemed both necessary and desirable, then I carefully placed my right hand on the very centre of her bottom, with my palm on the left cheek and my fingers on the right. There is stayed for several seconds while I took a deep breath and enjoyed the feel of my hand pressing into her yielding flesh. I raised my arm, waited until the faint mark left on her bottom had faded, then brought it flashing down to sink into the exact part I had aimed for.

The delicious softness of both skin and flesh imprinted themselves in my palm, even to the extent that I could feel the division between her buttocks. I savoured the almost liquid quiver of her flesh as my hand flattened out the rich curves, the ringing sound of the impact, and the pink patch flaring into view as I let my arm fall away to rest on her thigh.

Apart from a little jerk as the sting clawed into her, Bertha neither moved nor uttered a sound for several seconds. Then I just heard another little groan and noticed the subtlest of changes in the shape of her derrière as the tenseness of expectancy left her and she yielded to her fate, lifting her bottom to meet the next spank.

In the full and certain knowledge that she was in the throes of a warm sensual glow – apart from the fact that I knew her well, the first scents of her arousal had wafted into my nostrils – I devoted my full attention to the spanking.

I find a good rhythm important. Not that every smack has to be administered at equal intervals. My favourite approach is to cover the entire surface of the bottom with sharp little slaps delivered quite rapidly, then to pause for a moment or two before driving in six or so (rather depending on the size of the bottom in question) really snappy spanks with at least five seconds between each. Whether one is intent on pleasure or punishment, the variety makes it far more difficult for the owner of the bottom to let her (or his, for that matter) mind drift away. From my own experiences, I know full well that a prolonged assault in the same tempo allows you to go limp and let the waves of pain gradually spread through you, until you are almost in a trance. When, however, you are not quite certain of the nature and weight of the next series of spanks, you concentrate far more.

There was no sense of urgency, or even haste, in that spanking. I knew full well that Bertha was as sensually excited as I was, and that Mavis was quite content to watch her friend and colleague being spanked for as long as suited us both. She had a countrywoman's natural patience on the one hand and on the other an abiding interest in witnessing a pretty girl having her bare bottom soundly walloped. Therefore, once I had suffused the whole available area with a glowingly bright pink, I felt no compunction at all in pausing to enjoy the variety of sensations Bertha was offering me, from the warm softness of her skin as I gently stroked her, to the sight of her tiny little bottom-hole peeping out at me when I eased her cheeks apart to investigate this most private of areas.

Her soft sighs were music in my ears. Then, when I resumed the energetic fustigation, the ringing sound of the spanks provided a different music – Wagner as opposed to Chopin perhaps.

I noticed a portion of almost white skin at the very base of her posterior and made her spread her legs wide and cock her hips up in the air to make it more accessible to my fingertips. Then I spent several happy minutes reddening it.

At last, with an aching arm and a throbbing palm, I sat back, panting, but by no means weary. The dear girl slumped heavily over my lap and, as her head drooped towards the floor, her scarlet rump loomed up even nearer my face, the tight cleft opening somewhat to expose a line of whiteness separating the twin mounds of red. I leant forward and saluted her with my lips, brushing them softly over every little inch of intimate flesh within reach. Her skin felt hot and deliciously smooth and I kissed and licked to my heart's content, while my hands stroked the cool flesh of her back and thighs. My lips could feel her tremors and the scents of her excitement filled my lungs. Turning my head to the side, I rubbed my cheek against her, marvelling at the different feel of her bottom on that part of me. For some reason, one can touch the same object with different parts of one's body and receive varied impressions.

By this time my cunny was tingling steadily, and with my right arm no longer troubling me, Mavis's splendid haunches beckoned. I prised Bertha's cheeks apart and gazed at the wrinkled pinkness of the displayed orifice. So neat and pretty. I sensed that she was holding her breath in tense expectation of that most thrilling of caresses and, smiling to myself, I extended my stiffened tongue, leaned forward and stabbed the tip straight on to the centre of the raised ring of muscle.

She shrieked with joy and her buttocks writhed in my fervent grasp, making it hard to hold them open. I moved my left hand under her soft belly until it cupped her love-nest, while the tip of my forefinger rubbed the stiff and slippery little button until she reached an obviously very fulfilling climax. Sitting back again, I helped her to her feet. She staggered on her weakened limbs, holding her skirts up to her waist as, with a charmingly dreamy expression on her face, she applied one hand to her cunny and the other to her bottom, rubbing away with slow sensuality.

'I trust that I have spanked you to your complete satisfaction, Bertha?'

'Oh yes, ma'am!' she replied softly. 'It was really lovely. Oooh, my poor bottom's beautifully hot. Thank you, ma'am. Especially for the kisses at the end.'

'It was a pleasure, Bertha. As always. And I do believe that you have added a little to your curves. I swear that your bottom wobbled more than it used to. I heartily approve, by the way.'

'Thank you, ma'am. It's probably Mavis's good cooking what's done it. Are you going to spank her now, ma'am?'

I looked across and assumed my most solemn expression. 'I am not sure that I have the strength left,' I said wearily. 'Beating Bertha has rather drained me.' I paused and then the sight of poor Mavis's woebegone countenance was too much and I spoiled my little game completely by giggling like a schoolgirl. An answering grin of pure relief lit up her broad face and she uttered a loud, theatrical sigh.

'For one horrible moment, madam, I thought you were quite serious and that my bottom was not going to be treated in the way it wants so badly,' she declared.

'My dearest Mavis,' I replied. 'How could I possibly pass up such a golden opportunity to have your delightfully big bottom all bare? Now, ignore my teasing and lay yourself over my lap.'

I was charmed and flattered at the warmth of her smile as she rose to her feet and trotted across to my chair, where she bent forward, rested her hands on my left thigh (giving it an impudent squeeze as she did so), then lowered her centre portions into position, moving her hands on to the floor one by one and finally bracing her parted legs by pressing down with her toes. She was ready, and as I gazed down on the broad curves outlined by the thin material of her skirt, so was I.

I bared her in the same leisurely fashion and examined her bottom with just as much pleasure as I had Bertha's, enjoying the very different formation as much as the common elements of smooth, rounded cheeks, tight clefts and wide folds. Her skin was not quite as smooth as her predecessor's but her much bigger buttocks were warmer under my hand and shared that springy resilience which I loved so much. On the other hand, their breadth made for an even more satisfying target for any dedicated spanker and the rippling wobble which my first lusty spank produced was a feast to the eye.

Probably the most vivid difference was that Bertha's coloured up with almost indecent speed, whereas Mavis took several smacks on the same spot before her skin blushed in acknowledgement. For this reason, as much as a desire for variety, I altered my conduct of her spanking. Rather than let my palm dance freely over the available surface, I concentrated on one part until I had produced a pleasing pinkness, then moved to the equivalent part of the sister cheek. When her entire bottom was blushing nicely, I paused for reflection.

Her fortitude surprised me. I had realised early in my experimentations with Bertha that she shared my sensual feelings when it came to a sore posterior, but I had always felt that her elder colleague tolerated corporal punishment rather than relished it. I knew that she found the idea of a naughty girl being spanked for her sins absolutely normal and also that, in common with most country folk, she had a splendidly earthy appreciation of the usually hidden portions of the human anatomy. She had, for example, joined in our naked romps in the garden with quiet enthusiasm, applying her tongue to both Bertha and myself with no hesitation – and with every sign of enjoyment. She had also presented her own parts for our delight with no signs of false modesty and her sighs at her climaxes were as wholehearted as one could wish.

None the less, after I had devoted a further ten minutes to a steady barrage of crisp spanks and rendered the entire surface of her voluptuous bottom a brilliant, shining red, I stopped and busied my hands in the gratifying task of rubbing her better. Her little groans as I shifted her yielding mounds this way and that were very much as expected but when I pulled them wide apart and began to tickle her brown bottom-hole with the tip of my forefinger, she took me aback, in no uncertain manner.

'Oh please, not yet, madam. Can I have some more smacks first? Please?'

My jaw dropped. For a pleasurable spanking, it had been quite hard, and I had been convinced that she had had enough. Very little less than the submissive Bertha, in fact. Nevertheless, I did not let my amazement inhibit me for more than the briefest moment. I rested my left arm across the small of her back, took a firm grip of her fleshy hip and drove my aching palm with full force into the roundest part of her left buttock. She grunted and her body jerked as her entire bottom wobbled like a strawberry blancmange.

'How did that one suit you, Mavis?'

'Oooh, it was lovely, madam. Sorry, but can I just shift a bit? Stick my bottom up a bit?'

'Of course.'

She bent her arms to lower the upper part of her body and then brought her feet forward, the toes of her boots scraping horribly on the stone floor. Then she bent her knees inward and raised her hips so that only my left thigh was in contact with her body. Her big bottom loomed dramatically up before my face, bright red all over save the one darker patch on the nearer cheek, firm evidence of the effectiveness of my last spank. It was a most arresting sight and I gazed for some time until I noticed that the straining muscles of her thighs were quivering.

I administered another hard spank to the equivalent part of her other mound. Unfortunately, her elevation reduced the amount of travel available to my arm and therefore it was not quite as devastating as the previous one. Despite that disadvantage, however, I did not consider ordering her to resume her earlier position as the proximity of her bottom to my face had singular charms, especially when her musky scent wafted into my nose.

Delighted with her attitude, I flailed away to my heart's content, until the combination of the considerable pain and the strain on her limbs forced her to slump back over my lap. I lessened the force of my blows and increased the rapidity of their delivery, setting her scarlet flesh into constant motion as she bucked, writhed and roared in her pain and ecstasy. At last, my arm could take no more, and panting with a combination of lust and exhaustion, I thrust one hand beneath her until I could tickle her love-nest while with the other I massaged her hot cheeks. Very shortly, her cries reached such a volume that I knew her climax was nigh, whereupon I thrust a finger past the ring of muscle guarding the entrance to her back passage and into the warm, clinging depths.

When her shrieks subsided, I rested my hand on the relatively cool flesh of her upper thigh, watching the little spasms which rippled through her bottom, then glanced up at Bertha. She was standing in open-mouthed fascination, her pretty face red with her blushes. Her skirts were tucked up under her elbows while her hands seemed to be happily engaged in rubbing her presumably still-tingling bottom. I stared at her dear little cunny, the sparse hairs covering her slit, matted with her spending, and her plump bare thighs shifting noticeably in sympathy with the workings of her hands behind.

I was, for the moment, completely sated. The two vigorous spankings had exhausted me. I wanted peace to collect myself before deciding which of my many desires I would satisfy. But before I retired to my contemplations, I told Mavis to stand alongside Bertha with her skirts held equally high while I admired their thighs and cunnies. Then they had to turn round to let me see their red bottoms. I gazed long and with complete satisfaction, told them to rearrange their apparel. Then, ignoring their expressions of disappointment, I dismissed them and retired to my bedroom.

I flopped down and tried to concentrate on my major dilemma. I was now a woman of property and the lawyers had strongly hinted that apart from the house itself, Aunt Grace's legacy would be more than enough to see me through the remainder of my life in some comfort.

By the same token, Phillip seemed to be increasingly attracted to the life of a roving artist and, although I could not face the prospect of permanent deprivation, I was growing accustomed to living without him. My fortune would allow me to give full rein to my independent nature, so it was surely possible to find a satisfying course in life which would allow me to select my own path.

Shaking my head to clear away the doubts and apprehensions, I redirected my thoughts to my servants' bottoms. I thrilled to the memory of nice Mavis thrusting her hips up as she pleaded for more and harder smacks; I recalled the way Bertha bent over my lap with all her usual gracefulness; I remembered the intimate contact of the half-naked girls lying restlessly on my thighs. Unable to find any solution to my problems, I now desired distraction, so I rose from my bed, walked to the top of the staircase and called down.

'Mavis . . . Bertha!' After the briefest of intervals, two anxious faces peered up at me.

'Yes, madam?'

'Remove your clothing – everything mind, for I want you stark naked – and come up to my bedroom.'

'Yes, madam,' they chorused.

I leant over the banister rail and, with growing hunger, watched the two white bodies come into view, greedily eyeing the exposed flesh as their apparel was strewn all over the floor in their haste. Mavis turned her back to me to remove her stockings and the sight of her big pink bottom, changing shape as she bent, sent throbbing pulses of wild desire flooding through my vitals. Oh, I wanted them! Then they were trotting energetically up the stairs, breasts bouncing excitingly. I stood back to let them pass, smiling at their self-conscious giggles as they paraded their equally mobile buttocks down the corridor.

Having spent several moments admiring their nether rotundities, I made them lie face down on the bed so that I could kiss and stroke their bottoms in earnest, and in no time my fevered tongue was delving into the softness of their clefts, urgently seeking out the intimate orifices buried deep within them.

I then felt a strong urge to feel their hands on my naked person, so bade them strip me, a task they accomplished with consummate ease. I was soon burying my face in the bolster while four hands and two mouths thrilled me.

If I remember currently, more than two hours passed before we sank back, utterly exhausted. In that time, I had investigated every inch of their bodies as thoroughly as they had mine. We had found some new delights; all of us, for example, finding that having one's toes sucked is quite delicious! Perhaps the most thrilling moment for me was when I told Bertha to find the little box containing my six beautifully carved wooden dildoes, while I knelt up with my hips thrust as high as I could manage and with my bottom-hole tingling furiously at the imminent prospect of a good plugging. After a thorough laving with both tongues, Bertha oiled my entrance and passage with tantalising deliberation and then thrust the full length remorselessly deep into my fundament. Delectable!

At last, wearily, they prepared a bath and I gave expression to my gratitude and affection by letting them enter it before I did – and by washing them with great thoroughness.

The days sped by. The weather had yet to settle into the expected summer pattern and so we were unable to indulge ourselves in our naked romps in the garden, but there was plenty to occupy us and when I felt the need for fresh air and open spaces, I could saddle up my beloved mare, Matilda, and canter across the felds. I often returned soaked to the skin and spattered with mud, but I was always blissfully happy.

* * *

In the meantime, my thoughts for the future use of Aunt Grace's house were still no nearer to clarification and it seemed eminently sensible to discuss them with Elizabeth, whose wisdom, sympathy and experience I valued highly. I wrote, received a warm invitation to spend several days with her, and duly set off immediately after breaking my fast on a perfect morning, perched on my little dog-cart and in a fever of impatience to see my friend again.

I passed the spot where we first met and my bottom tingled at the memories. As I related in the second volume of my memoirs, Elizabeth had arranged my capture and imprisonment after she and I had collided when she had carelessly ridden her horse into mine. My instinctive lash across her derrière had enraged her beyond reason at the time and her revenge had been appropriate. For the remainder of the half-hour journey, my mind dwelt on the memories of the thrashings I had endured and then on the rapport which had developed between us subsequently.

So, as Matilda trotted up the long drive, I was already hoping that our time together would involve more than deep discussions on what I had already decided to name Redhand House.

I was not to be disappointed. I was greeted at the main entrance to her house by a pretty young maid, whom I recognised from the last meeting of The Society. She was a most comely little thing, with a sweet elfin face, twinkling eyes and the broadest of smiles – and I clearly remembered her chubby little bottom. Taking no notice of her strange discomfiture at my arrival, I greeted her with genuine warmth, bending forward to kiss her soft lips, which reacted most flatteringly to my touch.

'Mary, is it not?' I asked, pleased with my memory.

'Yes, madam.' She blushed most prettily at the compliment, which inspired me to kiss her again, this time drawing her close to me so that I could drop my hands down her back and reacquaint myself with the shape of her posterior. 'Oh, madam, that was a lovely surprise!' she exclaimed, when I eventually drew back.

'You like my kisses then?'

'Oh yes, madam, very much,' she responded.

'And how about the feel of my hands on your bottom?' I continued, squeezing away happily.

'Lovely, madam.'

'As is the feel of your bottom under my hands,' I said. 'Now, if you could tell her ladyship that I have arrived, I am sure that I will be able to find an opportunity to stroke your pretty bottom again. Although I shall undoubtedly demand that next time it is bare.'

The charming creature blushed again and lowered her gaze shyly to the floor. 'I would like that very much, madam. But her ladyship is still abed, madam. We were not expecting you until later in the morning . . .' Her voice tailed off in embarrassment.

I studied her gravely. 'That is hardly your fault, Mary. And I presume that you are concerned that your bottom will suffer if you wake her before the due and proper time.' Once again, a red stain suffused her face and she nodded. 'Well, I certainly do not wish to think that my early arrival was the cause of you being turned up to be spanked, however pleasant a sight that would be. I shall wake her. Now off you go, child.'

Ignoring her stammered protests, I handed her my cloak and my veiled riding bonnet, shook my hair free and hoisted my skirts. I then trotted up the sweeping staircase to the familiar bedroom, eased the door open and slipped inside on tip-toe.

My silent approach paid off handsomely. Not only was Elizabeth still fast asleep but she had obviously had a disturbed night, for she had kicked off the bedclothes and her contortions had dragged her nightdress up to her waist. I was thus greeted by the splendid sight of her bare bottom gleaming in the dim light and I crept silently up to the side of her bed to study it closely. Her limbs were sprawled in a most inelegant fashion, with her thighs widely apart, exposing the lower part of her cunny.

Holding my breath, I bent forward until my face was just inches away from her posterior. Elizabeth is generously curved and her bottom, although perhaps too broad for perfection, is none the less delightfully feminine. In that position, with the calm of sleep relaxing her muscles, it looked temptingly soft and perfectly posed for a spanking. I was just about to administer the first smack when my eyes were drawn to the cleft between her cheeks. Towards the lower end, a darker patch showed the position of her anus, inspiring an even ruder awakening. I adjusted my stance. A floorboard creaked. I stood still, holding my breath. She stirred, mumbled something and then subsided, but with her plump thighs even further apart. I held my flowing hair about my ears, bent down and thrust my tongue deep into the warm depths of her bottom. Her shrieks of alarm and delight were music to my ears, and transferring my hands to her writhing buttocks, I buried my face in between them and soon brought her to a noisy climax.

I then bathed her, happily submitted to a sound spanking on my bare bottom, and helped her dress. We then decided to take advantage of the pleasant morning and talk while we ambled through her delightful gardens.

After luncheon, we retired to her bedroom, undressed and lay nestling in each other's arms while we summarised our discussions.

'So Annie,' she began, gently cupping my bosom. 'You have this house – a house which has a reputation for disciplinary activities – and ample funds. You are an ardent lover of the rod. So, why do you not continue in the same vein?'

I reminded her of my reluctance to leave Petworth and ended my recital of its varied pleasures with a description of the joys I had found in my little schoolroom.

'Well, there is your answer, you silly goose. Turn the house into a school. I can just see you as a strict schoolma'am. A cane tucked into your belt and a bucketful of whippy little birch rods in the corner of your study! And you will have ample holidays.'

I laughed. 'That thought had indeed occurred to me, Elizabeth. But I feel that my enjoyment of girlish derrières reddening under my hand would, in fact, deter me from the path of proper discipline. I would always wonder if my tastes rather than justice dictated a girl's punishment.'

'Yes, I understand,' she said thoughtfully. Then she jumped down from the bed and began pacing up and down, the movements of her bottom, bosoms and thighs hardly distracting me in my excitement at her enthusiasm. She continued. 'Why not combine both aspects? Found an establishment which caters for those with a fascination for discipline and, at the same time, have a proper curriculum. In that case, your pupils will benefit from further education – in addition to enjoying as many spankings as they wish.'

I clapped my hands with glee. 'Elizabeth, I do believe that you have found the answer!' I cried. 'Now, let me think. No girl younger than eighteen will be eligible – and there will be no upper age limit. I see no reason why even grandmothers should be barred from proffering their bottoms if that is what they desire. The only criterion is that they do not physically offend.'

'As usual, Annie, you are right. I myself once whipped a woman of some fifty years – and a most satisfying experience it was. She had a marvellous bottom. Full, plump, surprisingly firm and with the softest, smoothest skin. And she presented herself with an admirable air of coquettish modesty.'

I smiled. 'Yes. Coquettish modesty is a fine phrase, Elizabeth.'

'Obviously you will not be able to fill the establishment immediately,' she continued, 'but I am sure that all the other members of The Society will volunteer without hesitation. Bernice and Thomasina will love it.'

'I agree,' I said in a low, steady voice. 'And how about you, Elizabeth? How would you feel if I summoned you to the front of the class and made you raise your skirts and lower your drawers in front of the others? I would make you stand there for several moments while I stared blatantly at your naked thighs and cunny, while your classmates stared equally hard at your bare bottom. Then I would put you across my knee and spank you until your fat buttocks were sizzling hot and bright red.'

She stared at me, pale and with parted lips, then blushed and lowered her eyes. I led her wordlessly over to a suitable chair and helped her into position, enjoying the unusual sensation of her naked front resting on my bare thighs, and then spanked her with a song in my heart. And a sense that I was on the first steps of a new and rewarding path in life.

The remainder of my stay passed in a similar vein. We talked and made love and the plans for my academy began to take shape. Then, just as I was about to depart for home, I learned a lesson which was more welcome in retrospect than at the time.

I was dressed for the ride home and had reached the hall – a little hurt that there seemed to be nobody to see me off – when dear little Mary appeared, pale and tense. Naturally I smiled warmly at her but before I could speak she stammered out something to the effect that her ladyship was waiting for me in the ballroom. Only a little puzzled, I followed her down the corridor, watching the enticing movement of her posterior under her tight skirt and chiding myself for not keeping to my promise to lay it bare.

It was no more than a passing thought, for we then arrived and she beckoned me through the open door. At the far end of the large and beautifully proportioned room was a row of chairs, all occupied. I recognised several of the servants and noticed one strange man before my gaze passed upward and on to the centre of the stage. I swear that my heart stopped. I certainly stopped breathing. My belly felt hollow, my palms were moist, and the skin of my bottom crawled with fear.

Up there, its back to me, was a solid, upholstered chair. Standing beside it was Elizabeth. She was flexing a long cane.

I tried to swallow and failed. My knees weakened and I swayed. Then Mary took my elbow, led me remorselessly past the audience and helped me up on to the stage. I had to force myself to meet my tormentor's eyes and their glittering darkness, coupled with the cruel smile on her lovely face reassured me not one bit.

I had felt her cane and the memory of its biting sting, plus the humiliation of having an audience of strangers as eager witnesses, frightened me. I wanted to turn and flee, but knowing that I had shown craven cowardice would outlive the pain of my forthcoming beating, however undeserved. Pulling my shoulders back, I met her eyes with all the fortitude I could muster.

'Remove your cloak and bonnet!' Her voice had the steadiness of true authority and my trembling hands did her bidding. 'Now pull up your skirt and tuck it into your belt.' I was not wearing a chemise so it was a relatively simple task. My drawers clung to my quivering cheeks. 'Unfasten your drawers.' I fumbled at the bow and they slithered inelegantly to my feet. 'Remove them.' Knowing that a display of maidenly modesty would only annoy her, I bent right down to disentangle them and fold them neatly, horribly aware that those behind me had a clear view of my splayed bottom and most of my cunny. 'Bend over the chair.' With tears pricking my eyes, I collapsed over the back, burying my scarlet face in the seat.

Her soft hands roved around my protruding rear, fingers pressing deep to test the resilience. I kept perfectly still until she suddenly pulled my buttocks apart, exposing my anus to the watching eyes. I gasped aloud and wriggled futilely.

I felt the cane press into the centre of my bottom, cool on my hot skin. It left me and I held my breath for what seemed to be an age until both buttocks seemed to explode with agony, driving the breath from my lungs. Then the blaze faded to a narrow band of fire across both quivering mounds and I braced myself for the second. It landed, slamming my front into the chair. I cried out.

Just as the pain was settling down to an insistent throbbing, the third cut landed across the base of my derrière and hurt even more than its predecessors, making me writhe helplessly. But then my natural defences began to rescue me. A welcome lassitude crept over me and my bottom seemed to act of its own volition, pushing itself out as though pleading for further visitations. My sobs died away and my feelings toward Elizabeth changed from fear and resentment to a state approaching adoration. It was now important to show my audience that I could summon up rare levels of courage so, not caring that my cunny would now be on display, I spread my feet and bent my knees inwards: bracing myself; offering myself.

Nine more times the whippy cane slashed across my buttocks. At each stroke I wailed, swerved my tortured hips to and fro and then proffered them anew for the next. And when my ordeal was finally over, it seemed totally natural to prostrate myself at Elizabeth's feet and press my tear-stained lips to her boots, heedless of the view which I was presenting to the silent watchers.

* * *

My journey back was exceedingly painful, until about half way, when the burning changed to an insistent and maddeningly delicious glow, suffusing the centre of my body. So intrusive was it that I had to guide Matilda into a field, tether her to a tree and hurl myself to the ground with skirt up and drawers down while I frantically frigged my love-nest, my naked bottom set afire again by the sharp blades of grass. My climax was as intense as any I had known.

Two

When I eventually arrived back home, I was once again in a fever of sensual excitement. My buttocks throbbed and ached and my frenzied diddling had done no more than dampen the fires in the core of my being, and that only temporarily. Those long minutes of sublime submission to Elizabeth's cane had somehow reawakened my dominant side and I wanted to impose myself on my servants.

As I unharnessed Matilda to begin the task of rubbing her down, my clothes suddenly felt horribly constrictive. I hastily stripped myself of all but stockings and boots, thankful that I was not a pampered aristocrat, for whom the task would have been all but impossible without assistance. As usual, I found the sensations of nudity most pleasing. The cool air lingered caressingly on my heated skin, particularly welcome under my arms and between my thighs. My naked breasts jiggled and my nipples flared into excited life as they brushed against Matilda's coat. I set to and the dust made me sneeze, filling my lungs with the heady scents of horse and stable. I bent to her legs, slowly, so that I could savour the separation of my posterior and the gentle draught in the division. I worked with a will and the shafts of sunlight shining through the small cracks in the walls filled with floating motes of dust.

Breathing hard but in far better temper after my exertions, I moved to Matilda's head and reached up to place my arms round her neck. She seemed fascinated by the unaccustomed feel of my naked skin and nuzzled my bosom. The velvety touch of her nose and the warm gusts of her breathing made me quite dizzy. Still naked, I led her out of the stable, across the yard into the paddock, and was about to set her free when a sudden surge of mischief welled up inside me. Clicking her to a halt and ignoring her puzzled whinny, I rested my hands on her withers and hauled myself with scant dignity up on to her back, indecently astride. She twitched nervously as I desperately tried to gain both balance and equilibrium. Her coat tickled those parts in contact with it and the bare cheeks of my squashed bottom throbbed anew. I soon settled and, gripping firmly with my thighs and knees, touched my heels to her flanks and urged her into a walk.

We moved as one. Her backbone pressed into my cunny and my buttocks shifted easily to her rhythm as we circled the paddock, once, twice, before my limbs longed for the assistance of reins and stirrups. I halted her, slid off her back and ambled thoughtfully back to the stable and my clothes, thrilled at having found another sensual pleasure.

My little equine escapade seemed to have cooled my ardour as effectively as my nakedness had cooled my flesh. I found a clean cloth and sponged myself down, then dressed and slipped quietly into the house, where I engaged my servants in small conversation while I enjoyed a cup of coffee. I then asked Mavis to prepare a couple of cold collations for me and gave them both the rest of the day off, explaining that I had a great deal of work on the London house to exercise me.

Comfortably ensconced in my study, I sharpened several pencils, found sufficient sheets of clean paper and settled down to draw up the skeleton of a curriculum. My academy must not be a sham. As Elizabeth had recommended, the pupils had to be offered the varied challenge of true education, otherwise I would soon find that false reasons for punishing them would lessen the satisfaction for all concerned. My immediate concern, therefore, was to establish which subjects I was able to teach with something approaching authority. Fortunately, my late mother had been a woman of several talents and, apart from the occasional spell in the (non-punishing) hands of a governess, she had been responsible for educating me. While I sensed that the time would come when members of my sex would be given the opportunity to pursue their studies to the highest levels, in 1893 most women of my background aimed to devote their energies and abilities to the taxing role of the ideal wife!

I am not of a rebellious nature and therefore it never occurred to me that I could challenge established ideas and attempt to advance the cause of female education. Even if I had had the necessary intellect, I lacked both the learning and the enthusiasm. No, if I planned a curriculum based on those subjects on which I could speak with some authority, I would feel much more at ease in my self-appointed role. And my punishments would carry far more weight if I could explain the erring girl's faults with due clarity.

I picked up my pencil and listed the areas in which I could fairly claim a degree of expertise: art; cooking; the gracious hostess; deportment; embroidery; the kitchen garden. At that stage, I came to a halt. My French was rudimentary and I did not feel that my knowledge of our own glorious language, or the many masterpieces which have been written in it, was sufficient to qualify me to instruct others. I had even less faith in my musical talents. After a brief pang of despair, I cheered myself up with the thought that it should not be beyond my abilities to find others more qualified than I who could take the lessons. Even if they did not show any signs of sharing my taste for spanking, then it would matter but little. I would ask for detailed reports on the progress of each pupil and carry out the punishments myself!

Settling down to collect my thoughts on each separate subject and to make preliminary notes, I worked steadily until I heard the clock strike six, at which point I felt that I had done enough. I tossed my pencil carelessly down on to the table, from where it bounced on to the floor and the point broke. Frowning in annoyance at my clumsiness, I bent to pick it up and immediately the lingering ache in my bottom flared up. I stayed in position, the tightness of my clothing against my protruding cheeks reminding me inevitably of Elizabeth's cane. Memories of the humiliation and fear and the searing bite of the rattan wand flooded through my mind. Smiling happily to myself, I wandered downstairs, opened a bottle of wine, finished it with my supper and went to bed at an unusually early hour, determined to be fully rested before what I knew would be an energetic day.

I awoke refreshed and full of vigour and was lying in bed waiting for Bertha to fill my bath for me when I realised that it would be impossible to hide my weals from her inquisitive eyes. A quick peep in the long pier-glass with my nightdress hoisted clear confirmed that they were easily visible. I considered sending her down to help Mavis with my breakfast and bathing and dressing alone, but knew that she would immediately suspect the reason for my unusual reticence. So the obvious decision was to let her find out and enjoy her concern.

Which is exactly what happened. As she took my peignoir and nightgown from me, she had an uninterrupted view of my bare bottom and dropped my garments in surprise.

'Really, Bertha, that was uncommonly careless of you,' I snapped at her. 'They will have to be laundered now. See to it, please.'

With a prim expression on my face, I climbed into the bath and sank back, blissfully inhaling the scented steam and feeling the hot water loosen the last of the knots. Opening my eyes, I watched Bertha bundle my nightclothes into the laundry basket and come back to the side of the tub.

'I'm sorry, ma'am, but –'

'But what, Bertha?' I interrupted.

'Your bottom, ma'am,' she stammered. 'It's all marked. Lines right across it!'

'Well, of course it is. Lady Elizabeth gave me a dozen with her whippiest cane just as I was leaving. In front of an audience of her servants. On my bare bottom. And not only were all present treated to the sight of my naked posterior under the lash, so to speak, but I was also made to raise my skirts and take my drawers down to my ankles, so that everybody had the clearest possible view of what I try to keep decently concealed!'

'You mean your cunny, ma'am?'

'Yes, Bertha, I do. And to make matters even worse, my limbs were trembling so much that I was terrified of losing my balance and tumbling in an undignified heap. To brace myself – this is when I was removing my drawers, you understand – I felt it far safer to place my feet some distance apart and also to bend at the knee. The obvious result was that the cheeks of my poor bottom were splayed wide and I have a horrid feeling that my delicate little bottom-hole was also exposed.'

Bertha's mouth formed an 'O' of sympathetic horror, an emotion clearly belied by the lascivious gleam in her green eyes. 'Oh, you poor thing, ma'am. I really feel for you.'

'Thank you, Bertha, but I am sure that my ordeal did me a great deal of good. Now will you please stop gawping and wash my bosoms.'

The dear little thing was even more solicitous than usual as she applied the soapy sponge to my breasts and shoulders and especially so when I stood to give her access to all those parts previously under water. I particularly enjoyed the tenderness with which she handled my buttocks. Although no longer painful, I still appreciated the lightness of her touch.

When I had been rinsed, dried and powdered, I led her down the corridor back to my bedroom, enjoying my nudity even more than normal as I saw in my mind's eye the stripes dancing to the stately rhythm of my buttocks. It was warm enough to retain Eve's costume while Bertha dressed my hair and painted my face. Still naked, I moved across to the long pier-glass and studied my reflection. My skin had an appealing pink sheen after my hot bath, and with my hair flowing over my shoulders I looked the picture of maidenly innocence, in complete contrast to my lascivious and domineering mood!

'My cunny hairs are a trifle straggly,' I announced after a careful study. 'Fetch a hairbrush and comb, Bertha, and tidy me up.'

Her actions did nothing to soothe the growing tingles pervading that region, especially when she bent her head to kiss me. I swivelled round, admired the lines on my bottom for a while, then told her to kiss me there – after she had stripped naked. She obeyed with admirable speed and then I could close my eyes and stand still, waiting with bated breath for the gossamer-light touch of her lips.

Five minutes later, I was sighing lustfuly. Bertha had traversed each weal with her moistened tongue before blowing gently on the still-damp path and the sensations were pure bliss. I slowly sank to my knees, thrusting my hips high in the air, and with a delightful giggle she spread me and applied her tongue with loving skill. Waves of hot ecstasy surged through me. Their intensity grew apace when my cunny yielded to the invasion of a finger, and when she touched my love-button my spending was so strong that I all but swooned away.

Not for the first time – and by no means for the last – I had cause to be grateful to the dear girl for her sympathy. She helped me to my feet, led me to my bed, laid me gently down and then settled beside me, holding my head to her plump bosom while I panted my way to full recovery. Her soft, silken warmth, her tender words of love whispered into my ear, and her soothing hands roaming about my naked body, were all delightful.

After a few minutes, my mind had cleared, my blood had cooled and, rather to my surprise, the tingles were once again making their presence felt. I wanted, above all else, to ravish my delectable slave and to repay her for all the thrills she had just given me. Wriggling out of her tight embrace, I turned her on to her back and lay on top of her, glueing my mouth to hers and pressing down with the middle of my body so that my dark gold cunny hairs mingled with her red ones. Her arms tightened around my back, squashing our bosoms together. Our pantings intermingled and our tongues fought for ascendancy. Our hands roved; squeezing, pinching, patting. We rolled around the bed, naked limbs entwined, while fingers probed and penetrated. Eventually, I pinned her face down, sitting on her shoulders, and gazed down on her squirming buttocks while I caught my breath. Of its own accord, my right hand rose, the palm stiffened and, eager for the stinging impact, I lowered it again. I wanted to spank her properly, with due ceremony, so I applied my lips to her divided moon instead.

Perhaps ten minutes later, I was holding her head to my bosom, breathing deeply to draw the lingering scents of her spending into my lungs. Then the spring breeze wafted the equally enticing smell of frying bacon into my nose and another hunger manifested itself.

I slapped her bottom. 'Come on, Bertha, let us see what the worthy Mavis has prepared to break our fast.'

She scampered to where her clothes lay in an untidy heap and I watched her tightly bent bottom as she gathered them.

'No, Bertha,' I laughed. 'Let us go naked.'

She peered back at me and her upside-down grin was

especially charming. 'Oh, madam, what a wicked idea. And will you make Mavis strip off as well?'

'Why not? Quick, tidy yourself up.'

Mavis's reaction to our appearance was memorable. With a plate laden with crisp rashers in one hand and a wooden spatula in the other, she turned at the sound of our footsteps. Then her jaw dropped, her eyes widened, and she dropped my breakfast, the sound of the breaking china shattering the quietness.

'I was eagerly looking forward to that, Mavis,' I announced in icy tones. 'You will set about another breakfast immediately. Only you will remove all your clothing first. I shall then be able to study your bottom properly while I decide how best to punish it. Severely.'

Red-faced and looking very confused at the unexpected turn of events, she began to scramble out of her clothes.

'Hold it there, Mavis. I want to have a good look at your bosoms.'

Staring fixedly at the floor, still blushing, she held her chemise around her waist while I stared equally fixedly at those trembling globes, the neat brown nipples puckering attractively before my eyes.

'Proceed,' I snapped, and she hastened to obey, pleasing me by turning her back when she took down her drawers so that I could see her bottom loom into view.

As she busied herself at the range, my two major hungers were titillated. The smell of frying bacon made my mouth water, while the quivers which rippled through her ample buttocks at even the slightest movement set my feminine parts tingling insistently.

I stole a look at Bertha. She too had her eyes fixed on her colleague with an entrancingly lustful expression.

With an excellent breakfast at last inside me, I sat back to ponder my next move. Clearly Mavis's punishment was the first priority but I was most anxious to do full justice to her, her bottom and my own desires. On the other hand, I did not wish to hurt her beyond her burgeoning levels of tolerance, nor did I want to mark her skin more than strictly necessary. I made her stand before me so that I could gaze closely at her rump while I deliberated.

I stroked each cheek, reminding myself of the smoothness of her skin, then I extended my right forefinger and pushed it into the plumpest part of each buttock, enjoying again the yielding quality of her flesh. My own bare bottom stirred restlessly on the wooden seat of my chair and the association of wood and naked skin inspired me to choose a hairbrush. As an implement, it may lack a dedicated sense of purpose, but does have a certain domestic charm.

'Well, Mavis,' I announced in the satisfied tones of one who has solved a tricky problem. 'It's time for you to receive your punishment. Bertha, could you please go up to my bedroom and bring down my spare hairbrush? The wooden one, not the one from my ivory set. Thank you.'

She trotted off obediently and I resumed my pattings and proddings while I decided on the position that would suit us all best.

Soon after Bertha had left, I determined that I could not resist putting Mavis across my knee and warming her up with a nice little hand spanking before applying the hairbrush. The feel of her bare cheeks, plus the prospect of holding her soft, naked body across my uncovered thighs was just too tempting. So I guided the trembling woman into position and immediately began a systematic slapping of her derrière, setting it quivering like an enormous jelly but causing only the slightest smart, for she remained both still and silent throughout. Her nervousness, however, was made obvious by the tense way she held herself.

By the time Bertha returned, I had rendered the target area a pretty pink and it was time to spank her properly, so I patted her thoughtfully and planned my next move.

'Right, Mavis, up you get and stand in the corner. Next to the dresser.' She walked the short distance to the chosen spot. 'I think that it would be a good idea if you stood there for another five minutes, Mavis. Until ten o'clock. When the clock strikes, you will get your spanking,' I announced.

'Yes, madam.' The cheeks of her bottom contracted; dimples flared up over the entire surface and the cleft tightened until it was no more than a thin line. Then, with a tiny sob, she relaxed it. I gazed at her with great pleasure. Ever since my first sight of the statue of the naked goddess in Aunt Grace's garden, the rear view of an unclothed woman had fascinated me. Mavis's bottom was not elegant. A life of hard physical labour had given it a muscularity which went well with her broad shoulders and strong arms and thighs. Not that she had cause to be modest about it (nor her bosoms, for that matter). Both sets of protuberances were beautifully feminine. So I spent the five minutes studying her with real admiration – and desire. But most important of all was the plain fact that I was inordinately fond of her. Her big, soft, warm heart appealed to me no less than her equally big, soft and warm bottom.

For an instant, I regretted the cruel way I was treating her. She had been flummoxed by my bizarre appearance and so the dropping of my breakfast should have been almost forgivable or, at the most, punished with a normal spanking on her bare bottom, rather than this far more extreme and lingering chastisement.

My regret lasted but a moment. My caning at Elizabeth's hands had taught me that the pleasure of corporal punishment – the searing smart which tests one's courage to the full; the pride in being courageous; the intensity of one's emotions when the smart mellows to a throbbing glow – are all made even more vivid when there is an element of real trepidation. I knew that Mavis was not like Bertha or myself. For us, a bare, sore bottom was naturally transformed into a sensual delight. She, by contrast, was having to learn how to enjoy pain.

As the clock struck and her big buttocks clamped themselves together again, I fervently hoped that what was about to happen to her would give her great joy in the end. I stood up.

'Come here, Mavis.' Her face was screwed up with fear but softened after her eyes had swept quickly over my nakedness. Her big breasts bounced gently as she stumbled towards me. She stood before me; trembling, naked, blushing. Delicious. I leaned forward and kissed her, then rested my hands on her shoulders and continued. 'Mavis, my dear. You have been a naughty girl and have earned a good spanking on your bare bottom. I confess that I shall enjoy smacking you. I love your bottom.' I paused and dropped both hands until they rested on the softness of her buttocks. I pressed inwards and my fingers sank into the flesh and brought her closer, so that the hairs on our mounts of Venus intertwined. 'And I love you.' Our breasts touched and my nipples sparked into life. 'Submit to me, my Mavis. Proffer your bare bottom to me in the full knowledge that I will beat it severely. By the time I have finished with you, it will be burning like the fires of hell. But you, my dearest, will be in seventh heaven. That is a promise. Know for certain, Mavis, that I know of what I am speaking. You will now salute your mistress. Kiss the hand that has already punished you and is about to wield the hairbrush; then the lap which has supported you. Last of all, kiss my bottom. As I shall kiss yours when I am done with it.'

'Oh, madam!' she cried, and sank to her knees, grabbing my right hand and smothering the palm with lovely wet kisses. 'I am yours. My bottom is yours. Beat it until it is as red as a ripe cherry.' She bent her head to my right thigh, just above the knee, and as her soft lips caressed my skin, I looked down at the smooth plain of her back below her dishevelled tresses and quietly enjoyed the touch of her lips on my skin. She halted when she had reached the top of my right thigh and then pressed her mouth on my cunny, making me quite dizzy.

Almost too soon, she had reached my left knee and I turned to present my striped bottom. Five minutes later, we were ready.

'Right, Mavis. Lie at full length on the table. We'll start you off like that.'

She obeyed, emitting a little squeak as her naked front came into contact with the cold wood. Not that I paid a great deal of attention as I was far too busy looking at her bottom as she clambered up and settled down. I picked up the hairbrush, pleased with its weighty solidity and noting with satisfaction that the flat surface was admirably shiny and would sting nicely. I moved over to my trembling victim, then walked slowly around the table, studying my target from every possible angle and thrilling to the way her large, firm hemispheres stood out in high relief as they swelled upward.

I finished my tour of inspection and stood to her left side, looking straight down on to her bare, trembling bottom. Then I rested my left hand on the smooth plain of her loins, took a firm grip on the handle of the hairbrush, and began what was to be the longest and most testing spanking she had ever experienced.

My initial spanks were light – wristy flicks rather than full-blooded swipes – but enough to produce a springy ripple in her flesh and to leave a pink mark in their wake. I concentrated entirely on her left cheek, working methodically from top to base and from flank to cleft until it was a pleasing shade of salmon pink. Then I crossed over to the other side and repeated the procedure. As soon as I had matched the colour of both halves, I resumed my original stance and took a firmer grip of my instrument.

'Right, Mavis,' I announced, 'I am now going to give you six proper spanks on each buttock. They will obviously hurt considerably, so it is perfectly in order for you to wriggle your bottom about after each one, but I shall not administer the next smack until it is perfectly posed. Understand?'

'Of course, madam.' Her voice was soft and low, but firm and clear. My heart warmed to her.

'Another thing. I love the way your fat cheeks wobble when they are spanked, so move your legs apart to make it harder for you to clench your muscles. Yes, that is perfect.'

'Excuse me, madam.' My right arm halted halfway up to my shoulder.

'Yes, Mavis?'

'Wouldn't it be better if I lift my bottom up a bit? Like this?'

I studied the new presentation and not only had to agree that the curves were even more enticing but also felt bound to express my appreciation of her willingness to submit wholeheartedly.

'That is indeed an improvement, Mavis. I compliment you.'

'Thank you, madam.'

We turned our heads in unison at that point, so that our eyes met, and the pleasure in her shy smile was as clear as day. I smiled back at her, then addressed myself to the task in hand.

WHACK! A bright red oval mark sprang up on the upper part of her left buttock. Both mounds shivered and shook before the biting pain made her clamp them together and grind her front into the table. Her pent-up breath whistled through her teeth and she moaned.

Inspiration struck. 'Please count out each stroke. Aloud.'

'Yes, madam. One.' Her bottom softened, rose and stilled.

I tapped the area immediately beneath the red mark.
WHACK!

'Owww! Sorry, madam. Two. Ohhh, that smarts.'

Four more times my trusty hairbrush rose and fell. Four times her wails of pain echoed shrilly in the silence and by the time the sixth stroke had bitten into the base of her buttock, she was sobbing quietly and it took some time for her to present her bottom properly. I crossed round to her other side, my eyes glued to her writhing two-coloured rump, and then attended to the other cheek.

With the dozen finally delivered, I gave her another pause to collect herself before another series of small smacks. This time I made her slide back to rest her feet on the floor, with her knees tucked in under the table. Her bottom was now considerably more open and more tightly curved, although to my surprise, it wobbled even more noticeably than previously.

Once again, I administered a harder dozen, after which she was moaning and gasping but no longer crying. Her courage and sensuality had overtaken the pain.

By then I was tired, so I resumed my seat, once again enjoying the sensation of my bare bottom settling on the hard, cool seat. Mavis was very flushed and breathing heavily but not seriously distressed. I gathered myself for the final stage, glancing across to Bertha. The yearning on her face made the prospect of dealing with her even more tempting than usual!

My voice broke the silence.

'Now move to the side of the table, facing me, Mavis. Then lie back and lift up your legs until your knees are pressed into your bosoms. Bertha, perhaps you had better help her.'

She turned, rested her behind against the table – wincing as she did so – then lay down. Bertha grasped both of her friend's ankles and raised them, standing well to the side to give me an uninterrupted view of the changing aspects of the buttocks and the slow widening of the deep cleft until her bottom-hole popped into view. Finally, Mavis wrapped her arms around her knees and hugged them to her bosoms.

I rose and walked slowly over to her, tapping the brush against my right thigh, and despite the attractions of the sight before me the sharpness of the sting at each tap caused me to admire and respect Mavis's courage and obedience even more. I came to a halt right behind her and studied the target with a beating heart. Quite clearly, this is by far the most humiliating posture any woman can be forced to assume for a spanking. One's buttocks feel so tightly stretched that there is not even the small comfort of yielding fleshiness to give some protection but, most of all, there is the awful knowledge that both delicate orifices are on full display. The feeling of utter vulnerability is made even worse as one can watch the instrument of correction hovering menacingly over the threatened parts.

She presented the most delicious of targets. Her straining buttocks were red, the wide division white, the wrinkled surround of her anus brown and its centre pink. Her cunny stared up at me between her bulging thighs, the pink inside of her slit in gleaming contrast to the hairiness of her fat lips. I ran the tip of the brush along the full length of her fork, from bottom-hole to mound of Venus. She groaned in fear and pleasure.

I then set about her, flicking at the strip of white flesh and then tapping at her anus very gently, having no wish to harm her. She moaned at the strangeness of it. I smacked her tight, pointed cheeks and the fleshiness by her hipbones. At last, she crossed the divide. Her cries changed; her hips bucked and jerked unrhythmically; the lips of her cunny opened wider, exposing the gleaming pinkness within; little pearls of love-juice shone on the brown hairs of her bush. As her climax began to overwhelm her, I tossed the faithful hairbrush aside and glued my mouth to her twitching anus.

As the echo of her shrieks died away, Bertha and I helped her to lie at full length and set about the happy task of easing her pain.

We applied cold wet cloths and then fetched some soothing lotion, which we applied with genuine tenderness. These were followed by lips and tongues and, after a half-hour or so, she was well on the way to full recovery. Bertha used the brush on her head and then passed it to me to untangle the hairs on her cunny. We both rouged her lips and cheeks and finally stood back and admired our handiwork. The good woman was quite transformed and even prettier than she was in her normal, unadorned state. Without any bidding from me, she paraded her naked form up and down the kitchen, wiggling her red posterior like a saucy maiden and making Bertha and I clap and laugh with pleasure.

It was time for Bertha's bottom to be reddened. I decided to follow the same procedure, with the same implement, and so the pleasure of the morning's activities was doubled. Her smaller buttocks were no less charming and quivered deliciously. Her smaller, pinker bottom-hole looked even sweeter peeping out at me between her splayed and very red cheeks for the last few smacks, and her climax at the end was equally violent.

She needed far less soothing than Mavis and so I did not have too long to wait before I could lead them up to my bed and present my yearning openings to their hands and mouths.

In the ensuing weeks, we were kept busy. The house needed its annual cleaning, my kitchen garden needed a great deal of preparation and there was a significant amount of work on Redhand House to occupy my quieter hours. Nevertheless, we diverted ourselves with our accustomed sensual enthusiasm whenever the mood struck us. Although the weather was often wet and chill, I had no compunction in making either or both work naked so that I could sit quietly and enjoy watching the view!

Our lessons continued, albeit irregularly with one small difference. I bore in mind their request to be spanked on the bare bottom, so made them remove their drawers before we commenced, thus making the preparations speedier, if rather less entertaining. I also took heed of Mavis's comments after her spanking with the hairbrush, when she had told me that being made to count each stroke had made her concentrate far more effectively. 'You can't just lie there and let it all wash through you, madam,' she had said shyly. 'You really do have to keep your mind on your bottom and the spanking and when it's getting nice and sore, that's quite hard to do.'

I took full advantage of the opportunity to bring out my full array of implements and to use them as often as warranted, both in and out of the schoolroom. My hairbrush, one of Phillip's old leather slippers, my Scottish tawse, a French martinet and a constant procession of fresh rods, cut from the profusion of weeping birches which graced our lovely garden, all left their mark.

I was whipping Bertha with the martinet one morning when I added another refinement to the counting discipline. She was kneeling on the long footstool, her naked buttocks thrust high in the air so that the twelve strips of leather could kiss the sensitive cleft. I paused to examine the pattern of pink stripes and dots.

'I think another dozen will do you, Bertha,' I told the gasping girl. 'And you will count each one aloud. But I think that I want your bottom even tighter. Arch your back. Yes, that is a better presentation. Now your knees further apart. Excellent. Right, that is how I want you for each stroke. You may wiggle in between if you wish, although that will of course prolong your chastisement, but you will indicate your readiness to receive the next smack by posing properly. And, when you are ready, you will tell me so in a clear voice. Understand?'

'Yes, ma'am. Please give my bare bottom the first one now.'

THWICKKK!

'Ow! Owww! One, ma'am ... Please give my bare bottom the second stroke now, ma'am.'

THWICKKKKKK!!!

And so on. Her compliance pleased me and her own contribution to the occasion in the repeated use of one of my favourite phrases – 'bare bottom' – brought a happy smile to my face.

And so by the time I received another invitation to stay with Elizabeth, I had not only considerably advanced my knowledge of the art of corporal punishment but also had an even clearer idea of how to make The Academy, as I had decided to call it, more exciting for me and the pupils.

I arrived at her old house, its faded stonework somehow adding rather than detracting from the perfection of its proportions, and climbed a little stiffly down from the elegant little trap I had recently purchased to replace my clumsy old dog-cart. I alighted, smiled at the handsome young stablehand who was steadying Matilda, then walked briskly up the stone staircase to the open door and into the magnificent hall, relishing as always the perfection of the family portraits on the walls. As I did so, I remembered the state my poor bottom had been in when I had last descended the same flight. My first reaction was to dread the prospect of another such beating. My second was to hope for one!

Elizabeth's greeting when I was conducted to her drawing room sent any such thoughts fleeing from my mind. She rose hurriedly, strode towards me so that we met before I had crossed even half the distance between doorway and her chair, then flung her arms round me and kissed me passionately on the mouth, an unsisterly approach which warmed the cockles of my heart. I returned it in full, thrusting my tongue between her full lips and into her warm, wet mouth. In unison, our hands dropped down to the seats of our skirts and, gasping for breath, we drew our heads back to gaze at each other. I kneaded away at her derrière and her eyes closed.

'Oh, Annie, for some reason I have longed even more than usual for the touch of your hands on my flesh. Ohh, that *is* tantalising!'

I forced the tips of my fingers into the division between her cheeks, pressing her clothing hard against her anus so that she moaned softly. For the first time with her, I felt in complete command, and the blood sang through my veins in expectation of fresh delights with this forceful, aristocratic, beautiful and elegant woman.

I made her lead me upstairs and remove every stitch of clothing before undressing and bathing me, instructing her in great detail on how I best liked my bottom and cunny washed. She dried me and then laid me across her bare lap to powder my bottom like a babe in arms. While I was lying there, enjoying the touch of her hands, I planned how best to fill the hour or so at our disposal before luncheon. She had admitted that she was thirsting for my caresses and I had every intention of obliging her. However, my needs for her caresses took precedence over hers for mine, especially when she gently rubbed the soft powder into the cleft between my buttocks. My tightening throat made my voice sound strangely high.

'Right, Elizabeth, I feel sufficiently pampered. And thank you for your expert ministrations.'

'It has been a pleasure, Annie,' she replied softly.

'I am delighted to hear it,' I continued, wriggling gently on the delicious fulcrum of her soft thighs, 'because your touch has excited me. You will continue to caress me – under my directions – until I have spent at least twice.' I paused for a moment, then settled firmly on her lap, straightening my limbs until I had adopted a perfect spanking pose. 'But first you will smack my bare bottom until it is a nice shade of pink.'

Her left hand pressed down on my loins and her right slapped down across the centre of my arched derrière, setting the cheeks deliciously a-wobble. The warmth fanned the flames of desire and my gasps had nothing to do with the slight pain her slaps caused me. All was pleasure. I had almost forgotten how delicious a sensual spanking could be. Every element, from the lovely sound of flesh on flesh to the feel of her round thighs supporting me – even more enticing when they were also naked – had my cunny weeping with joy. Her expertise made any instruction from me superfluous and I lay at ease, sighing and moaning as the waves spread slowly through me.

Eventually she stopped and the pink mists which had clouded my mind faded away. I concentrated on my buttocks. They were throbbing quite satisfactorily but I still felt the need for more.

'That was exactly what I desired, Elizabeth. My bottom is lovely and warm, with just the right degree of smart. It is, I should imagine, beyond pink, is it not? A distinct red?'

Her hand smoothed over the upthrust mounds. 'Not really red, Annie,' she replied, after due consideration. 'More a salmon pink.'

I bent my elbows and drew my feet inward, thus projecting the parts under discussion even further. 'Let me see,' I pondered aloud. 'I think that a further dozen should set me up nicely. Yes, six on each side, low down. On the sitting portions. But before you start, you will pull the cheeks apart and examine my anus. I like having it looked at.'

She obeyed instantly and my excitement stilled my breathing. Perhaps this part of me is especially sensitive, for I do not share the usual discomfiture in having it exposed and scrutinised – as long as the action is being carried out by a lover, of course. The feeling of fingers pressing into the inrolling of the twin mounds and the slow opening of the cleft until cool air wafts into the inner recesses always thrills me.

When I was forced to exhale, Elizabeth took my gusting sigh as a signal that I was ready to receive the final dozen, and before I could anticipate the burning pain, my ears rang to the sound of her stiff palm landing right on the base of my left buttock. I squealed and jerked at the smart but managed to keep my bottom properly posed for the second spank, which followed a minute later – allowing me to enjoy the bite, absorb it, feel it fade and prepare myself for the next.

By the time the last one sank into my ample flesh, I had indeed enjoyed a sharp little climax. I struggled to my feet, rubbed away at my smarting rear, kissed her with real passion and then ordered her to lead me to my bedroom, where she gave me my second climax with her customary expertise.

I then repaid her, both in kind and in full, before we dressed and went down for luncheon. As we sat in the small family dining room, I felt more at ease in her company than I ever had before. Up until then, I had always felt rather in awe of her, but the events of the morning had shown that we were now equal in her eyes. I was therefore able to take her even further into my confidence and, to my secret pleasure, she rewarded me by confiding in me.

Over luncheon, The Academy was the main topic of discussion and I elaborated on my concern that I was insufficiently learned to do justice to the pupils.

Elizabeth suddenly held up a hand and silenced me in mid-speech. 'Annie, I have a solution. My old governess, Miss Parfitt, is coming to stay here for two weeks. She is widely read and an excellent instructor. I am sure that she would be happy to help.'

My forkful of roast mutton halted halfway to my lips and I stared at her. Realising that I was looking faintly ridiculous, I moved the food to my mouth and chewed away, my mind racing. I swallowed and at last could speak. 'Oh, Elizabeth! What a kind thought. But surely she will be expecting to enjoy a quiet holiday and will not wish to exercise herself?'

'Oh pish!' she retorted. 'There is a huge difference between trying to drum multiplication tables into the reluctant brain of a seven year old and imparting one's knowledge to an intelligent and willing adult. No, I am sure that she will enjoy educating you.'

'But it will mean extending my stay, Elizabeth. I hate to impose unduly on your hospitality.'

'Again, pish!' she said, laughing. 'Apart from the indisputable fact that I enjoy your company, Annie, we have some unfinished bedroom business!' There was a steely glint in her eyes and I blushed. Then I addressed myself to my plate and we finished our repast in companionable silence.

The conversation resumed in the drawing room, where we treated ourselves to a cup of tea, and I soon realised that I needed more clothes than I had with me. Elizabeth kindly offered to send one of her stablehands to my home to collect whatever I needed, including she added, some plain skirts, blouses and undergarments. 'I think Miss Parfitt would appreciate it if you appeared demurely dressed, as befits a serious pupil.'

I soon penned my note to my servants, then we changed into our riding habits and set off to the stables, where my dear Matilda awaited me, already saddled. Both Elizabeth and I were accomplished horsewomen and we enjoyed an exhilarating ride through her magnificent park, ending with a furious race back to the house. I was thrilled to win handsomely, especially as I accomplished this notable feat by setting Matilda to jump over a fallen tree, thus gaining several yards. I can still recall the glow of triumph as we sailed through the air, with my balance perfect throughout.

As I reined to a halt, panting and laughing, Elizabeth rode up alongside and we trotted back to the stables. I sensed her eyes on me and a quick glance confirmed my suspicions. At first, I wondered if my dashing jump had aroused a surge of jealousy in her, for I did not imagine that many of her friends would have been able to outride her so easily, but then I dismissed the thought as unworthy of her. Correctly so, because as she regained her breath, she asked me to give her some lessons!

I agreed enthusiastically and, feeling that our horses had gained a second wind, suggested that we retraced our steps and used the lower parts of the same tree. An hour later, I handed Matilda to a waiting lad and we walked arm in arm back to the house, carrying our veiled hats and breathing in the clean air.

Two days after that, soon after a light breakfast, I was making my way nervously to the old schoolroom. Miss Parfitt had arrived the previous day and had welcomed my enthusiasm for scholarship. She was a pleasant woman, if a trifle severe, some 50 years old and with a quiet but authoritative manner, which had even subdued Elizabeth – rather to my amusement. However, as I ascended the narrow staircase, my heart was beating rapidly. I was not in any fear – it was more that I sensed that she would be an exacting task mistress and I rather doubted my adequacy.

After a general discussion on the subjects most relevant, we settled on Latin, French, history, geography, literature and mathematics, with the intention of giving me a sufficient grounding in each to enable me to further my knowledge on my own.

Miss Parfitt was patience personified and by the end of our first morning, I was captivated by her. She had a dry humour and was able to bring subjects to life by describing aspects which most pedagogues would have considered superfluous. For example, in addition to explaining the role of the senate in ancient Rome, she could describe the type of man who would have been a typical member, and make comparisons with our own parliament. Like a flower opening up to a long-awaited shower of rain, I buried myself in my work, to the extent that I fear I was in danger of becoming a bore at meal times, when I regaled my hostess with the extent of my wisdom. Had Elizabeth not taken me up to my room after the second spoiled dinner and spanked my bare bottom quite soundly with my own slipper, I feel that our friendship would have been in jeopardy!

Unfortunately, I must have relaxed too much! The following morning saw me far less attentive and unable to do justice to the short essay Miss Parfitt had set me. She read it quickly and looked up at me. I did not notice her stern expression.

'This so-called essay, Annie, is disappointing to say the least,' she announced in her usual low and steady tone.

Seeing no cause for alarm, I defended it, whereupon she dissected my efforts ruthlessly. 'Furthermore,' she continued, 'I believe I asked you to outline *Wellington*'s accomplishments, not those of the Duke of Marlborough!'

'Oh,' I responded feebly.

'Annie, I did say to you that I would treat you exactly as I would any other pupil and, if I remember correctly, you concurred. Come here!'

I stared at her, mouth agape. I was speechless. There was an ominous scraping as she pushed her chair away from her desk. She was going to spank me! I began to protest, saying that I was 22 years old and therefore it was only appropriate to chide rather than chastise me. Her steely blue eyes held my rapidly blinking gaze and she pointed at her lap.

Gentle reader, you may well be puzzled that I, Annie Milford, proud possessor of a bottom which was known widely in both West Sussex and south-west London as one which was not only very spankable but also one which loved being spanked, should not have prostrated myself willingly across her thighs. The reason is simple. Every spanking I had received until then had contained an element of sensuality. Even on the rare occasions when my husband had been given cause to correct me for some failing in my wifely duties, I had known, as I gritted my teeth to contain my cries of pain, that he loved my derrière and would, sooner or later, caress me. Miss Parfitt, by contrast, showed no sign of any emotion other than anger. My mind dwelt only on the shame and pain, knowing that there would be no pleasure.

Needless to say, my protest availed me naught and I stumbled to her side and lowered myself clumsily into the time-honoured position.

'Lift your hips.'

I obeyed instantly and held them raised while she whisked up my skirt and petticoat, leaving just my drawers and shift to protect me. Suddenly I hoped fervently that she would leave those in place and lowered my body until it was resting on her lap once more. But this was to no effect. I felt her nimble fingers undo the ribbons and my drawers were firmly pulled down to my knees. Again surprisingly, I dreaded the prospect of having my shift raised.

'Please, Miss Parfitt, do not bare me entirely. This is already utterly shaming. I am not a child with little sense of modesty and my chemise is thin – it will offer but slight protection.'

She slapped my thigh hard. It stung. I squealed.

'You have behaved like a child and will be treated as one. Now lift up again.' I could not help emitting a little sob as I obeyed, and in the twinkling of an eye my plump, womanly bottom was laid bare before her. I settled back down, staring at the rough wooden floor while tears of pure shame and misery trickled down my cheeks. I closed my eyes and waited, my skin crawling in expectation.

Those expectations were met. In full! She slashed her right hand down across both cheeks, making me cry out with pain, and immediately continued in the same vein, covering the entire surface with ringing spanks. In no time I was sobbing in earnest and the relief when she stopped was genuine. Alas, it was but a temporary cessation in hostilities.

'Stop making such a fuss, girl. And keep your legs still.'

'I am sorry, Miss Parfitt.'

The small interval in my punishment was enough to enable me to regain some composure. I bent my elbows a trifle, brought my feet a little closer, then parted them sufficiently to give me more stability. This action naturally raised my bottom to her, an unconscious but unmistakable gesture of willing submission.

'That is much better, Annie. Hold yourself like that as well as you can.' That said, she continued, with markedly longer intervals between each blow, although her pace was significantly faster than that I used on my servants and my buttocks had barely a chance to still themselves from the effects of one spank before the next set them into rippling motion once again.

I bore the punishment with as much fortitude as I could muster, but she spanked so hard that my tears were soon in full spate again and I could hear my small voice pleading for an ending to the torment. At last she desisted, and whereas in normal circumstances I would have lain across the punishing lap to savour the period of recuperation in pleasing intimacy with my chastiser, on that occasion I could not wait to struggle to my feet and cover myself. She did not permit this, however. Instead I was made to stand in the nearest corner with my red, bare bottom on display so that I could contemplate both my shortcomings and the consequences thereof. With little to distract me, I contemplated to good effect!

From that moment, hardly a day passed without a session across her lap. I was beginning to think that I had misjudged her and that she did have something of a penchant for my hindquarters, but I was disabused of this notion when she showed such congratulatory delight on the occasions I did not earn a spanking. I realised that she took no pleasure in punishment but simply shared my feeling that there was no better method of educating a spirited young person.

It became the norm for her to mark my work and if I failed to reach the required standards, I was given six hard smacks per mistake. To receive these, I was made to rest the upper part of my body on the top of my desk, bare my own bottom and thrust it out, so that the two mounds were nicely separated. Then I was given the six spanks and had to give the correct answer. If I erred again, I was smacked again.

There was still no enjoyment in my punishments. I had overcome my initial reservations about exposing myself to her and completely accepted the pain and embarrassment as the most effective possible way of improving my abilities – and dedication. I also very much appreciated her attitude. As soon as a punishment was over, it was not referred to again. When my sore bottom was covered up and restored to its seat, the lesson continued in the same mature atmosphere and our shared enthusiasm ensured that my education proceeded at great pace.

It was not all work, however. Elizabeth and I grew ever closer and we were able to pass many a happy hour walking or riding in her extensive estate, discussing all manner of topics. An unexpected benefit of my lessons was that I found myself far more capable of matching her intellect and this meeting of minds complemented what had always been a unity of sensuality. Our friendship blossomed.

We also spent the nights together, sleeping without night attire, and I loved lying half awake as the dawn light stole through the gaps in the curtains, listening to her soft breathing before waking her by gently stroking whichever part of her body came most easily to hand. Not surprisingly, my first choice was always her deliciously smooth bottom! (Although it is fair to say that her plump bosom pleased me nearly as well.)

I think that we both gained equally from that fortnight together. Elizabeth's tastes had previously leant towards the active role, although she had always submitted quite willingly during meetings of The Society. During this period, however, we both agreed that it would not be a good idea for me to present Miss Parfitt with a bottom showing signs of previous chastisement, so any spankings which I received had to be mild, almost token ones. Not that I found these anything but pleasing. To lie across Elizabeth's broad thighs, with her hand gently slapping my naked curves, always induced the most pleasurable sensations, even if the sharp seasoning of pain was absent. And the vigorous kneading to which my buttocks were always subjected sent the blood coursing through my veins nearly as effectively as a sound chastisement.

So, if Elizabeth was denied the pleasure of spanking me as soundly as she wished, I did my utmost to find different ways to please her.

One fine afternoon, for example, we had ridden far and fast and had arrived breathless at a large copse on the boundary of her estate. Confident that we were unobserved, we tethered the horses, wandered into the shade of the trees, tossed our veiled bonnets aside and lay down under a large beech tree.

'Oh, Annie, that was quite exhilarating. I am aching

all over – and I am sure that my poor derrière is black and blue.'

I rolled over on to my stomach and peered down into her flushed face. I kissed her gently and tantalisingly. Then I turned her head to one side and moved her raven-black tresses aside. 'Oh, Elizabeth, your poor, delicate, little bottom,' I whispered, licking the inside of her ear to ensure that I had her full attention. 'I know just how to look after it. I shall turn you over, arrange your clothing so that only your bottom is bare and then –' I pushed my tongue back into her ear and placed a hand on her plump bosom '– spank you until it is *really* black and blue!'

Ignoring her squeals of protest, I turned her over and loosened her skirts until I was able to ease them down to mid-thigh. I then walked around her, describing the delectably indecent picture before me, followed by a detailed account of what I was about to do to her. Half an hour later, her bottom was bright red. I then turned her over, pressed her knees against her breasts and, before I set to work on her openly displayed charms, again walked around treating her to a lurid description of the sight before me. By the time the sounds of her climax had faded I was seething with lust, and having stripped, made her lie flat on her back, then stood astride her head, letting her feast her eyes on a worm's eye view of my charms, before lowering my bottom on to her mouth.

Eventually sated, we walked around the wood in nothing but stockings and boots, at one with nature and at peace with ourselves. My memories of that afternoon are clear, not only because it was a pleasing experience on its own account, but also for the aftermath. Before our naked walk, I had told Elizabeth that I had to see Miss Parfitt at four o'clock, but she had persuaded me that the afternoon was yet young and that there was no cause for unseemly rush. With only the slightest qualm,

I had fallen in with her desires, had shared her enjoyment of our surroundings and had even agreed to a further loving before we dressed and rode back home.

Needless to say, we were late, and were both summoned to Miss Parfitt's room as soon as we had bathed and changed. We arrived at her door at the same time and exchanged guilty glances. I know that I felt very remorseful at having neglected my studies, whereas I think that it was our lack of manners which grieved Elizabeth the most. Miss Parfitt did not believe in wasting time on repetitive lectures. We were asked to explain ourselves and as soon as it became obvious that we had no good excuse, she pronounced sentence.

'You both disappoint me,' she announced grimly. 'You, Lady Elizabeth, know full well that Annie's studies are of paramount importance to us both. And yet you actively encouraged her to play truant.' She turned to me. 'You, Annie, should have stuck to your guns. If you wish to instruct others, your own character must be of the strongest. I shall whip you both. Tomorrow morning, so that you have time to contemplate both your lack of concentration and the painful effects. And before you report to the schoolroom, you will both cut a suitable birch rod. Until nine o'clock, then.'

Neither of us slept well that night and were awake well before dawn, snuggling up tight in our nervousness. Strangely, however, as the sun rose, my determination to benefit from the forthcoming whipping rose as well. I knew that I had been most remiss and that I deserved every stroke and I felt a growing exultation at the challenge ahead. From the many spankings I had already received, I knew that there would be no pleasure, but did sense that I would achieve great satisfaction from displaying proper fortitude. My repentance would be true.

After we had dressed and swallowed a cup or two of cocoa, we armed ourselves with sharp knives and found a suitable weeping birch tree. We soon agreed that Elizabeth's broader buttocks merited a longer, less bushy rod than would suit my pert curves, and then at nine we knocked on the schoolroom door, our trembling hands clasping our rods.

True to form, Miss Parfitt wasted little time on preliminaries and almost before I had drawn breath, I was watching Elizabeth hand over her rod, walk to the main desk, raise her skirts and lean forward, resting on her elbows with her parted knees bent inward. Suddenly my fascination with the sight before me quite overcame my own fear and I leaned forward to obtain the best possible view. Her silk drawers were so tightly wrapped around her thrust-out rear that the division between the twin mounds was clearly visible and I could see how well her bottom was presented. Then Miss Parfitt leaned over her victim, untied the waistband, carefully drew them down, then surprised me by refastening them just two inches below the buttocks. Like that, they hung neatly down and covered most of her thighs. Elizabeth looked quite lovely. Her clothes framed her bare bottom most elegantly and the position she had adopted was both graceful and effective, in that her cheeks were soft and relaxed yet projected perfectly. She was a picture of compliant femininity.

Miss Parfitt patted each cheek and, apparently satisfied with the degree of quiver she produced, picked up the rod, laid it across the full width of pale, gleaming flesh and let fly.

I had watched a number of birchings, but seldom with such avid attention. Miss Parfitt wielded the rod with consummate grace, raising it well above her head before bringing it whistling down to sink into the soft, spread flesh of the Lady Elizabeth's naked bottom. At each stroke, her buttocks quivered and a trace of bright red weals appeared almost instantly on her fine skin. Every time, as the twigs fell away, she squealed and wiggled her hips, adding to the fleshly agitations. The first six rendered the target a dramatic pink and the second reddened it all over. She was crying softly and in obvious pain, but her hands still gripped the edges of the desk, and apart from the jerks and wiggles she kept quite still.

After that first dozen, Miss Parfitt paused and leaned over the suffering derrière to assess the damage. I had already noted that the right buttock had suffered more than its sister, especially from the sharp tips, which had left crimson dots all over the flank. This was rectified by a lighter assault on the left side to even things up.

She ended the whipping with a further dozen, beginning on the outer parts of Elizabeth's left buttock and taking a small inward step after each stroke, so that the whole surface was evenly treated. By this time, my friend's courage had been stretched almost to its limit. She was sobbing loudly and had slumped forward, not caring that her new position caused her suffering posterior to project itself rather lewdly. And when Miss Parfitt announced that her whipping was done, she straightened up painfully, then amazed me by falling to her knees and kissing the punishing hand, sobbing out her apologies and thanks for her sound and well-earned correction, tears still pouring down her flushed cheeks.

My turn was nigh! With a wildly beating heart I watched my friend's clumsy rearrangement of her clothing and then, when she had regained her composure and was standing beside me, I approached Miss Parfitt to hand her my rod. I curtsied and spoke my mind. 'Miss Parfitt, I formally apologise for my thoughtlessness and for the inevitable inconvenience I caused. The blame lies more with me than with Lady Elizabeth, so please whip me even harder than you did her. I deserve it.'

Miss Parfitt smiled at me, transforming her expression. I felt a rush of warm affection for this elegant, grey-haired lady. Offering her my intimate and sensitive flesh for her to assail as vigorously as she wished seemed so appropriate a penance for my misbehaviour.

I raised my skirts and laid the front of my body on the top of the desk, then parted my feet and folded my knees inward, feeling the thin material of my drawers tighten across my out-thrust buttocks. I knew that the supple twigs would sting even more on tautened flesh: I was also fully aware that they would bite into the softness of my widened cleft and add noticeably to my torment. All well and good.

In silence, Miss Parfitt untied my drawers, tugged them down and refastened them just below my jutting bottom. I felt her hand pat each cheek. The rod rested against my bare skin, cool and prickly. I held my breath and closed my eyes. A faint whistle. Then that familiar liquid, stinging swathe of fire across the centre. My pent-up breath whistled through my clenched teeth and I braced myself, more determined than ever to behave in an exemplary manner throughout my well-merited whipping.

It was certainly as painful as any I had endured, and this time there was no underlying excitement to alleviate the burning – only my contrition. I gripped the desk and pressed my feet into the floor with all my strength as the pain washed through me. The fact that I cried out was unimportant – a girl is entitled to express her femininity when she is being whipped. Then I heard Miss Parfitt telling me that it was over and I only just managed to prevent myself falling down, so weakened were my limbs.

Two very chastened women spent the morning comforting each other!

Three days later, very much wiser and with a new perspective on the complex subject of corporal punishment, I guided Matilda homewards, delicious memories of the previous night's energetic activities in Elizabeth's capacious bed flitting through my mind. I stopped as soon as I could, found the two dildoes which had played such a prominent part, and holding the reins lightly in one hand, caressed them with the other, pressing them to my lips, sure that I could sense the lingering traces of her scents on the polished wood. Every detail of her ravishment came back. I had tied her wrists to the rails at the head of the bed, fastened silken cords to her knees and pulled them upwards and apart, then tied them in turn, so that all her secret parts were on view. I had blindfolded her, anointed her straining anus and pushed the smaller of the two dildoes steadily and remorselessly up her fundament. Once her shrieks of outrage had died away, I had diddled her clitty, all the while moving the wooden pego in and out of her bottom, and had finally thrust the larger one into the glistening pink depths of her love-nest. It was debatable whether my climaxes were noisier than hers when she eventually treated me in the same way, or vice versa!

Three

I arrived home to a happy welcome and found a letter from the lawyers informing me that I could take possession of Redhand House. Thrilled at this unexpected news, I wrote to Phillip's cousin, Arabella, and made all the necessary arrangements for another long absence, alleviating my devoted servants' distress by promising that they could both come to London as soon as it was practical. At last, I could make my escape.

With mounting excitement, I said farewell to a tearful Bertha, then Mavis drove me the several miles to Petworth Station, where we waited in uncomfortable silence for the arrival of the train.

Arabella, who still lived in her great aunt's house in Richmond, only a half-mile from my new home, greeted me with great warmth, and it was not long before we were talking and laughing like a pair of schoolchildren. By happy coincidence, her aunt was visiting other members of the family, so we could behave with our normal irresponsibility. With a simple supper consumed and the servants dismissed, we could retire in privacy, snuggle into bed and talk to our hearts' content, with Arabella understandably as excited about the idea of my academy as anyone. I was too weary after my journey for energetic loving, so we settled for a delightful session in the *soixante-neuf* position and gamahuched each other until we spent. Then we slept happily intertwined until well after sun-up.

By mid-morning, having dressed informally and

breakfasted hastily, we climbed into Arabella's carriage and set off for Redhand House, my excitement at revisiting my first major possession almost too much to bear. Cook and the maids greeted me effusively and I suggested that they congregated in the kitchen, while I found the key to the cellar and took out half a dozen bottles of hock, which we placed in a tub of ice. While we waited for them to cool, I outlined my plans for the house, assuring them not only that their employment would continue if they so wished, but also that they would not lack the kind of sensual diversions so dear to all our hearts!

'Plenty of spanking, I hope, Mrs Milford?' asked Elspeth, as impudent and as lovable as ever.

'Of course, my dear. In fact, probably even more. And I see no reason why I should not start as I intend to continue. Bring your cheeky little bottom here, bare it, bend over and grasp your ankles!'

'Oh thank you, madam,' she replied, completely unabashed. She trotted up, whisked her skirts up, took down her drawers and bent right over to present a drum-tight and open little bottom – one which I smacked most heartily to the delight of one and all.

With my hand still glowing and with Elspeth's red posterior still thrust nakedly in the air, I told Cook to uncork the wine and give all but Elspeth a glass. Ignoring her muffled protests, I raised mine and bade them to toast the future success of The Academy, but rather than drain it in one, I drank only half and then dashed the remainder straight into the depths of the naked, yawning bottom to my left. The owner squawked at the icy douche but managed to stay in position. I then knelt behind and licked every drop of wine from her flesh, to a rousing ovation from the others and shrill squeaks of pleasure from my victim.

On that happy note, Arabella and I went methodically around the house, making careful notes of all the alterations and additions I required. I had already decided that the basement would remain essentially untouched. What had been the theatre for Aunt Grace's entertainments would provide a perfect arena for public punishments and the other small rooms would still serve their original purpose – facilities for private and demanding punishment sessions.

The ground floor would also stay the same and I would keep Aunt Grace's apartments on the first floor, with Uncle George's bedroom and dressing room converted into the main guest rooms. The library needed no more than additional furniture to transform it into a classroom, with the conservatory and the small dining room as others.

The maids would still be quartered in the attic, which left the second floor the only one needing serious rearrangement. We decided that it should be possible to provide eight small but adequate bedrooms and three bathrooms, depending on the builder's advice.

We met him the following day and he turned out to be a respectable and helpful man. He raised no silly objections to my plans and suggested a number of practical improvements, the most notable of which was a complete revision of the kitchen to incorporate a far larger range. That, he explained, would be capable of providing all the hot water such an establishment would need. Even better, that water could be sent through pipes into the bathrooms and straight into each bath. I clapped my hands with joy at the delicious prospect of being able to bathe so easily, and again when he said that the water could also be sent to iron 'radiators' in all the rooms on the ground floors, keeping them beautifully warm.

'You will still need fires on the really cold days, Mrs Milford, but you see hot air rises, and so the upper floors will be warmed up as well.'

I thought for a moment. 'It does sound most tempting,

Mr Percival, but I cannot help but think that the cost will be quite horrendous.'

'It would not be cheap, I grant you, madam. But probably not as dear as you think. Now let me see –' He gazed out of the window, stroking his rather straggly whiskers '– I did similar work for Mr and Mrs Anderson in Twickenham. Not long ago. Taking everything into account, the bill was in the region of four hundred guineas.'

I kept my expression as impassive as I could. 'That seems quite reasonable, Mr Percival.' I also stared out of the window in deep contemplation. On the one hand, I fully intended to ensure that the girls would be kept warm by frequent applications of some suitable implement to their rumps. On the other, it would do no harm to offer comfort – and a warm house was far more conducive to nudity than a cold one. 'Yes, I agree. Include the work on your schedule and send me an estimate of your charges as soon as possible. Once I have agreed it, when can you start?'

'Very soon, Mrs Milford. Fortunately, we have just completed a major work – much sooner than planned – and have several weeks before the next.'

'Excellent. I look forward to receiving your letter.'

'You shall have it on the morrow, madam. And my thanks for your custom.'

I dismissed him, rejoined Arabella, and we repaired to the garden, where our first port of call was the statue of the naked goddess which had been so instrumental in awakening my interest in the female form. She was showing signs of neglect, so we did not linger and returned to the kitchen where Cook had a pot of coffee awaiting us. I told her to get one of the maids to scrub my statue with soda to get rid of the green stains and, fully satisfied with the progress, we returned home.

That evening, after supper, Arabella sat alongside me on the sofa and admitted that she had noticed a great change in me. 'You have a new air of authority about you, Annie. A great confidence. What has caused it?'

I thought deeply, surprised. 'I think that it is probably many things: marriage; becoming a woman of property; The Academy in prospect; having to manage in Phillip's absences. Growing up. But please do not think that I have lost one iota of the love I have always felt for you!'

'I *was* thinking that, Annie. You have been here two days and have not even threatened to smack my bare bottom for me!'

Love, remorse, desire and passion swept through me like a tidal wave. 'Oh my darling Arabella, I am so sorry. So very sorry.' I clasped her soft little hand. 'I shall put you across my knee immediately and give you the most loving, lingering spanking ever. On your bare –' I leaned forward, kissed her and breathed the last word into her open mouth '– *bottom*! Then I will place myself in whatever pose you demand and you can do the same to me.'

With great joy, we indulged ourselves to the full in our favourite pastimes and continued to do so until I had agreed all the details of the reconstruction with the worthy Mr Percival and it was time to return home.

If I had set out on the journey back home in a confident frame of mind, I arrived with the future looking even more rosy. My chosen compartment was mercifully empty when I climbed into the rather stuffy interior, so that I had welcome solitude to linger over the many events of the past days. As you can imagine, I was not best pleased when two passengers joined me at the second halt, although my spirits lifted somewhat when I saw that they were both female. I studied them with mild interest.

The older of the two was a woman in her mid-30s, dressed plainly but with some quality. I instinctively eyed the seat of her skirt when she turned to place her folded cloak on the seat beside her and noted a pleasingly feminine breadth to it, but apart from that she made little impression. The younger one was considerably more interesting. With hair as dark as Elizabeth's, large eyes, a full and kissable mouth and the fairest of complexions, she was more than just pretty, with only a sulky and bored expression spoiling her attractiveness. Even so, I did not feel in the mood for light conversation and buried my nose in my Latin primer.

To my growing irritation, they started squabbling almost immediately, clearly continuing a long-running dispute. I did my utmost to block my ears to their shrewishness, succeeding reasonably well until the older woman's high-pitched voice cut through like a knife.

'... Jane, I am most tempted to give you a sound spanking!'

I could not stop myself lifting my eyes from a fascinating passage on the usage of the ablative absolute, and inevitably they met Jane's. She yawned, blatantly and rudely. My right palm tingled. Holding my gaze, she responded to the threat. 'My dear Aunt Maud, I have lost count of the number of times that you have threatened me thus and I doubt if you have the strength – or the will – to turn me up, especially as I am sure that the good lady opposite harbours no desire to witness an undignified brawl.'

She slumped back against the seat, yawned again and treated me to what she clearly imagined to be a conspiratorial smile, although it seemed to me more of a cocky leer. Gloating inwardly at this unexpected turn of events, I carefully marked my place, set the book down and turned my gaze towards Aunt Maud.

'Mrs . . . er?'

'Miss. Miss Brown.'

'How d'ye do, Miss Brown. My name, by the way, is Milford. Mrs Milford.' I looked at her closely and saw that despite her naturally troubled air, she had a nice, gentle and pretty countenance, and my sympathy for her grew. 'Far from taking your niece's part in this affair, you have my full support.' Her expression changed and she returned my smile with a sweet one of her own. I turned to the open-mouthed youngster. 'Jane, I have seldom heard such disagreeable tones and that is no way to treat your elders and betters, let alone a close relation. Far from preventing your aunt from awarding you a well-merited chastisement, I shall do everything in my considerable power to assist her.' I held up an imperious hand and stilled her protest. 'Now, as I see it, you have two choices. The first is to submit and lay yourself across your aunt's lap and the second is to continue in that rebellious vein, and resist. If you take that option, you will undoubtedly suffer additional hurt in the struggle and, on top of that, it is most likely that other passengers will hear the disturbance and investigate. In which case, I have no doubts that they will approve. *And* will wish to watch!'

I sat back and waited calmly for her response while she stared at me in horror, twisting her fingers in her lap and with her mouth still unattractively agape. 'You would not dare!' she stammered.

I leant forward and stared straight into her face, which reddened angrily. 'Are you entirely sure? Can you reasonably doubt that I shall not carry out my threats? Or that I shall not support your aunt to the hilt?'

She stamped her feet petulantly and then heaved a deep sigh. 'Very well, I shall submit. But under protest and because I have no wish to draw attention to my humiliation!' Glaring at me, she rose to her feet, tottered as the train swayed round a corner, steadied herself by resting a hand on the window, and turned to face her aunt. Her dress was fashionably full and loose at the back so that I could glean only a vague impression as to the shape of her posterior, although there seemed to be a promising swelling in that region. After a brief silence, she continued, her voice tight.

'I assume that you wish me to place myself across your knee?'

I could just see Miss Brown's face and noted that she was swallowing nervously, clearly concerned that somehow her devious and arrogant niece would get her revenge. She nodded and the girl sprawled inelegantly into the desired position. Her aunt gazed rather helplessly at the seat of Jane's skirt, then raised her right arm and brought it down with contemptible feebleness somewhere in the centre of the supine body, eliciting an annoyed 'Ow!' and a jerk of the hips. I felt my lips compress in my own annoyance but bided my time. Perhaps a dozen equally light smacks landed in the next minute, none of them making enough noise to be heard over the creaking of the carriage and the clattering of the wheels. At each one, Jane protested volubly, although even to an eye far less practised than mine, the so-called victim could hardly have felt them, especially through so many layers of clothing. I was none the less taken aback when Miss Brown called a halt, unable to credit that even so weak a woman could have considered that any form of punishment.

'Well, Jane, I hope that that has taught you a lesson. You may resume your seat now.'

The girl clambered to her feet, smiling triumphantly, and then sat down with a theatrical sigh. I cleared my throat and leant forward to address the flustered aunt.

'My dear Miss Brown,' I announced grimly, 'I am not without experience in the complex and challenging art of bringing arrogant young ladies to heel. Believe me, what you have just administered will do her no good at all ... Silence, Jane, I am talking to your aunt ... and, in fact, will only encourage her to maintain her deplorable behaviour.'

The poor woman flushed scarlet at the vehemence of my criticism. 'Oh dear, Mrs Milford, I thought that for once I had managed to exercise some authority over the impossible child, but clearly –'

'I am *not* a child!' Jane interrupted. 'I am eighteen years of age and –'

'Be silent, child!' I snapped at her. 'Your position is already parlous enough and I would earnestly advise you not to make things worse. I would not have the slightest hesitation in having a quiet word with the conductor at the next halt and explaining that you are in dire need of a sound spanking in public. Now sit still and hold your tongue.'

To my amazement – and secret joy – she stuck out the offending organ and deliberately held it between the thumb and forefinger of her right hand. Ignoring her, I turned back to her aunt.

'Miss Brown, you strike me as a gentle and refined woman and I fully sympathise with your distaste for confrontation. I fear, however, that unless Jane is brought to heel immediately, she will soon be uncontrollable. That situation will be tragic for all concerned, not least to herself. May I ask your indulgence and make a few suggestions?'

'Please do, Mrs Milford. I own that I was on the verge of giving up with her. She used to be the sweetest and most amenable of children but since her parents went to South Africa she has been quite impossible. I appreciate that the separation has not been easy for her and perhaps it is this which has made me too lenient.'

I smiled inwardly at the rather lame excuse but felt that it would be tactless to suggest that it was her mild and ineffectual character which was most to blame. 'I am sure that you are right, Miss Brown, but, as I have just stated, unless she is thoroughly chastised soon, you – and her parents – will have an unmanageable hoyden on your hands. And what chance would she then have of making a suitable match? Few men would be tempted, despite her beauty.'

I glanced across to the subject under discussion. She had let go of her tongue and was staring at me in horror. My implacable approach at last seemed to impress her, for she plucked up the courage to give voice.

'Er, Mrs Milford ... um, dearest aunt, I offer my most humble apologies for my behaviour. I agree that the chastisement I have just received was unduly light but I do assure you that it had the desired effect. I promise that I shall be a good girl from this moment on.'

We both stared at her and I could instantly sense that Miss Brown's resolve was beginning to waver. Mine was not. I freely confess that I was most reluctant to pass up the opportunity to watch her bottom being treated in the due and proper manner, but had I felt that her apology was in any way genuine I would certainly have proposed that she be given a second chance. There was, however, an unpleasant shiftiness in her attitude and a crafty gleam in her eyes. Before her aunt could intervene on her behalf, I continued as though she had never spoken.

'If you give her a proper spanking now, Miss Brown, and nip her rebellion in the bud, I am convinced that it will save you the trouble of introducing harsher measures at a later date.' I looked back at Jane for a second. She had turned quite pale. 'I can, for example, imagine that you would not find it easy to apply a birch rod to her. So, if you take my advice, madam, you will put the insolent little baggage across your lap again, raise her skirts, lower her drawers and spank her as a grown-up girl should be spanked by a close relative. On her *bare bottom*!'

Those two words never ceased to send a little thrill through me and there is not the least doubt that Jane found them as threatening as I had hoped. Her hands flew to her mouth and her widened eyes stared at me.

'I have never heard of such a thing!' she spluttered. 'Oh, Aunt Maud, please tell this awful woman to keep her counsel. I have apologised and promised to mend my ways. As far as I am concerned, that is the end of the matter.' She sat back, folded her arms under her plump little bosom and stared pointedly out of the window, her nose stuck up in the most impudent manner.

Miss Brown and I looked at each other. I raised an eyebrow eloquently and saw a new resolve in her. She squared her shoulders, set her mouth so that its usual soft weakness was transformed into a thin line of determination and then reached out to grasp her erring niece's wrist. She tugged hard so that Jane had little choice but to rise to her feet, and in an instant – perhaps too surprised to struggle – she was whirled round to her aunt's right side and flung over the waiting lap, squawking indignantly until the impact drove at least some of the breath from her lungs. By the time she had collected herself sufficiently to attempt to clamber back up, her skirts and petticoats were in tangled disarray about her waist and a fair portion of naked flesh protruded from the slit of her drawers, gleaming whitely in the subdued light and quivering softly with the combination of her wrigglings and the coach's swaying. The stillness lasted but a second, because as soon as Jane felt the fresh air on her intimate skin, she howled in outrage, reached back and pushed her clothing down, before redoubling her efforts to get free.

It was clearly time for me to intervene again. I swiftly moved to sit by the writhing girl's head, grasped a wrist in each hand and forced them up to her shoulder blades, pinning her down.

'Ow, that hurts, you horrid woman,' she panted. I pulled a trifle further upward and she cried out with the pain, but her struggles died away as she realised the futility of further resistance.

'There, Miss Brown,' I said calmly. 'Do not concern yourself with her kicking – she can do you no harm and her efforts will only tire her more rapidly. You should now be able to bare her bottom easily.'

And, to give her due credit, she did so with brisk determination, ignoring the strident protests. There was then a long pause. My view of the naked posterior was limited to the upward swelling of the twin buttocks from the small of Jane's back, and although I gazed long enough to gain a clear impression of her clear, white skin and to note that there was a pleasing breadth to the cheeks, I found my attention drawn to Miss Brown's nice face as she looked down on what I could fairly presume was the first mature female derrière she had studied. Certainly there was a distinct blush on her face, but as I watched her, the realisation that a pretty feminine bottom was pleasing to the eye caused a notable change in her expression. Her right hand fussed nervously about the deranged clothing above and below the expanse of quivering flesh and I sensed that she was fighting a natural desire to touch.

Once again, I felt that it was time that I came to her assistance.

'Are your arms paining you, Jane?'

'Yes, they are.' Her voice was sulky and resentful.

'Well, I have a solution. As far as I am concerned, the only pain you should experience is in your nether regions. I shall sit alongside your aunt so that you are lying across both laps. That will be a great deal more comfortable for you, but if you move your hands anywhere near the target area I shall hold you down again and cause you additional pain and discomfort by doing so. Do you understand?'

'Yes, Mrs Milford. Could we then proceed with this ordeal so that it is over before we arrive at Petworth?'

'All in good time, my girl. And I would advise you to be slightly less impertinent.'

With a theatrical sigh, she raised the upper half of her body and allowed me to slide underneath her until my hip was nicely pressing into her aunt's.

'A distinct improvement,' I continued, 'and I have a

much better view!' At the realisation that two women – one a complete stranger – were gazing avidly at her bare bottom, Jane groaned and clamped her cheeks together in shame, tightening the long cleft until it was no more than a thin line separating her dimpled mounds.

I was by now far too excited to let Miss Brown continue in her amateurish and ineffective way, so continued with her instruction.

'She does indeed have a good bottom, Miss Brown. Worthy of our very best attentions. I suggest that before you commence her chastisement, you remind her of her humiliating and vulnerable situation. Stroke her bottom ... all over. That is good. You see the feel of your hand on her naked skin may well be soothing in different circumstances but, in her present state, does no more than reinforce her exposure. Her skin looks delightfully soft and smooth. Is it?'

'Yes indeed,' she replied eagerly. 'Just like silk.'

'May I feel it?'

'Please do.'

'Oh yes, admirable, quite admirable.' It was indeed pleasing. 'And now it is a good idea to test the consistency of her flesh by pressing and squeezing all over ... like this. See how my fingers sink in? Especially here, where the curves are ripest.'

I watched Miss Brown's nice hands roam freely over her niece's bare buttocks and her growing confidence was obvious. At first they probed very tentatively but soon were kneading and patting away with gay abandon. I stole a quick glance to my left to see how Jane was reacting to this unaccustomed and obviously unwelcome treatment. Her head was turned away so my view was restricted to little more than a blushing cheek and a closed eye. It was enough to make it quite clear that she was very unhappy! I looked back at her bare bottom – in the circumstances a far prettier sight!

Miss Brown was beginning to pat the mounds more

vigorously now, so it was clear that she was ready to begin the punishment. I still felt that she needed guidance and therefore did not hesitate to proffer further advice.

'I am sure that you have noticed the welcome change in her demeanour, Miss Brown,' I said. 'This is partly due to her basic intelligence but one can never underestimate the effect of being forced to display one's naked posterior, especially when it is subjected to a prolonged handling. However, I do consider that it is time to proceed to the next stage and suggest that you begin her spanking now.'

She tore her eyes away from the tempting expanse of white flesh, beamed happily at me and raised her right arm. I, in the meantime, rested my left hand on Jane's shoulders, my right on her bare loins, and pressed firmly down, eliciting a little wail of dismay from the trembling maiden.

Miss Brown certainly showed an improvement in her approach. The ringing sound of her flattened palm striking the left cheek was easily audible over the background noises as we rattled downhill, and the imprint showed up clearly on Jane's beautifully fine skin. There was a brief pause while the effects were studied.

'Well done, Miss Brown!' I enthused. 'I am sure that she felt that one.'

'I did, I assure you!' Jane cried out plaintively from our left. We ignored her completely and continued our contemplation of her bottom.

The second smack sent the sister cheek into agitated convulsions, and then Aunt Maud settled into a reasonably brisk rhythm, while I watched with growing excitement. Now that I had managed to dominate them both, I could settle back and enjoy the sights and sounds.

The most unusual element was, of course, the background noise. There were the creaks and groans from the carriage; the rhythmic, steely clatter of the wheels; the frantic puffing of the engine as it raced along. Otherwise, the sound of flesh on flesh and the anguished cries of pain were both familiar and delightful. An additional pleasure was that the irregular jerks of the train transmitted themselves to the mounds of soft, naked flesh, so that even when they were not shuddering under the impact of a spank, they rippled and wobbled most charmingly.

And, with time to look at it properly, I noted what a very pretty bottom Jane had. My own palm began to itch and somehow my desires must have communicated themselves to my companion, for she suddenly slumped back, panting and clearly weary from the unaccustomed exertion. In unison we gazed down at the squirming posterior, and while she ruefully massaged her hand, I stroked the hot skin and then found myself quite unable to resist running the tips of my fingers down the length of her cleft, possibly the most deliciously soft and silky part of any girl's bottom. Her reaction to my caress caused me to hold my breath. Instead of shrinking at the invasion, she pushed her hips upward, so that my fingers probed into the division itself. My cunny tingled. Just as I was about to speak, Miss Brown's voice broke into my reverie.

'Well, I do declare that your ideas on punishment have succeeded beyond my wildest expectations, Mrs Milford,' she announced, slightly breathlessly. 'I cannot believe how well she took her spanking. Look how red her posterior is – it must be exceedingly painful!'

'I am sure that it is, Miss Brown,' I replied, deciding not to correct her ignorance on what a *really* sore bottom looked like. Hopefully she would find out for herself in the fullness of time. I turned to address the naughty girl, whose sobs were beginning to fade as the smarting receded. 'Jane, my dear, I heartily endorse your Aunt Maud's compliments. I assume that this is the first time that you have had your bare bottom smacked?'

'I-I think so, Mrs Milford,' she stammered. 'My mother may have administered some sort of similar punishment when I was still in the nursery, but I have no recollections of it.'

I stroked and squeezed her cheeks for a moment or two. Then Miss Brown finally proved that she had indeed sensed what I desired so strongly. 'My dear Mrs Milford,' she began, in a voice ringing with new authority, 'I am so grateful to you for your sound advice that I have entirely forgotten that Jane was unpardonably rude to you as well. I can see that she has a fat and resilient bottom and I think that justice will be done if you administer further punishment. I hope that you will not consider this an imposition.'

'By no means,' I replied, 'and thank you for your consideration. But it is her first proper spanking, so I feel that we should give her more time to recover. May I suggest that we make her kneel up on the opposite seat, facing the wall, and with her bottom on full display? Not only will that allow the cool air to speed her recuperation, but it will also serve to remind her of the consequences of her naughtiness.'

The worthy woman clapped her hands gleefully, and in a short while the erring girl was kneeling uncomfortably opposite us, her skirts tucked under her arms and her drawers drooping forlornly about her ankles. It was a most charming sight. The movements of the train were again transmitted to her relaxed buttocks, making them quiver spasmodically. I stole a glance at my companion and knew for certain that I had made another convert to the cause of fair punishment of the female bottom. Her eyes were gleaming, her lips slightly parted and her cheeks pink. The ensuing conversation confirmed my opinion.

'Clearly you have considerable experience of girls'

posteriors, Mrs Milford. To my inexpert eye, Jane seems very well endowed in that area. Am I correct?'

'You are indeed, Miss Brown,' I responded warmly. 'She has a truly delightful bottom. Her buttocks are full and round and the folds at the junctions of cheeks and thighs are especially attractive. As you remarked earlier, her skin is as smooth and soft as the finest silk.'

Jane was obviously disturbed by our comments, wriggling and shifting about on her knees, but too subdued to protest. I noticed after several more compliments that her pleasure at our praise overcame her natural modesty, for she projected her bottom noticeably, as though instinctively soliciting further favourable comment! Alas, she was to be disappointed. I could wait no longer.

'Well, I think you are ready now, Jane,' I announced with deceptive calm. 'Come here!'

At the reminder that she was due for another painful session, her buttocks tightened and she looked back at me over her shoulder.

'Please, Mrs Milford,' she pleaded. 'My bottom is still very sore. Could you not let me off? I sincerely apologise for my impertinence and swear that I have learned my lesson.'

I bestowed my warmest smile on her. 'Come here, my dear, and sit on my knee.' She obeyed, nervously, and when she had settled, I stroked her cheek. Some of the tension left her and I immediately surmised that one of her problems was that she had been starved of the physical gestures of affection which should be the right of every child. Including a warm, loving spanking when needed! My heart softened. Collecting my thoughts, I continued. 'Jane, the improvement in your behaviour has been, to say the least, dramatic. And most encouraging. But you must learn that sins have to be paid for in full. Even the sincerest of apologies can be false. I shall spank your pretty bottom, but with affection, not anger. It will not be too hard, I promise. It will smart and may bring tears. Let them flow, for there is no shame when those tears are the result of remorse and contrition.'

The sweet girl blushed very prettily and her voice was so soft and low that I could only just hear. 'Yes, I understand, Mrs Milford. Would you like me across your lap?'

'Yes, dear.' I turned to her aunt. 'Miss Brown, may I suggest that you move a trifle further down? You will help her by holding her ankles – and will also have an unusual and pleasing view of her bottom.'

Aunt Maud blushed in her turn and shuffled along the seat until she was pressed up against the side. Jane then placed her knees on the seat to my right, lowered her middle until it was resting in the centre of my lap, straightened her legs and then charmed me by pulling up her skirts and petticoats to expose her own bottom to me.

Once again, I helped myself to an unhurried inspection, both visual and manual. At last, and after a deep sigh of satisfaction, I patted her left buttock. 'Are you ready, Jane?'

'Yes, Mrs Milford,' she replied softly.

During the interval, much of the redness had faded and so the effect of my first spank was immediately evident. I did not strike her with any force, relying instead on a fast pace to renew the discoloration, revelling in the softness of both skin and flesh. As is my wont, I altered the rhythm periodically, delivering six harder smacks, with several seconds between each, to the lower portions. Before long, she was squealing prettily and bouncing her bottom around on my lap, but by pressing firmly down on her loins, I kept her under control and could administer each spank exactly on the selected spot.

Inevitably, she soon burst into real tears and, after a final dozen, I decided that she had had enough.

I helped her to her feet and she tottered wildly before the train lurched. Losing her balance, she sat down abruptly, leapt up with an anguished wail as she contacted the hard seat, tripped over her drawers and ended up sprawled inelegantly on my lap, her bare bottom thrust up in a wanton manner! Slapping it affectionately, I asked Miss Brown to help me and we guided her into a kneeling position, where we could both soothe her with the gentlest of strokes. Very soon, her snuffles and gasps died away, and we helped her arrange her clothing and replaced her bonnet. Then we sat back, all enjoying the greatly improved atmosphere.

For the remainder of the journey, I told them about my plans for The Academy, and before we reached Petworth, I had not only invited them to visit me but had also agreed to take Jane as a pupil.

As we came slowly into the station, I saw Mavis waiting patiently with Matilda and my new trap, so I bade them farewell and organised the unloading of my cases.

For the first part of the journey home, I listened to Mavis's gossip with half an ear, but as we trotted through the hamlet of Tillington and turned up the hill, I could hold back no longer.

'Mavis, my dear, you would not believe what happened in the train!' Then I made her wait until we arrived, so that I could tell Bertha as well!

The ensuing weeks saw me very happy and contented. Although we had our fair share of wet and windy days, the weather was generally warm and the sun appeared frequently enough to prevent any low spirits lasting for longer than a few hours. Mavis and Bertha were flatteringly pleased to have me in charge and the house rang with our laughter. There was more than enough to keep them busy and when I wearied of my studies, I occupied myself in the garden, my physical exertions successfully refreshing my brain.

Our lessons became of real value to me, while continuing to provide ample scope for my favourite form of exercise. As I have related, only Bertha had received any kind of learning – and that had been cursory to say the least – but neither she nor Mavis could be described as stupid. It became, therefore, increasingly rewarding for me when I introduced something approaching the curriculum I was envisaging for The Academy, and they responded eagerly to the challenge. My hesitant attempts to introduce them to the intellectual demands of Latin were admittedly a failure, but they loved history, geography and poetry. Perhaps the most eloquent testimony to the change was that many a lesson passed without either needing a smacked bottom. And none of us minded!

If I needed further diversion, there was always my beloved Matilda. As our land was insufficient to provide a proper ride, I had perforce to travel the surrounding lanes and fields, so had to be dressed suitably. On my return, however, I always removed my clothes and unsaddled her, then cantered easily around the paddock, loving the freedom of nudity and the feel of her back under my bare bottom.

There was the occasional social event. The only one I can remember with any fondness was a dinner party at some near neighbours where I was placed next to a most charming young naval officer who flirted outrageously – although never stepping beyond the bounds of decorum. That was one time when I missed Phillip most grievously and not even Bertha alongside me in bed could quite compensate. Well, not at first. She was an intuitive little creature and sensed that her fingers and tongue were failing to give me the usual satisfaction. She softly suggested my largest dildo and pushed it into my yearning love-nest, diddling it in and out with some skill. The sensation of being stretched and filled certainly eased my pangs of loneliness!

A more significant event occurred late one evening,

just as Bertha and I were about to have supper. Mavis had left for home at six o'clock – her normal time – and so we were both surprised when she reappeared suddenly. One look at her troubled face was enough to change surprise to concern, and we helped her off with her outer garments and bonnet, sat her down, poured her a glass of wine and begged her to unburden her soul. It transpired that she had found that her worthless husband had helped himself to her savings and had drunk them away in less than a week.

'You poor girl!' I exclaimed, with real sympathy. 'What an unprincipled swine he must be. You must stay here. My bed is comfortably large and will take the three of us easily. Oh, Mavis, we shall soon take your mind off your troubles.'

'Oh, madam, I would be grateful. Just for tonight, mind. I don't want to impose,' she replied softly.

'Stuff and nonsense, woman. For as long as you wish. And if you still want to be here when my husband is back in residence, then we can see whether we can extend Bertha's quarters to make room for you both. And, of course, I will compensate you for your loss. Can you remember how much it was?'

She looked up at me, aghast. 'You cannot do that, madam, it was no fault of yours. No, I refuse to accept any money.'

I looked over to Bertha. 'I call that base ingratitude. Do you not agree?'

The frown on her face indicated that she was not absolutely certain of my meaning, but decided that the most sensible course was to nod her head vigorously.

'There you are, Mavis,' I continued, glowering fiercely at the troubled woman. To my horror, she burst into tears.

'Oh, madam, I am really thankful, honest I am. I didn't mean to sound otherwise. But it's not fair that you should have to pay for his crime.'

I drew her to her feet and held her tightly, severely troubled that my little jest had caused such distress.

'Oh, my funny old Mavis,' I whispered. 'I was only teasing you. About being ungrateful, I mean. And his crime was not your fault either. So, please accept my gift. I cannot bear the thought of you having to start saving all over again. And, my dearest friend, your love and loyalty since I arrived here have been beyond praise. Would fifty guineas cover your losses?'

Her arms tightened around me and her body was again racked with sobs. 'That is far too much, madam.'

I moved my head back a trifle so that I could kiss her tear-wet mouth. 'Then fifty guineas it is, Mavis. That is my final word on the matter. Now, you must rest, so Bertha and I will prepare supper. But first let me open a bottle of good wine.'

'No, madam!' she cried. 'I cannot sit idly by and watch you work. It seems all wrong.'

'Either your bottom stays on that chair, or I shall make it too sore for you to sit on it at all,' I said firmly. Then I took all the sting out of my words with a tender kiss.

Both Bertha and I worked in harmony to bring some cheer to our dear friend, and by the end of our repast she was looking far less haggard. Even so, an early night was evidently called for, and while I cleared away the supper, Bertha filled the bath and we retired.

I thoroughly enjoyed pampering dear Mavis, and as she lay in my arms, the soft rain of tears on my bosom was from happiness and relief, not desperation.

The far more active evenings and nights which I was now enjoying so much made my quieter moments even more precious. On one lovely morning, Mavis and Bertha had taken the trap into Petworth and I revelled in the peace and solitude, stripping quite naked and walking all around the garden before settling under our tree. I lay back with my limbs indecently splayed, and with the pleasure of the fresh air caressing my exposed cunny in the background of my awareness, let my thoughts roam.

Three notable events had advanced my knowledge of corporal punishment significantly. First, my caning at Elizabeth's hands; next, my tuition under Miss Parfitt, culminating in the birching; and last, but by no means least, Jane's spanking on the train.

I brought my caning into focus and recalled the intensity of the emotions which had flooded through me at the time. It occurred to me that the key element had been the suddenness of it all. I had not had the slightest inkling that I was about to be beaten and Elizabeth had given me no time to prepare myself before ordering me to bare and bend. My fear had almost overwhelmed me. It had flooded my mouth with its acrid sourness; my limbs had weakened instantly and my very breathing had involved no small effort. The eager gaze of the audience, consisting as it had done of my social inferiors, had made the skin of my bare bottom crawl. As I awaited the first biting cut of that slender wand, I had felt utterly sickened.

Then the pain had seared through my vitals like a cleansing douche. As the thin line of fire across my buttocks had settled from scalding to throbbing, I had felt a surge of love for my tormentor which exceeded anything I had felt before. Moaning and whimpering, I had locked my joints into the position which offered maximum exposure and accessibility, and silently willed her to thrash me to the very limits of my endurance.

She had done, but because of the special atmosphere, my endurance had been far lower than if I had been given due warning and therefore had time to strengthen my resolve. My submission to her had been absolute and, in the end, very satisfying.

Would The Academy attract women of similar inclinations? Would I derive any satisfaction in enforcing complete submission to my will, rather than applying pain for the sole purpose of giving pleasure? Was I capable of punishing a pretty girl with severity? I pondered for a while and thought that I would find it within myself, but only if by doing so I made her mend her ways.

Then I moved forward in time and mused over the incident of Jane in the train. For all her beauty – of face and bottom – the satisfaction had come from imposing my will on both her and her aunt and the change in her demeanour had been very rewarding. The punishment had been very moderate. When we parted, she had thanked me shyly for her 'lesson'. Was I correct in assuming that there had been a wistfulness in her eyes? Was she potentially submissive? When she was properly enrolled as a pupil, I would be able to test her at some leisure.

Lastly I mulled over my several sessions across Miss Parfitt's experienced lap. I was still certain that she did not have any great sensual feelings about the female posterior but was equally confident that she had not found spanking mine a distasteful experience. I had noticed that when she was preparing Elizabeth for her whipping, there was a soft expression on her face as she looked at the bottom she had just bared. Deeper reflection served merely to confirm my original thought that she was a firm believer in corporal punishment as a disciplinary measure. If she also found some pleasure in the feel and sight of the denuded target area, then she regarded that as no more than an additional blessing – not as the primary motive for selecting this method of keeping her pupils up to the mark.

The idea of Mrs Milford's academy was suddenly more appealing than ever. My own experiences as a teacher had proved that I had some ability and that I could rise to the challenge. I would mainly punish to correct but would always seek to find those who could learn to enjoy my attentions to their bottoms. After all, the maids were all confirmed devotees, so I could always turn to them!

Jane had served to convince me that my powers of persuasion were not negligible. I felt confident that I would be able to judge which of my pupils would have the potential for greater things and more confident since then that I would be able to persuade them to take the first, faltering steps on that steep and occasionally rocky path. Beginning with the fair Jane!

Satisfying my own submissive needs posed more of a problem. Then I realised that I had Elizabeth, Arabella and cook, all of whom knew my desires well enough!

Sighing deeply, my contented mind summoned up a kaleidoscope of images. All the bare bottoms I had chastised swam into my awareness. Plump, white, divided mounds of gloriously feminine flesh, quivering, wobbling, turning pink then red; soft clefts opening and closing; folds appearing and vanishing as the hips bucked and heaved. Suddenly I became aware of an insistent tingle in my secret places and realised that my right hand had stolen between my thighs, cupping my furry little love-nest, rubbing my spot. The images faded as the red mists filled my head.

In some subtle way, Mavis and Bertha became more like friends than servants. Perhaps sharing my bed was the main cause of the change, because there is such intimacy there. I found it much easier to open my heart to them and share my innermost thoughts.

I found that I was happy to ignore convention and play a full part in running my household. At first, my offers of help were greeted with indignant refusals, but with persistence I was soon pulling my weight.

For instance, a great deal of the pleasure I derived from my kitchen garden came from the knowledge that my own hands were mainly responsible for its creation and maintenance. If, on a warm day, I laboured in Eve's costume, then I indulged both my liking for physical exertion and my smaller lusts. If the three of us toiled naked, the enjoyment was even greater – and the progress even more satisfying. So by sharing at least part of the work in house and garden, I was far less the mistress than would have been the case normally.

This atmosphere helped me in several ways. First and foremost, my occasional pangs of loneliness vanished. I no longer subscribed to the theory that women are much less capable than men at organisation. Our great country had reached a position of immense power and influence in world affairs, with a woman's hand on the tiller. And I felt sure that if our queen depended rather more on the advice of her ministers since the untimely passing of her beloved Albert, she was still our guiding light. In an infinitely more humble capacity, I felt few qualms as to my ability to run my academy with some success. There can be no denying, however, that I had often wished that Phillip were with me, so that I could discuss various worries and problems with him. Now that my two friends felt sufficiently free to disagree with me, I felt more confidence in my judgement.

If I remained very much in charge in the classroom, our new relationship meant that I was no longer in complete charge during our less conventional activities.

For example, one day we were naked under our tree, replete after a delicious picnic accompanied by two bottles of champagne. I was lying on my back, nearly asleep, when Bertha broke the silence.

'I feel like a few good mouthfuls of bottom,' she said dreamily. 'Yes, to look down on a nice, plump bare bottom, choose the spot, open my mouth to suck in a goodly amount of flesh and then nibble it, would be really nice. The thing is, whose bottom will I choose? Yours is the biggest, Mavis . . . but I'm so full that it had better be yours, ma'am. Could you turn over please?'

A week before I would have just told her to lie down and leave me in peace until I felt like having my buttocks nibbled, but on this day I rolled over on to my belly. Without regret, I must add, for the soft touch of her lips, followed by her hot, wet mouth and then the sharp nip of her teeth easily compensated for the disturbed snooze!

Later on, it was Mavis's turn. Declaring that I was far too dozy for my own good, she sentenced me to a brisk spanking. Although little could have pleased me more, I made a pretence of resistance and took to my heels, whereupon they both gave chase.

If walking about without clothing is satisfying, running as fast as one can is quite thrilling. One cannot help but be aware of the fleshy bouncings and wobblings fore and aft, and the agitation of such intimate flesh seems to send lovely tingles throughout one's body. Needless to say, I was eventually captured – my pleas for mercy totally ignored – and led back to the tree. There I was forced on to my knees, with my tingling bottom thrust high in the air, and soundly smacked. Then, while Bertha held my buttocks further apart, Mavis gently smacked my anus as a final humiliation.

That little episode was instrumental in making me think even harder about the subtleties of spanking. Before Phillip's departure, my reactions had been instinctive, but recent events had led to a change in my attitude. As Mavis and Bertha had led me back to the tree, my emotions had been similar to those I had experienced prior to my caning, although obviously to a lesser degree. I had been terribly conscious of the movements of my bare bottom as they hustled me along and I had been hollow and tingling in anticipation of the spanking I was shortly to receive. I had felt utterly in their mercy.

We had enjoyed many similar romps and they had smacked my bottom on several occasions, but I had always been in control. That time, there was an implacable determination in both and I knew that it would have been wrong to have reverted to the role of mistress.

I had knelt and proffered my bottom in the certain knowledge that Mavis wanted to dominate me, for all the initial levity. Her spanks had stung and my mind had welcomed the pain and the submission as intensely as my flesh had always done.

Being dominated had made the enjoyment less superficial and therefore even more memorable and I saw no irony in the fact that I enjoyed the subsequent periods of domination over them more than ever before.

I admitted this to them in bed that night and told them that I was to be subjected to the same levels of discipline as they were. It would do me good. They understood me perfectly.

Some days later, my resolution was put to the test. I have forgotten the details of my wrong-doing but shall always remember the calm authority with which they sentenced me to a good spanking with the hairbrush. I was told to fetch it from the bedroom and stand in the corner for five minutes.

It seemed an age before I heard the scraping as a chair was dragged into the centre of the kitchen, and my nervousness changed to real fear. It was very similar to the atmosphere with Miss Parfitt – I was being punished for a real fault. There was no play-acting. I draped myself across Bertha's lap. She was younger than I, which made the abasement yet more pointed. She tucked up my skirts and pulled down my drawers. My bare bottom cringed. I could hardly breathe. My hands were hot, my buttocks cold. My teeth chattered.

She reminded me of my faults, patted my bottom with the brush and then began to spank me. It *hurt*. Even more than I had feared, but knowing that I deserved it, I welcomed the pain and raised my hips for each smack. She also proved that she had absorbed all the lessons I had taught her. Just as the burning smart had begun to dominate me completely, she paused so that I could regain my equilibrium. The colour of my bottom was described to me – she would give it a soothing rub and then ask me if I was ready for some more.

I could then make myself ready. I would press down with hands and feet, steady my breathing. Closing my eyes helped me concentrate on my bottom; anticipate the pain to come; do all I could to keep in position for her. It was important to be spanked with the same gracefulness that I administered a spanking. I willed my feet to stay planted on the floor and not to wave around so that I was reduced to an undignified sprawl over her nice lap.

She reduced me to tears and then stopped. I apologised to them both and kissed the hand which had wielded the brush so well and so lovingly.

I was forgiven and we all felt a surge of mutual love.

It seemed a good idea to hone my skills with the variety of implements at my disposal, especially those which I had not used to any great extent. We used to give one another one or two proper strokes with each and, with the experience of feeling their effect on my own skin, soon achieved a satisfying level of expertise with cane, martinet, tawse and riding crop.

So, by the time I had to visit Richmond to check Mr Percival's progress with my house, my knowledge was greatly advanced. In the main, what we had practised had simply confirmed my instincts, but I had been able to establish firm guidelines. For example, for formal and more leisurely punishments, I would draw out the interval between pronouncement of sentence and administration of the first stroke as much as practical, including an interval between the positioning of the culprit and the laying bare of her posterior.

I would, in most cases at least, use the tawse and the

martinet on tight, parted buttocks and the hairbrush, cane and birch on less severely bent ones.

Many light blows were preferable to fewer, heavy ones.

Using a suitable implement was just as exciting as using one's hand!

Four

In complete contrast to my last journey, I arrived without a single exciting memory to compensate for my dusty apparel, headache and stiff posterior! None the less, my pleasure at seeing Arabella again was as intense as ever. Clucking over my travel-worn appearance, she immediately ordered one of the maids to run a bath for me and, as I let the hot water ease my stiffness, I regaled her with a lurid account of my adventure with Jane and Aunt Maud.

'Annie Milford!' she exclaimed when I had finished. 'I have never known anybody on whom Dame Fortune smiles so readily. I am consumed with envy. Now stand up and let me sponge you. No, wait! I do not wish to splash my new gown.' She began to fumble with the buttons and fastenings, so, sighing theatrically, I stepped from the tub, quickly dried myself and helped her. It would be false to suggest that my gesture was in any way a sacrifice. First of all, I fully sympathised with her desire to protect a very elegant silk creation in deep red, which set off her lovely colouring to perfection. Secondly, she was by far the most beautiful of all my friends, so to ignore the chance to fondle her charms as they popped into view would have taken self-denial to ridiculous limits!

I love being bathed. Immersion in hot water seems to add notably to the sensitivity of my skin, so even when the only object is hygiene, it is a pleasing way of being pampered. When the person in charge of the washing is beautiful, naked and has a passionate desire to dwell on every inch of your body, the sensuality can be quite breathtaking.

As soon as I had settled back in the tub, she took hold of my hand and applied soap, carefully working it between each finger before slowly moving up my arm. She repeated the process on the other side while I lay back, my eyes closed and purring with contentment. Then under that arm and back again to the first, tickling me unduly, to the extent that I felt perfectly justified in ordering her to turn round and stick her bottom out so that I could give a juicy wet spank on each perfect buttock.

'Oh thank you, Annie!' she exclaimed after the second, shaking her hips around and making the full cheeks wobble like twin blancmanges.

'Not at all, my darling,' I replied smugly, and lay back, awaiting the next move. She decided that my feet were in need of special attention and to facilitate this, clambered into the tub. She straddled my knees, bent down, grasped my right ankle, raised it until my calf was trapped between her upper thighs, and began to apply the soap.

I was torn between several temptations. The feel of her slippery hands on my foot was unbelievably sensual and made me want to lie back and revel in it. Against that, the sight of her bottom quivering gently as she massaged my sole, held my wide-open eyes like a magnet. Finally, the silken pressure of her thighs against my limb had been a delight, but when she tugged it right into the fork of her body so that I could feel the soft crispness of her hair, I all but swooned.

My breasts were subjected to a lingering lavage and my nipples felt as if they would burst.

Then I stood and the attentions to my shoulders, back and thighs calmed me a trifle.

I bent to proffer my buttocks and the tingles started anew.

Lastly, she pressed me to my knees, my bottom thrust out, and the tingles surged as her slippery fingers delved into the open cleft and found my bottom-hole. Once that had been thoroughly washed, she moved downward to my throbbing cunny and I was done – and undone!

One of the many things that I loved about Arabella was that our thoughts were so often in perfect harmony. After my bath, I felt in the most languorous mood. So did she. We walked slowly down the corridor to her bedroom, side by side and content in our nakedness, and I discovered another little pleasure. It had seemed perfectly natural to rest my hand on her naked bottom as we strolled along and the smooth rolling of her hemispheres against my palm was, to say the least, interesting. Especially when I cupped the nearer cheek, and when her leg was stretched back, the tips of my fingers were momentarily trapped in her gluteal fold.

I loved her in a calm and relaxed manner, without allowing my passions to take control. Laying her on her bed, I attended to every inch of her. I kissed and licked her ears and toes; I stroked her shoulder blades and calves; I rubbed my bosoms against her knees and hips; I sat on her bottom, rocking to and fro while her fleshy mounds shifted easily against mine. Lastly, I laid her on her back, feet apart and knees up and kissed the soft firmness of both thighs, front and inside, until I was eventually lying prone between her limbs, staring closely at the core of her womanhood.

I loved her sweet little cunny. The hair was the colour of ripe corn and was surprisingly sparse. Even the triangle covering her mount of Venus was covered in little more than a downy fur. The shape of her plump lips was clearly discernible and the slit in between almost bare. As I stared, she stirred in her expectation and her thighs fell further apart, exposing a slash of glistening pink.

My hands were on her, parting the lips, opening her up. Complex folds of pure femininity, hot and slippery faced me. Her clitty peeped shyly from out of the protective shelter of its tiny hood, darker than the surrounding flesh; beckoning me, tempting me. I stroked it with the ball of my thumb, gently and with all my love. She moaned: her hips jerked. I bent my head and kissed her there, breathing deep of her fragrance. Her hairs tickled my lips and my nose as I slipped a stiffened tongue as far up the moist tunnel as it would reach, while rubbing my upper lip against her spot.

She panted; groaned; called out my name; and in hoarse, disjointed phrases, told me that she loved me. Her thighs pressed against my ears and her hands held my head against her writhing love-nest. I pushed my free hand under her pumping bottom and pressed the thumb into the tight division until I felt her tiny bottom-hole open up for me. With no apparent effort on my part, the top joint was enveloped in the clinging heat of her back passage. Then her cries became shrieks; it was all I could do to keep my mouth glued to the proper place. I could feel the spasms of her anal muscles clamping around my thumb as she spent with joyous abandon.

Wriggling free, I lay on my back beside her and she turned to rest her full length upon me, her face buried in my shoulder and her whooping exhalations fanning my tangled tresses. As I stroked her bottom I marvelled yet again at my good fortune, and waited patiently for her to make a full recovery. At last her breathing was back to normal and she raised her head so that she could look at me.

'You did not kiss and lick my bottom-hole, you naughty girl,' she announced earnestly. 'You know how much I love that. Especially when I know that it is your lovely mouth doing it.' She kissed me, then reached down to take my hands in hers. 'And when I know that it is these soft little hands which are holding the cheeks of my bottom apart.'

I widened my eyes in mock dismay. 'Oh, Lady Arabella, how terribly remiss of me. I apologise from the bottom of my heart.'

'An appropriate phrase,' she interjected, 'considering that we are discussing the heart of my bottom!'

I tried and failed to suppress an inappropriate giggle, then composed my features until the correct degree of remorse was writ large upon them. 'I am quite sure that you will wish to punish me,' I continued. 'And afterwards I shall of course make amends by worshipping your beautiful little bottom-hole until you are completely satisfied with my devotion.'

She looked down at me solemnly and, as our eyes locked, I could plainly see the reawakening of her lust. 'Yes, Annie, I shall indeed punish you.' Her voice was slightly hoarse; tight in her growing excitement. Thrilling. I squirmed a little under the soft, warm weight of her naked body. She raised her torso so that her dangling bosoms brushed against my slightly flattened ones. My nipples hardened and throbbed. Then she slid off the bed and stood over me, hands on hips, as powerful and proud in her nakedness as I was humble and submissive in mine. I risked a downward sweep of my eyes before looking straight into hers again, and even that brief glance was enough to give me the clearest reminder of her extraordinary beauty.

Her golden hair hung in disarray about her shoulders; her blue eyes were gleaming; her parted lips showed the white, even perfection of her teeth; her firm breasts shifted a little with her breathing and their stiff pink nipples pointed threateningly at me. Her belly was firm and round, and the small, deep button was like a third eye, glaring at my trembling nudity.

Her cunny hairs were dark and still damp from the plentiful effusion of her love-juices, bringing back memories of her scent and her delicious, intimate taste. Tingling all over, I waited.

Her nostrils flared in anticipation as she pronounced sentence. 'I shall smack your body. But before I begin, I want you to parade it for me. Rise up from the bed and walk slowly to the far end of the room.' I obeyed at once, and as I began the shameful display of my femininity I felt a surge of exhilaration. Even though I was well used to nudity, her manner added a new dimension. Even though I knew that she loved my physical appearance, her reasons for parading me were different to the usual seizing of an opportunity to feast her eyes on my intimate flesh. She was going to slap me – and presumably cause me no little pain – and was quietly assessing me.

'No, Annie.' Her voice rang with authority and broke into my reverie with harsh abruptness, forcing me to devote all my consciousness to my poor body. 'I want you to saunter along as though you are strolling down Bond Street . . . That is better. Swing your hips. I want to see your fat bottom wiggle. That is it. Now, twice more.'

The room was large and the journey to the far end took time. I felt the coolness of the polished floorboards beneath the soles of my feet, but otherwise I was virtually nothing but a swaying and very naked derrière, warmed by the intensity of her gaze upon it.

She made me repeat the exercise several more times, latterly walking just behind me. Obviously distance did not lend enchantment!

Then again and again, but this time walking fast, as though late for a secret tryst. The new pace agitated both pairs of fleshy globes so that the bouncing of my bosoms distracted me somewhat from the jostlings behind me.

At last, when my limbs were beginning to ache a little, she called me to a halt by the window and made me stand still, feet apart and hands on head. The sunlight bathed my body and the fresh air cooled me. I closed my eyes, steadied my breathing and waited anxiously for the next stage.

My anxiety was not misplaced! If I had found walking up and down embarrassing, having to crawl on hands and knees was a great deal more so! My buttocks felt horribly prominent and there was the certain knowledge that the after-portions of my most intimate place would be visible between my thighs.

Happily, before my aching knees began to dominate all the pleasing feelings, she halted me and crouched behind me, examining my elevated rear at leisure. By this stage, I was so under her spell that I instinctively lowered my arms and head, so that my bottom rose even more blatantly into the air. I knew that she was peering right into the yawning division, for I could feel the gentle zephyr of her breath in its depths. The knowledge thrilled me anew. Then her hands pressed into the taut crowns of my bottom cheeks and moved them apart. My breathing stilled and my anus tingled. I felt a weakness steal through my limbs and had to make a conscious effort to stay still. As the tip of a finger probed my exposed rosebud, I exhaled in a gusty sigh of ecstasy.

My relief was premature. The close view of my secret charms was not enough to divert her from the course of action she was clearly enjoying to the full. Perhaps the sight of my bare bottom-hole inspired the next torment: or perhaps she had already determined it. I was made to repeat my traverse of the room. Again on all fours and this time with my nose to the floor, as though I was using it to push a marble along. I immediately recalled that exciting incident at Aunt Grace's – one which I described in the first volume of my memoirs – when Cook, the maids and myself had romped naked in the garden and had raced each other pushing a croquet ball in the same manner. We had been caught in the act and the punishment had been severe. As I crept across the floor, all my secret places in full view, the tingles were intensified by the memory.

At last I was made to stand up, again with feet apart and hands placed on my head. I closed my eyes and waited for the stinging pain which I knew was about to visit me.

She started on my breasts, which caused me no small degree of alarm. My knowledge of anatomical detail was sketchy to say the least, but I knew enough to be aware that while the female buttocks consist of little more than muscle (delectably covered with a layer of yielding flesh), the breasts are considerably more complex and fragile. However, after the first few smacks, I realised that she intended these delicate organs no harm and was slapping them with due care. Then I could still my fears and enjoy the way she made them wobble and smart. I even opened my eyes and looked down, seeing her hand flash into view, land on whatever part she had selected as a target and then the smart blazed through my chest an instant after I had seen the rounded orb shake under the impact. I noted that my nipples were standing out like mulberries. My curiosity satisfied, I closed my eyes again and let the pain wash through my torso.

She moved from my bosom to my chest, thence to my stomach and to the fronts of my thighs, where the firmness of the flesh allowed her to add extra vigour to her smacks. Then down to my feet. I sensed that she had moved behind me and the tingles of expectation down the full length of my back complemented the soreness of my front to perfection.

She worked steadily down to the beginning of my bottom, then passed over those yearning mounds to set about the back of my thighs, continuing her relentless downward path.

She straightened and there was a brief respite while she gathered her breath. I took stock. Only the insides of my thighs and my bottom were as normal. Everywhere else stung notably. I felt her hand on the back of my left knee. It pressed in and, in sudden understanding, I raised it until it was crooked and my thigh was parallel to the floor. My heart pounded as I felt the softness of her belly against the outside. I gritted my teeth, sensing that the skin she was about to assault was especially sensitive. And so it proved. I could feel the individual imprint of her fingers on the softness and, for the first time, began to moan with the pain as my darling Arabella covered every inch from knee to cunny. I had to rest an arm on her shoulder, so weakened was my supporting limb, and was duly grateful that she did not chide me.

Then the other thigh was treated in like manner and was eventually returned to the floor. I stood, gasping and panting. The pain in the recently visited parts overwhelmed the quiet throbbing which was all that remained of her earlier attentions, but that soon faded sufficiently for a crawling dread to suffuse the untouched skin of my posterior. I gave it my full attention, knowing that she would feel free to strike with uninhibited enthusiasm. The cheeks were well used to hard slaps and the quality of the flesh there made them relatively invulnerable. She would use most of her strength and, for a moment, I was afraid, conquering that fear by trying to envisage how she would place me.

Clearly the same question was exercising her mind, for she squatted behind me and I felt her hands roam all over the twin hemispheres as she assessed them carefully. Her touch always thrilled, but the certainty of a painful spanking in the very near future made the thrill even more intense. I closed my eyes again and my mind drifted lazily.

'I think that I shall begin with you across my knee. Not only does that position suit your bottom admirably but I shall also enjoy the feel of your bare skin on my thighs. After that ... Now let me think. Yes, I have it. As you are being punished for ignoring my bottom-hole, I shall chastise yours!' My heartbeat increased and my hidden anus tingled in tune with the surrounding and enveloping cheeks. 'You will therefore position your bottom so that the hole is easily accessible. I trust that I have your full agreement, my naughty little Annie?' She moved to stand in front of me.

'Yes, Lady Arabella, you do.' The use of her title seemed perfectly natural. And the import of her calling me 'little' was not lost on me. Standing before her, stark naked, her lovely face filling my vision, I felt so much smaller than her. Except for my bottom, which gave the impression of being more than twice its usual size; softer and even more vulnerable.

I watched the sway of her posterior as she walked across the room to fetch a suitable chair, and then her bobbing breasts as she returned. She placed it carefully on the floor, sat down and patted her lap. Swallowing convulsively, I stumbled over to her and floated down across her plump, slightly parted thighs. There was a brief awareness of their softness against my front, then of the cool wood of the floor on the palms of my hands. After that, I consisted of little more than a naked, upthrust bottom.

One which was stroked, prodded and patted for an age before the first ringing spank put me out of the misery of anticipation. As I had suspected, she used the full force of her arm and my whole derrière wobbled as her rigid hand sank into the fleshiest part of my right buttock. I squealed at the smart and bounced my hips around on the steady fulcrum of her lap in a desperate but vain attempt to shake the pain from me. The second blow on the sister cheek had less effect, as my mental defences took command. I absorbed the third, fourth, fifth and sixth without crying out or wriggling, and then the burning spread from my buttocks and the pleasure began.

At last the first phase was over and Arabella helped me to my feet and I stook shakily between her thighs, rubbing my hot posterior and watching her as she massaged her right hand. There were attractive pink splotches on her thighs, where I had rubbed against them in my writhings. I knelt down, and kissed her lap in thanks. Then I seized her hand and pressed it against my lips. My bottom throbbed hotly behind me and its inner recesses tingled with foreboding.

She rested a hand under my chin, raising my face and bending down to kiss my lips. I saw that her face was soft and gentle again. As I knew full well, an energetic spanking rids one's soul of most, if not all, one's built-up anger and frustrations – and she had spanked me *most* energetically!

'Well, my darling,' she said softly. 'How shall we arrange your bottom for the finale?'

Resting my head on her lap, I pondered. Her hand stroked my hair and a feeling of deep peace and calm stole through me. The prospect of arranging my body in a way which would not only expose my anus but also make it accessible to her punishing fingers was now exciting rather than embarrassing. I spoke my thoughts aloud.

'I know my own bottom reasonably well, Arabella,' I said slowly. 'My cleft is deep and the hole well buried within it. If I kneel down, with my back arched and my hips raised to their fullest extent, the division is sufficiently open to expose me. However, I believe that the gap between the cheeks will not be enough to allow you to smack me effectively . . . I could reach back and hold myself widely open for you, if you like. Or I could lie on my back with my knees pressed to my bosom. That should do it.'

Once again, she raised my head and kissed me and this time her hot, wet tongue forced its way between my lips and thrust into my gasping mouth. Panting, we drew apart and I ran the ball of my thumb over her lips to dry them. She smiled. 'Why do we not do both? Go over to the bed and kneel up on the side facing the window.'

'With pleasure, my dearest,' I replied, and trotted to do her bidding. Slowly, in order to display myself as tantalisingly as possible, I assumed the most blatantly exposed position of which I was able and, while she looked on from afar, reflected.

It had all been a little game, from start to finish. Even her anger had been feigned but, despite that, I had been truly dominated. Her spanks on my bottom had been anything but playful and had hurt quite as much as Miss Parfitt's. The essential difference, of course, was that there was no real punishment here, so that I could devote all my thoughts to my sore bottom rather than to those errors of omission or commission which were the cause of the soreness.

As I knelt, the metallic taste of fear was again on my tongue. I trusted her implicitly and knew for certain that she intended no harm to the delicate little orifice so rudely exposed. I knew equally well that even light smacks on that small place would deliver a peculiar and unaccustomed pain. Knowing what she was about to do to me also made the pose I was adopting more humbling and shaming. From the beginning of our relationship, we had both loved looking at the other's bottom-hole and having our own under close and detailed examination. We both loved kissing and licking each other there and found even greater pleasure in being kissed and licked. Parting a pretty girl's plump cheeks to display the innermost secrets always gave me a special thrill. But no girl of my acquaintance owned an anus which could match Arabella's for prettiness and no other's eyes gazing upon mine pleasured me as much. Yet, kneeling on that bed, waiting nervously for the smacks to come, my belly felt full of butterflies. I was trembling, dry of mouth and moist of palm.

The floorboards creaked as she approached. I closed my eyes, lest I be tempted to turn and look at her nudity and thus distract myself from the trepidation which I was enjoying so much. I sensed her face close to my exposed charms; her breath made the tightened skin of my bottom tingle; a fingertip brushed against my tail-bone and I shuddered. It slowly began a downward path, inscribing little circles on the sensitive skin at the deepest inrolling of my buttocks, skirting my anus. I whimpered in my longing for her touch on my rosebud. She caressed the ridge leading from my anus to my cunny. I moaned. Suddenly I wanted her to smack me there and my fears were vanquished by a tide of pure lust.

A soft, warm hand pressed against each cheek and pushed them as far apart as they would go, stretching the ring of muscle and making it prickle for a moment or two, before a thrilling ache suffused my fundament. I pushed my hips back against her hands and the ache intensified. With a surge of relief, I remembered that I had packed my dildoes and knew that she would willingly thrust the one of my choice right up my bottom. Her hands left me and only my disjointed breathing disturbed the silence.

'You are right, Annie,' she whispered. 'Even bent as you are, your plump cheeks protect your bottom-hole. So will you please reach back and hold yourself open for me.'

'Of course,' I replied, and did as I was told. Her hands had felt infinitely more exciting than my own but, in compensation, my awareness of my anus was even more intense. Her first smack landed, making me gasp aloud. The slight sting came as no surprise but what did affect me was a jolting ache which seemed to penetrate deep into the passage. I must have eased the pressure of my hands and let the division close up enough to protect my hole, for the second slap landed mainly on buttock-flesh.

'I am sorry, Arabella,' I gasped, and spread my knees even further, at the same time gripping my cheeks as tightly as I could and forcing them apart once more.

'You have earned extra!' she said ominously, and administered the third, which landed dead on target. The smarting ache was more pronounced and I had to grit my teeth in my desperation to maintain a dignified silence. Then she stopped. I stayed in position, holding my breath, half-hoping that my ordeal was over but also wanting her to continue. 'Stay exactly how you are,' she ordered, and I heard the soft padding of her bare feet as she left the room.

I exhaled in gusty relief and let go of my bottom so that I could stroke my throbbing anus. There was more than the normal warmth there and as I soothed away with the tips of my fingers, the pain ebbed and the desire for a different assault grew. I heard her return and my hands flew back to my globes and forced them apart.

'You moved, Annie, did you not?'

'Yes, Arabella, I did.' I cringed inside. Her hand cracked down on my left thigh, just below the buttock. I cried out in shock and again when she treated the other with the same vigour.

'Right. Your disobedience has earned you an additional spanking. On your buttocks. Tuck your hands under your bosoms and stick your bottom out!'

In no time at all my palms were comparing the feel of soft bosom flesh to that of drum-tight bottom!

The ensuing spanking was very painful. My skin was still smarting after the previous chastisement and her hand lashed into my flesh with renewed enthusiasm, so that it was all I could do to remain silent. As my little mewings were threatening to become audible over the regular sound of flesh on flesh, I opened my eyes, turned my head to my left and the energetic movements of her naked form provided a welcome distraction!

By the time she had vented her anger on my protruding rear, it was blazing merrily away behind me and I was actually looking forward to a resumption of hostilities on my bottom-hole.

There was, however, a prolonged interval before then. I had not noticed that she had fetched a selection of silken scarves, some fine cord and a broom handle, all of which she laid carefully on the bed before my widening eyes. For once, her sensual imagination had surpassed mine, because although I immediately guessed that I was to be tied up so that my anus was completely accessible – the prospect alarmed and thrilled me equally – I could not see the purpose of the broom. Unless she planned to thrust it up either or both of my secret passages. At the thought of such a crude ravishing, my heart sank. Fortunately, she broke into my thoughts.

'You will now lie at full length, Annie.' I obeyed with alacrity, revelling in the easement of my muscles and appreciating the sensation of my anus reverting to its usual sheltered lair between my softly enveloping cheeks. I lay with my head buried in the silken coverlet, my bottom throbbing as the rest of my body glowed with the aftermath of her slapping, and waited, knowing that she was studying my pink and red flesh with her usual fervour.

'Your bottom is beautifully red, Annie,' she announced with justifiable pride. 'How does it feel?'

'Very hot indeed, Arabella,' I replied truthfully. 'And smarting most painfully.'

'Excellent!' she replied, reinforcing her satisfaction with a crisp spank across both sides. 'Now I must reduce your bottom-hole to the same condition. Turn over.'

I groaned but did as I was told without demur. Then she took hold of my nearer wrist and bound it firmly to one of the brass rails at the head of the bed. I watched the bobbing of her bosom as she tied the knot with surprising expertise, then enjoyed a brief glimpse of her bottom as she walked around to attend to the other hand. The cords were tight and a tentative tug proved the strength of my bonds. The fluttering in my middle grew worse.

She clambered up on to the bed and knelt with her back to me to deal with my feet, first spreading them wide. Curious, despite my nervousness, I raised my head to watch. Comprehension dawned as she slid the broom underneath my ankles, took hold of the right one and tied it to the wood with one of the scarves. Having accomplished that task, she swung a leg over me and started work on the other side, treating me to a delectable view of the lower portion of her posterior.

Soon both limbs were securely bound and she was carefully knotting a length of rope to the centre of the broom. This was then passed around the lowest horizontal rail of the bedhead and then she began to pull at her end of the rope.

The broom was drawn inexorably towards the head of the head, raising my feet as it moved. My knees bent and my bottom was lifted up, its twin halves slowly tightened and separated. She did not cease until the soles of my feet were pressed against the rail and my knees against my sides.

I lay utterly helpless, like a trussed fowl. In the background of my mind, I was aware that it was hard to breathe and that my knees and the backs of my thighs were painfully stretched. Not surprisingly, however, the awful feeling of complete exposure dominated. My buttocks were forced widely apart and my two precious and vulnerable orifices were chilled by the fresh air, which now had easy access to them. In fact, so bent and distended was I that I sensed that even the lips of my cunny had been forced apart, though I own that my excitement had contributed.

For the second time, her fingertip traced a tingling

path down and around the division between my cheeks. And again, I closed my eyes and savoured her touch.

She stopped and I tensed in expectation of the first smack. Nothing happened. I opened them, peering down at the strange view of my lower half and then up at Arabella's face, pleased at the tight expression on it as she gazed fervently down at the treasures on display. The pink tip of her tongue peeped out from between her lips and ran round both in a gesture of pure lust before slipping back inside. Then she noticed my gaze upon her and smiled at me triumphantly. Her right hand came into my sight, holding a length of cord some six inches long.

'Oh *no*!' I shrieked. 'Oh, my darling Arabella, please do not whip me there. I promise that your smacks stung like the devil. Owww!' This last exclamation was caused by a ringing spank on my left buttock and my protest died away. I felt a hand rest on the crown of my right cheek and then my pouting little anus caught fire as she flicked the cord into my yawning cleft.

It hurt. Not as much as I had feared perhaps, but none the less, enough to make me writhe and tug against my bonds. Uselessly, for I could do nothing to alter the awful exposure and my poor bottom-hole lay openly and helplessly before her. Soon, even my fortitude was tested to the limit. Her free hand pressed into my right buttock and my cleft gaped even more. This seemed to open my anus, because there was a sharper quality about the pain of the next few flicks, penetrating my back passage more quickly and sharply.

Then, just as I was losing myself in the blissful torment, a new sensation invaded me. Opening my eyes briefly, I saw that she was slapping my cunny with an open hand. It caused no pain – just pleasure. The impacts made my lips quiver and waves of ecstasy surged into the core of my being and I spent copiously.

We did not exchange a word as she untied me – the

sole communication was my groan of relief as the blood began to flow freely through my cramped limbs and joints. Then she was lying face down, with her trembling bottom before me. My hands rested on her cheeks, splayed thumbs digging into the yielding flesh on either side of the deep division, prising them apart until her delicate rosebud was staring sweetly up at me. Sighing with pleasure, I bent to salute it and her, stiffening my tongue so that I could push it past the tightness and into the velvety interior.

She knelt up so that my hands were free to roam beneath her, while my mouth could stay glued on her writhing bottom. She spent quickly, but soon recovered and laid me on my back, squatting over my face so that she could rock to and fro and offer her two orifices in turn. By the time the sounds of her second climax echoed round the room, I was all but exhausted and was more than content to lie in her arms while we gathered our senses. I remembered that I had wanted her to thrust a dildo up my bottom but no longer felt the same need, so dreamily promising myself that I would suggest it when we next engaged in similar activities. Then I determined to do the same unto her. With those happy thoughts bringing a contented smile to my face, I snuggled up to my darling and kissed her.

When we eventually arrived at Redhand House to inspect progress, I was in a calm and relaxed frame of mind. In view of the chaos which greeted us as we entered the hall, this was more than fortunate! Mr Percival was engaged elsewhere and his foreman, a Mr Fletcher, had to bear the brunt of my wrath. I silently stared at the bare walls, the missing floorboards, the naked pipes snaking hither and yon through enormous holes in the walls and then glared at him.

The poor man twisted his cap in his gnarled hands and shuffled his feet in embarrassment. 'Er, we weren't expecting you, ma'am.'

'That is perfectly obvious, Fletcher,' I replied icily. 'I am sure that if you had been, you might actually have made some effort. I was given to understand that the work would be close to completion by now.'

He looked around him, shuffled and twisted again and began to stammer some sort of excuse when, to his obvious relief, his employer entered. 'Mrs Milford, Lady Arabella. How good of you to come.' While distinctly more prepossessing than his underling, his ingratiating smile did little to reassure me, revealing nothing of his emotions and little more than a glimpse of yellowing teeth beneath his straggly moustache.

'I am sure that you do not mean that, Mr Percival. Had the work been further advanced, then I may have believed you. As it is, I feel that my presence must have come as a particularly unpleasant surprise.'

His eyes widened. 'But Mrs Milford,' he replied earnestly. 'I assure you that I am delighted with the progress we have made. Please follow me. This way, ladies.'

My ill temper began to fade, and by the time we had completed our tour of inspection, my confidence in him was fully restored. Most of the rooms had indeed been completed and the results exceeded my wildest expectations. He promised me that the unpleasant smell of fresh paint would soon disappear – especially as the fine weather allowed them to leave the windows open for the best part of the day.

The final reassurance came when we returned to the hall and the men restoring the plaster had started, with two of the gaping holes already repaired. My only lingering doubt was the newfangled radiators, which seemed excessively ugly. Again, Mr Percival raised his stature in my eyes by suggesting that they could be painted to blend in with the walls – in the main rooms, at least. The pupils' bedrooms were unimportant.

* * *

Although I was tempted to return to Sussex, Arabella's earnest plea to tarry a while longer was irresistible, and when I eventually climbed into the stuffy interior of the train, I did not regret my decision one iota! Apart from a few leisurely walks, one in Richmond Park, where we had flirted outrageously with a very handsome captain in the Household Cavalry and the rest by the River Thames at the bottom of Richmond Hill, our time had been spent alone with each other. Arabella's extraordinary beauty never failed to thrill me and just as pleasing to me was the joy she took in my body. I reflected that, had our love for each other become common knowledge, we both would have been cast out from society. This would have affected her more than me but even so, my life would have been made more difficult. Yet our consciences troubled us not one bit.

I was aware that my sensual desires were far stronger than most. While other women of my age, class and status may have peeped flirtatiously from behind the shelter of a fan at some handsome male, I cannot imagine that many would have happily speculated on the shape of his bottom and the size of his pego. Yet both Arabella and I had shared a little fantasy over our captain. We had openly agreed that it would be quite thrilling to be spanked by him and then to kneel in blatant submission, proffering our reddened bottoms to be comprehensively buggered – with the other watching his bottom thrust to and fro, encouraging him to greater efforts by spanking him.

And I could not imagine that many females would cast a lingering eye on the seat of a girl's skirt, assessing the shape and movements of the swelling rotundities beneath and longing to place the owner in the time-honoured position for a sound spanking; slowly to bare her bottom and to apply the stiffened palm until her whiteness had become 'one red'.

Furthermore, as Arabella pointed out as we were

sprawled naked on her bed (after we had put all my dildoes to their intended use, both fore and aft), very few have the opportunity to transform their fantasies into reality.

'Annie,' she whispered softly, her big blue eyes but inches from mine. 'When your academy is properly established, you will still come and see me, I hope.'

I propped myself up on an elbow and stared down at her in total disbelief. 'How could you think that I shall ever be so preoccupied that I shall not be able to spend time with you? I love you. It is as simple as that.'

'And I love you, Annie. With all my heart.'

Tears sprang to my eyes as we kissed with the same tender fervour that I experienced with my husband. Then I rolled her over and slapped her plump bare bottom lest our emotions overwhelm us both. Later, we discussed The Academy and she raised a problem which had been exercising me from time to time.

I had not been able to plan how to satisfy the two main categories of pupil. In other words, I wanted to provide useful education for some and unlimited opportunities for chastisement for those whose tastes ran in that direction. I had been vaguely conscious that it would not be easy to accommodate both satisfactorily.

'As I see it, Annie,' she said, 'if you were to summon up a pupil who is there purely to be thrashed and beat her as she wishes to be beaten, you will horrify those who are there to learn and who would expect little more than a reasonable spanking when they are slack.'

She had summed up my doubts with her normal precision, and while I gave myself time to reflect, I wriggled down until I could use her bottom as a pillow. Unable to think of an immediate solution, I turned on to my front and began to kiss and lick the first inch or two of her bottom-cleft, just by her tailbone, where the skin is so deliciously soft and smooth.

After a silence punctuated by her little sighs of

pleasure, she continued. 'I remember overhearing my elder brother talking to nanny after he had been made a prefect at Harrow and telling her – with no small relish – that he was allowed to beat the younger boys. I was only sixteen but old enough to be consumed with jealousy at the thought of being able to order some comely youth to let down his trousers and bend over to have his bottom caned. Only the Beaks were allowed to wield the birch, by the way. He also said that one of the disadvantages was that any misdemeanour on his part was punished with extra severity.' My heart pounded as I appreciated the import of her tale. 'So,' she continued, 'why do you not appoint the submissive pupils prefects. You may not wish to grant them the privilege of punishing the other girls, but you will have every excuse to whip them in private, without causing the least concern elsewhere.'

'Arabella, you have the answer. I am impressed. Now, how can I reward you for your cleverness?'

'Umm. Let me see. First you can kiss and lick my entire derrière –'

'With the greatest pleasure,' I interrupted.

'And secondly, you can make me a prefect. At the appropriate time.'

I gasped. 'Oh, Arabella, of course I shall. And you will be allowed to punish the other girls, I promise. The sole condition will be that I shall witness the chastisements.'

'I accept,' she said, laughing. 'Now, I have a perfectly posed and completely bare bottom waiting for your attentions. Get busy!'

I did.

I returned to Petworth in the highest of spirits and after a day spent quietly to recover from my various activities, I was soon busy. I had planned to open The Academy formally on 1 June, which gave me some six weeks to make my final preparations. My first task was to plan the most effective way of attracting new pupils. As a start, I wrote to Miss Brown informing her that I would expect Jane to present herself on the appointed date and what she would need in the way of clothing and personal effects. This led me to the thought that members of my academy should have appropriate uniforms, and after I had given the matter some thought I raised the subject with Mavis and Bertha that evening, when we were enjoying our post-supper cup of chocolate.

'Well, ma'am,' Bertha said, after a brief period of contemplation. 'Obviously you want them to look nice. And young. Like schoolgirls, even if they are in fact too old. So that'll mean nice, short skirts, won't it?'

'Correct,' I agreed.

'And as you'll be giving them lots and lots of spankings, you won't want to waste a lot of time getting their bottoms all bare, will you, ma'am?'

'Also correct.'

'So,' she continued remorselessly, her green eyes shining at her sensual imaginings, 'they mustn't be too tight, otherwise you won't be able to whisk them up quickly.'

'I agree whole-heartedly, Bertha. And they should be nice and short, showing a reasonable amount of bare thigh. If they are also made with a flare, raising them will be delightfully easy. Yes, I can see them. Little tunics – in good quality cloth, mind – tight round the bosom so that the upper charms are discernible and in black, I think. That will show up the whiteness of their naked skin to even greater advantage. Excellent.'

'And with a coloured sash round the waist,' Mavis chimed in. 'Then you can tuck up the back of the skirts if you want to make her stand in the corner with her bare bottom on show.'

I clapped my hands with delight. 'Mavis, that is a lovely idea. Well done.'

For a moment we all sat quietly, our minds dwelling

on the thought of a pretty girl on view, knuckling her eyes to stem the flow of well-merited tears.

'And what about drawers, madam?' Mavis broke in. 'Will you make them go without all the time?'

'Oh, I do not think so,' I responded immediately. 'No, lowering a girl's undergarment is such an important part of the proceedings ... But what sort of drawers would be best, girls?'

'How about those new ones of yours, ma'am?' suggested an eager Bertha. 'You know, the ones you wear under your tight dress. All in one piece and only just covering your bottom. Shall I dash upstairs and get them – oh, wait a minute, I think that they have just been laundered. Yes, I know where they are.'

She scampered out and was soon flying back through the door, the tiny garment in question borne triumphantly aloft. It then seemed logical to go upstairs to my room so that I could put them on and examine the result in the looking-glass, something which I had unaccountably failed to do since I acquired them. They proved to be ideal, clinging to my curves and dipping into the division so that the shape of the twin mounds was clear. I made Bertha try them on and then put her over my knee to see how easy they were to take down. The drawstring was threaded through the waistband and the ends emerged by the right hip, so it was a simple matter to untie them with my left hand, loosen the tape with the right and then whisk them down to her knees. Naturally, the sight of her sweet little bottom pouting nakedly up at me proved irresistible and I was soon making it wobble!

Unfortunately, they were too small to accommodate Mavis's more ample proportions. But I spanked her anyway.

I then remembered that Aunt Grace had used a local dressmaker and corsetière, who had shown obvious pleasure at the sight of my nervously naked person when I was being measured for a new wardrobe. Her name was Mrs Savage and the next day I penned a note to Arabella, asking her to find out if the worthy woman was still in business and, if so, to call on me on the occasion of my next visit.

The remaining days flew by. Twice I journeyed to Richmond, where Arabella and I spent many a happy hour watching Redhand House respond to the finishing touches being applied by Mr Percival and his merry men. We also summoned Mrs Savage. To my relief, if not my surprise, she was delighted to act as official dressmaker to The Academy, and when I declared that I needed several additions to my wardrobe, her pleasure was doubled. She was prettier than I recalled, although her rather mousy appearance was completely at odds with her surname. And, when I began to remove my clothing to be measured, the anticipatory glint in her eye was even more obvious that it had been the first time she had seen me.

I enjoyed watching her attend to Arabella's naked body as much as I had enjoyed her attentions on mine, and was delighted when she accidentally pricked my friend's bottom with a pin. A sound spanking was the obvious response and we soon had her displaying a surprisingly well-rounded pair of buttocks, with an especially tight cleft between them. She was clearly not used to corporal punishment and squealed loudly from the onset. Not that her wails deterred us in the least and we made her complete her business in just her stays, with a very red bottom still bare for us to feast our eyes upon.

The event which lit up that period more than anything was another meeting of The Society, an organisation which I described fully in the second part of my memoirs. Elizabeth kindly asked me to act as Mistress of

Ceremonies and suggested that an educational theme would be particularly appropriate.

I made my preparations with my usual care and have every reason to believe that a good time was had by all. I had naturally begun on the basis that I would be the mistress in charge of the 'classroom' but then had second thoughts. I would soon be fully involved in that role and had already prepared myself for it. The part of a pupil would be more exciting and I felt that the passive side of my nature needed satisfying more than the active.

As usual, we met for dinner, dressed as exotically and provocatively as we could. I had stipulated masks. Not ones that covered the entire face, as I wanted to be able to kiss all my friends properly, which was less satisfying if one could not stroke the other's cheek. Otherwise, our only apparel was stockings and shoes, gloves and jewellery, and stays. In black, leaving bosoms, cunnies and bottoms quite bare. As we gathered to drink champagne before moving into the dining room, my heart thrilled to the sight of the seven beautiful women, their charms in full view, the brilliant masks adding mystery and rare excitement to their looks. I also warmed to the intimacy of the atmosphere, personified by the couple nearest to me. They were talking with great animation, looking smilingly into the other's eyes, one hand holding a glass and the other lovingly stroking her friend's naked bottom.

Naked servants, male and female, padded around the room attentively, ensuring that no glass remained empty for long. Heaving a sigh of utter contentment, I moved forward and joined them.

After a delicious dinner, I called the meeting to order and asked them to move into the ballroom, where they could digest the magnificent repast and enjoy a small entertainment. As soon as they were comfortably ensconced I slipped away to change into a rather drab day dress I had carefully hidden. Stripped of my mask and jewels, with my hair tied up in a bun, I assumed the role of the harassed mistress of a normal household. My partner was one of Elizabeth's maids, a tall and willowy girl called Stella, whose bottom had fascinated me since the first time I had clapped eyes on it. Seen from directly in front, her hips were boyishly narrow and there was little promise of anything exciting behind. That impression was totally erroneous, for although the narrowness was equally apparent when she turned to present her rear view, the amazing jut of her tight little buttocks was pure femininity. As was the deliciously fine and long cleft.

The two of us put on a little play for my friends, having already equipped the stage to resemble a drawing room. I was obviously the mistress with Stella suitably clad as a maid. We opened with me seated at my desk, chiding her wearily for a succession of misdemeanours and finishing by fining her ten shillings. She gasped in dismay.

'Oh, madam, I have a mother and three young sisters to support,' she wailed most convincingly. 'That money represents a month's food for them. Please, madam, I know that I have been a very naughty girl and deserve to be punished, but can't you find another way? Please, madam?'

I buried my face in my hands in despair. 'But what other punishment could possibly have the desired effect?' I said plaintively. 'I have chided you again and again and my patience is at an end. That is the end of the matter, Stella.'

There was a pause before a soft voice broke the silence. 'Why don't you spank me, madam?'

I looked at her, aghast. 'Spank you? *Spank you?* How could you suggest such a thing? You are a grown woman, not a child. And, unless I am very much mistaken, a spanking is administered to a part of the body which is not even discussed in polite circles, let alone handled. No, it is out of the question.'

She frowned, seemingly puzzled, then her expression cleared. 'Oh, you mean my bottom, madam. Well, of course that's where a girl should get spanked. There's nothing wrong with that. Honestly. I've often had mine smacked. My last mistress used to turn me up at least once a week.'

I let my jaw drop in horror. 'You mean that she would apply her hand to the seat of your skirts?'

'Oh no, madam.'

I clutched my bosom in relief. 'Thank heavens for that.' There were a few giggles from my audience, which I studiously ignored.

'No, she made me pull up my skirt, petticoats and shift before laying myself across her knees.'

'Oh, you poor child!' I exclaimed.

'Then she'd untie me drawers and pull them down to me ankles.'

'I do not believe that any woman could be capable of such depravity!' I cried.

'That's as maybe,' she announced primly, 'but Mrs Farmer – my previous employer – always said that a girl weren't properly spanked unless it was on her bare bottom. And she would feel it all over before she started smacking it.'

I slumped back in my chair in a swoon, fanning myself vigorously. 'No wonder you left her employ.'

'Oh, it wasn't because of the spankings, madam. It was 'cause they went to India. No, if I was a naughty maid, I wanted to be well smacked. And on my bare bottom. I've got a nice bottom, madam. Well, Mrs Farmer always said so. Let me show it to you and see what you think.'

So saying she sprang to her feet, turned her back on me and exposed the part under discussion. I stared at it, inwardly revelling in the display, outwardly showing an embarrassed fascination. Feigning reluctance, I leaned forward until the plump divided mounds filled my vision. 'Touch it, madam,' she urged softly. 'Feel how soft and smooth it is.' I did and it was. 'Now, why don't I go across your lap and then you can try a few spanks and see how nice it all feels.'

Tentatively at first, but with growing enthusiasm, I spanked her until her firm cheeks were the colour of a ripe cherry. Throughout she encouraged me to greater efforts: 'Oooh, I felt that one, madam. Perhaps another six just like it ... Now the same on the other side, please.'

When I eventually finished, she clambered to her feet with a rueful grin on her face and rubbed away at her naked curves with great energy, making them shift and wobble far more than my hand had done. To a burst of applause, we took our bow and left the stage. I thanked Stella sincerely for her bravura performance and quickly removed my clothes.

Thence to the main event. I had asked Cynthia, perhaps the prettiest of all, to play the part of the mistress (and had no reason to question my choice). While we were all changing into our schoolgirl costumes, the stage of the ballroom was being furnished with suitable desks, a blackboard and a long footstool. Half an hour after my right hand had sunk into Stella's bare bottom for the last time, we assembled in eager expectation, immediately taking advantage of 'teacher's' delayed arrival to partake in some suitably juvenile horseplay, for which we were properly punished on her arrival.

I loved my role as one of the naughtiest of the pupils. Berenice, Thomasina and I liked a sore bottom more than the others, and Cynthia arranged matters so that our fate was largely in our own hands. We were set a series of fairly simple exercises and were punished according to one's results. If, therefore, one felt like being summoned to her desk to be spanked or whipped in front of one's unsympathetic classmates, all one had to do was pretend to be stupid.

For some reason, my bottom's natural resilience was greatly enhanced that evening and I spent many minutes presenting my rear end to the full variety of implements at her disposal. The smacks and blows seemed as light as thistledown, despite the clearly felt quivering of my flesh at each impact, and I thoroughly enjoyed peering backwards and seeing the rapt expressions on the faces of my beloved friends as they watched the spreading redness.

Even my hardiness was tested by the finale. We three submissives were sentenced to a sound birching – 'for persistent wickedness' – and I was to be the last to be whipped. I had, therefore, the added torment of watching first Thomasina's small bottom, then Berenice's much bigger and amazingly firm one being thrashed scarlet before proffering mine. The pain of the birch is like nothing else and nothing else can bring about the same feelings in the core of my being. The bite of the cane is initially fiercer but the birch's effects accumulate in a more leisurely fashion. The burn lasts that much longer and one's skin seems to get impossibly hot. In addition, the flexibility of the little twigs ensures that the inrolling of the cheeks and the folds at their base are all visited most effectively.

Cynthia made us lean over the front of her desk, so our bottoms were moderately bent; soft and yielding. To commence with, that is. All three of us could not restrain ourselves from gradually leaning forward, further and further, as the fustigation progressed, until we were thrusting our blazing rumps out as far as we could.

From the sounds that my two companions made towards the end, they spent copiously with the pleasure of the pain. I certainly did.

During an initially quiet breakfast the following morning, Elizabeth asked me to tell the company about my plans for The Academy, and to my intense pleasure, all of them showed great delight at the idea and insisted on a visit at the first possible opportunity.

Five

Arabella and I, accompanied by Mavis and Bertha, completed our tour of Redhand House and then repaired to my new drawing room. Two bottles of vintage champagne rested in a cooler, so I opened the first, filled four glasses and handed them round. My three friends looked at me expectantly and I realised that a small speech and a formal toast was called for.

'My dear friends. All of you have had a part in the inspiration which brings us here on this auspicious day. Each one of you has, in her own way, fanned the flames of my desires for loving female company, for beautiful female bottoms and for the sensual chastisement of the female bottom. Tomorrow, Cook and the maids will return from their holidays and the day after that, seven friends of mine from Sussex will be here for a visit. Then, on the first of June, our first pupils will be enrolled. There are busy, but exciting times ahead. Now raise your glasses and let us drink a toast to The Academy – and all the lovely bottoms which will grace it.'

We drained our glasses and I refilled them. Then Arabella rose and spoke. 'It is my turn to propose a toast. To Annie Milford, proud owner of the most beautiful bottom in the world –'

'Hear, hear!' interrupted Bertha and Mavis in unison.

I glared at them and Arabella grinned broadly. '– and, of course, bosoms, thighs and a cunny to match! May her right hand never tire of bringing joyous pain to all those who want it: may her unique abilities as a corrector of wayward females never wane. And may she never lose the desire to present her own naked buttocks to the many who derive great pleasure from smacking them!'

They rose and drank to me, while I blushed and wriggled modestly. I opened the second bottle and then suggested that on such a fine, warm evening, it was absurd to suffer the restriction of clothing. I ordered the two servants to strip completely. Arabella and I watched avidly as they did so and then I told them to act as ladies' maids and undress us. Which they did, with some unseemly – and quite thrilling – gropes and strokes as our more prominent areas were uncovered.

Much refreshed, I decided that a tour of the garden was called for and I led a giggling column through the conservatory and into the fresh air. As soon as I felt the cooling embrace of the breeze, I felt a glorious sense of freedom. I shook my hair free and danced round the main lawn, revelling in everything, from the feel of the newly mown grass under my feet to all the wobblings and bouncings. After a suitable interval, my three friends joined me and my pleasure was intensified by the sight of their lovely white nudity. We recreated that happy afternoon soon after my arrival in Richmond, when Cook and the maids had joined me by the fountain. I had been contemplating my statue and had undressed to be at one with her nudity and the others had also stripped. Soon my reservations had been overcome by my curiosity and my fascination with the naked female form had begun.

As then, the four of us cooled our bottoms in the fountain's waters; again, I arranged running races and we played croquet. Only when the sun began to sink and I felt that we had been exposed to its rays for long enough did we traipse back inside.

The new range immediately proved its worth by supplying hot water at the turn of a tap and so the depth of our baths was no longer limited by the strength and endurance of a maid's arms.

After a light, cold supper, we decided that we should christen the huge new bed which Mr Percival's carpenter had constructed especially for me, and after our ablutions I made them don their nightdresses and we made our way into the bedroom, the gas lamps and candlesticks filling it with a seductive and warm light.

We all enjoyed a splendidly torrid night, marred only by the knowledge that Mavis and Bertha would be leaving before long. In view of this, I did all in my power to ensure that their stay was memorable, and certainly started on the right foot by insisting that they let Arabella salute their bottoms. Both were initially awkward at receiving such an intimate caress from a member of one of the land's greatest families, but such was her skill that they soon forgot all reservations and climaxed as loudly as ever.

Needless to say, both were most appreciative of the compliment and thanked Arabella very prettily before repaying her!

The next day was bedlam. Cook arrived in time to prepare a hasty breakfast for us and the maids soon followed. They greeted Bertha, who had once accompanied me on a visit to Aunt Grace and was therefore known to them, and made Mavis welcome. I did, however, notice that Cook treated her with some reserve, presumably concerned that she was facing a rival to her authority. I had a quiet word in her ear, assuring her that Mavis's main role was in looking after the Sussex house, and after that the two of them worked in perfect harmony.

There was a great deal to do. The whole house needed a thorough clean; the bedrooms for the members of The Society had to be made ready; provisions had to be ordered and stored. Thanking my lucky stars that Cook was such an able assistant, I could concentrate on doing something to repay Mavis and Bertha for all their devotion. Once I had seen that my supervision was no longer necessary, I had a quiet word with Cook, called a Hansom cab, and we departed for a day in London.

It proved to be an inspired idea and we all had a day to remember. Our driver was worth every penny of his fare, showing us all the famous buildings and thoroughfares, finding us a perfect spot in Hyde Park for our picnic and being a veritable mine of information. I shall never forget my friends' shining eyes at the sight of Regent Street's elegant buildings and the gay, cosmopolitan crowd. For my part, I loved St Paul's Cathedral more than anything. That dome! The crypt, where so many of our country's heroes are laid to rest. I was so moved by Admiral Nelson's tomb that tears sprang to my eyes.

Mavis and Bertha seemed to find it difficult to decide which had been their favourite sight. Both had stood in awe outside Buckingham Palace, breathless at being so close to our great queen, but they had also gazed speechless at the sophistication of the riders and strollers in Hyde Park.

Neither could credit the number of houses and the crowds of people. I sympathised with them, telling them that my first impressions had been the same, despite my acquaintance with large towns such as Leicester.

We arrived back home, tired but happy, and to my intense pleasure I found that everything had been done to my complete satisfaction. At about six o'clock, I told everyone to go upstairs, change into more formal evening wear and gather in my drawing room in an hour's time.

I waited for them to arrive, which they did as the clock struck, and Cook, Mavis and I poured out the wine. We toasted the future and I reminded them of my expectations.

'My friends. I hope that you are all ready for the fray and have enjoyed your holiday. You all know about my plans for The Academy but may not be fully conversant with the role you will be playing. In short, the best part of the day will be spent performing your normal household duties. As before. And, as Aunt Grace did, I shall do all I can to take care of you.' I paused as my eyes swept round the room, pleased at the happy expression on every face. 'For example,' I continued, 'I shall always be more than happy to see you privately, so that we can discuss any problems which you have and to do what I can to help. I know that each one of you enjoys presenting your bare bottom for a good warming and I promise that you will not be neglected on that score!' Again I paused and smiled warmly at each one in turn. The glow in my heart intensified as they responded with clear excitement as they looked into the immediate future with keen anticipation. The brief interlude gave me time to collect my thoughts. There was much to tell them, but little time.

'As this is a completely new venture, we cannot – or rather should not – make too many detailed plans in advance. In the beginning, at least, flexibility will be our watchword. All I can say with certainty at this stage is that I intend to attract two main categories of pupil. The first will be those whose parents or guardians feel that a taste of disciplined education is the best solution to whatever problems they are experiencing. These will provide me with the opportunity to teach and correct, but they will seldom be of interest to the rest of you. Unless, of course, their behaviour warrants public chastisement, in which case I may well invite you to witness the punishment.'

Once again, I surveyed my rapt audience: Cook, broad of face, bosom and beam and handsomely gentle rather than pretty; Elspeth, fair and elfin; the quiet, darkly plump Maria; Connie, with her apple-like breasts at odds with her generous bottom, and the alabaster skin which showed off her black hair to such effect. Vera's bottom was also satisfyingly plump and her olive complexion contrasted well with her best friend's; Bridget was sitting on the floor with her knees drawn up under her chin and her glorious red hair flowing loose from under her cap. Hers had been the first bare bottom-hole I had ever seen and I felt a flaring desire to gaze again on the neat, delicate, wrinkled pinkness nestling between her small buttocks.

All of them so pretty and all so sweetly friendly. My emotions made my throat constrict and I had to clear it before finishing my little lecture.

'I also wish to open this establishment to any lady with a taste for the rod. They will be separate from the other pupils – for most of the time at least. We shall appoint them prefects, following the traditions of our great public schools, where the senior boys are responsible for the junior ones. Our prefects will be in different uniforms and will be subjected to the sternest discipline. I hope, of course, that some of the juniors will show sufficient character to join the ranks of the seniors. Give suitable encouragement, of course!' We all laughed and I made my final point. 'I may continue Aunt Grace's admirable tradition of formal dinners with some form of entertainment afterwards, although not necessarily copying her exactly. We shall see. Now, let us recharge our glasses.'

I was too preoccupied to encourage the orgy of Sapphic indulgence which I sensed they all desired, and after a light and informal supper in the kitchen took Mavis, Bertha and Cook to my bed (Arabella had excused herself as she was occupied with some family dinner). Watching Cook and Mavis pleasure each other, all the while holding Bertha's silken nudity close against mine, proved a delightful experience. Such amplitude of rounded feminine charms, quivering in abandoned ecstasy as they delved and kneaded each other, was memorable!

We all fell asleep in united contentment and rose at the crack of dawn, helping the maids make the final preparations for the arrival of my friends from The Society.

At ten o'clock, two carriages rattled up the short drive and my seven eager friends climbed down and looked about them before turning to the drivers and encouraging them to unload their cases as fast as possible. A flurry of maids emerged from the front door and I saw seven pairs of eyes greedily appraising their charms, drinking in the bosoms bobbing freely under the white blouses and lingering on the curves of thigh and buttock, which their tight skirts revealed so tantalisingly.

I waited in the hall, my heart thudding and my breathing short and laboured. My bosom ached, my stays constricted, while my bottom tingled and my cunny felt moist and open. I knew that the next two days would test my sensual stamina to the full. Would I have any strength to welcome the three pupils due on 1 June? Elizabeth led the chattering throng through the door and my nervousness vanished as she clasped me to her breast and kissed me.

One after the other they followed her example. Jemima Ford's lovely face swam into my vision. Tendrils of fair hair had escaped from her bonnet but her blue eyes were glistening and her full red lips puckered delightfully as they reached for mine. I dropped my hands to the swell of her buttocks, remembering the womanly breadth and the tightness of the dividing cleft.

Then Berenice. Dark hair and eyes. A smaller mouth but a much bigger bottom. Such firmness down there. It squirmed under my hands, communicating her longing for hot punishment.

Cynthia. Perhaps the prettiest of them. Elfin and slender, with rich brown hair. Eyes and mouth which always seemed to be smiling, even when she was crying out in the ecstasy of pain as her dear little bottom quivered under the lash.

Then Rachel. Fair and freckled. A bottom as neat and sweet as Elspeth's.

Alice and Thomasina. Quiet and the least eye-catching, but both with pretty and soft posteriors.

I led them on a rapid tour of the ground floor, then the first and second floors, leaving out the attic out of respect for the maids' privacy and the basement out of a desire to keep the best until last. We returned to the conservatory, where they all gazed longingly at the desks which silently awaited their first customers. Then I quietly ordered them to strip.

'I want you all absolutely naked girls. There is a sun bonnet for each of you by the door over there and that is the only item of clothing you are allowed.'

'Oh bliss!' sighed Elizabeth. 'I think that the arduous journey has left us all horribly hot.'

There was a chorus of agreement and then hands flew to fastenings and in the twinkling of an eye, naked white flesh began to appear. More quickly than I would have believed possible, all seven were in Eve's costume, stretching and groaning with relief as the fresh air cooled them. They stood in a semi-circle around me, completely at ease but staring pointedly at my red silk gown. I laughed apologetically and undressed.

Five minutes later, we were by my beautiful statue, lowering our naked derrières into the water, before lying back to cool the rest of our bodies.

Refreshed, we repaired to the shade of the summer house, where bottles of champagne waited in buckets of ice, with various pies, dishes of quails' eggs in aspic, cold new potatoes steeped in mayonnaise, and other treats, all of which were quickly demolished by my starving friends.

After another dip in the fountain, I ordered them to go to their bedrooms and change into the school dresses which we had used at our last meeting – and which I had commanded them to bring with them. I donned my working apparel (a narrow black skirt and white blouse) and we then filed into the library.

The atmosphere was notably different to that which characterised the meetings of The Society. My tests and questions were much more challenging and the 'girls' were far more serious in their behaviour. Even so, they were all spanked to their hearts' content and Berenice and Thomasina willingly proffered their naked rumps for a brisk birching at the end of the 'lesson'.

After dinner, I took them down to the basement and showed off both the theatre and the four small rooms, each newly equipped with the wherewithal to administer proper whippings: the first with a ladder bolted aslant to the wall; the second with a traditional whipping bench; the third with a wooden bar set back from the far wall and with rails set into the wall and floor for wrists and ankles. The fourth contained my *pièce de résistance*: a specially-made stool, sloping down towards the head and with a padded platform on which the victim would kneel in some comfort. Several cushions of varying thickness and length allowed for sufficient adjustment to accommodate victims both tall and short. In each room, a variety of canes, straps and whips hung from the walls, and I had just had time to complete a series of watercolours, each of a pretty girl fastened to the relevant apparatus, her bare and scarlet bottom the central point of the painting. I had hung them on the walls just before my guests' arrival.

We returned in thoughtful silence to the theatre and the evening's entertainment began.

I told them all to sit in the seats originally reserved for Aunt Grace's guests, pulled the bell rope concealed behind the curtain and, as if by magic, Cook, my two servants and all the maids appeared and tripped lightly on to the stage, standing in a line with their backs to the audience.

One by one – and without a word from me – they removed their lower garments completely, walked briskly around the front of the platform and laid themselves across my lap for a spanking. Then back to the further end of the line, where they stood with their reddened bare bottoms on display. Some 30 minutes later the sequence was complete and, leaving them in place, I joined The Society and we gazed appreciatively at the row of pretty posteriors, quietly commenting on the variety of shapes, sizes and shades.

As soon as my hand had cooled and my arm no longer ached, I returned to my desk and summoned the penitents up to receive a light dose of the birch. In the same order and with the same willingness, they presented themselves over the end of the desk and the whippy twigs reddened their plump curves all over again.

To warm and genuine applause, they gathered their discarded clothing and trooped back upstairs, with my full permission to soothe each other in whatever way suited them!

I then turned to my friends.

'I think, my dears, that I shall dispense with the preliminary spanking which I had planned. Each one of you had your bottom well warmed this afternoon and so we shall proceed without delay to more serious business. Follow me to the first punishment room. But first, please remove your gowns and chemises.'

Seven beautiful women soon faced me, clad as ordered, with softly trembling breasts supported by their corsets and with white thighs gleaming nakedly between stockings and drawers. We crowded into the designated room and one by one, they tried the ladder. I tied their wrists and ankles, lowered their drawers and gave each three strokes of the cane, three of the birch and one with a riding whip. Except for Berenice and Thomasina, who were already finding the atmosphere most exciting and pleaded for a double dose.

In the second room I made them remove their drawers entirely and lie on the bench. It was long enough to accommodate each one at full length and the straps in the centre and at each end fastened them quickly and securely. The prone position showed off their bottoms to excellent effect and the clenchings and bouncings as I applied the birch were most enticing.

To the third. The bar. One at a time, they had to press their bellies to the smooth wood, move their feet widely apart and then lean forward to grip an iron rail set into the wall. Like this, their buttocks formed a smooth curve and were sufficiently parted to provide a target consisting of two separate mounds. After I had demonstrated to one and all the feel of the cane in this pose, I used Thomasina and Berenice to show how the same device could be used to present a bottom even more humiliatingly – and vulnerably. I made them grasp another rail set well below the level of the bar, then quickly tied a silken cord to each knee. Each cord was run through a ring in the wall and back to the upright poles supporting the horizontal one. I could then easily pull their legs up and apart so that they were as bent as a hairpin.

I applied a nine-thonged whip to each yawning bottom and the shrieks were eloquent testimony to the effectiveness of both pose and implement. When I had let them down, each capered about in the restricted space with fingers pressed into her cleft, where the central parts of the thongs had bitten into the tender skin.

Last but by no means least came the stool. The basic position was with the torso sloping down, the knees tucked in and the bottom the highest point of the body – perfect for all the implements at my disposal and with the added advantage that the buttocks were parted.

Wearily we moved back to the theatre, where more champagne awaited us and its refreshing qualities were especially welcome. After half an hour or so, bottoms were gently throbbing in the background, dry throats were back to normal and seven pairs of eyes turned on me. Smiling, with my own flesh tingling and my heart pounding furiously, I stripped to stockings and shoes and led a silent procession to the first room.

Elizabeth took charge, fastened me tightly to the ladder and announced that they would each give me one stroke in each room, and that they would use the strap in the first, the birch in the second, the whip in the third and the cane to finish me off!

I paled at the severity of my sentence and the taste of my fear was metallic. But my cunny wept in eager anticipation!

By the end of my ordeal my bottom burned like a furnace, and when I was released from my final bonds, my trembling hands flew behind me and gently fingered my smarting cheeks. Even the softest touch relit the fires and I was amazed at the roughness of my skin back there as the myriad of weals cross-crossed the ample mounds.

That night, I slept alone and very deeply. True to form, my bottom was much recovered by the morning. The redness had faded and only some lines and dots marred the whiteness. It ached and throbbed, of course. And, after my close inspection, the memories of the night flooded back into my mind and the little slit of my cunny seemed to open up as the desire surged through me. I lay back on my bed and spread my thighs. My right hand stroked the silken skin of my inner thigh, the palm brushed over the moistened fur, and then my middle finger delved into the hot interior, found the pleasure spot and I spent copiously.

I lay back, exhausted. Then dear little Bertha trotted in with my morning tea tray, gasped when I turned over to show off my bottom, and set about the task of soothing it. She began with her tongue and ended with a liberal coating of ointment. She then asked me to kneel up so that she could apply her tongue to my bottom-hole and her eager hand to my love-nest. My second coming completed my recuperation.

All of my guests proved to be in a similar state to myself – sated from the exertions of the night – so we spent the morning in calm conversation, sitting in and around the fountain, gently soothing our aching bottoms. After a light luncheon, their carriages arrived and, amid firm promises of further visits in the near future, they departed.

The following morning I was in my study awaiting the arrival of my pupils. A girl named Mary was the first, led in by her elder sister. Arabella had brought The Academy to their notice, telling me that Mary had been placed in the charge of her newly-wed sister and was proving a nuisance. Apparently she showed no interest in the normal social whirl and, for a girl of eighteen, even less in attracting sufficient attention from the opposite sex to have any chance of making a good match.

The sister – The Honourable Mrs Tavistock to give her her full title – was an intense, dark woman who dismissed her sibling's abilities and character in a few, short sentences, gave me a bankers' draft for a month's fees, wished me luck and departed before I had even had time to ring the bell for the duty maid to see her to the front door.

I turned to Mary and studied her. She was plainer than her sister, albeit not without charm. Her hair was a nice, deep brown, her retroussée nose and neat little mouth were definitely pretty, and her slender figure was not without promise. She returned my gaze steadily.

'So, Mary,' I said after a suitable pause. 'You like neither men nor parties, I understand.'

She blushed and looked down to her lap, on which her hands twisted nervously. 'No, not much, Mrs Milford.'

'I see. Well, what does give you pleasure?'

She shrugged. 'I enjoy reading ... I miss home ... I had friends there.'

I smiled at her, sympathising with her obvious loneliness, then I rose, walked around the desk, took her hand, and led her to the *chaise-longue*. We sat down side by side. 'There now, is this not friendlier? Tell me, which is your favourite book?'

She smiled for the first time and, like a flower opening up in the morning sun, she began to tell me all about Charlotte Brontë's *Jane Eyre*. I approved her choice and the intelligent person whom I suspected lurked behind the shy and timorous façade slowly emerged.

I eventually dismissed her and rang for Elspeth to escort her to her bedroom and help her unpack. As she trotted out behind the equally slender maid, I fixed my eyes on the seat of her skirt and noted that there was hardly a trace of feminine mobility to be discerned. I did not expect to derive a great deal of sensual excitement from smacking her bottom but then she had not struck me as being a girl who needed much in the way of physical correction.

Jane was the next. Miss Brown bustled in, dressed as drably as she had been the first time, but with a new sparkle in her eyes and a perceptible air of confidence. I rose to my feet, kissed her warmly and then turned to her niece, holding out my arms to her.

'My dear Jane,' I said happily, and not altogether untruthfully, 'how nice to see you again.' She blushed in her surprise and proffered her cheek for me to peck. I led them across the room, sat Miss Brown on an easy chair and Jane on the sofa, and filled three tumblers with lemonade. Then I sat beside the youngster and we talked with some animation about nothing of any importance. After another two glasses of lemonade had washed the dust of their journey from their throats and the soft cushions had presumably eased the aches from their soft posteriors, I brought up the subject most dear to me, first resting my hand on Jane's knee.

'Judging from Jane's greatly improved demeanour, Miss Brown, you have taken heed of my advice and smacked her bottom again!' I was smiling broadly as I spoke but both blushed and wiggled in their seats. And I clearly felt a tremble in Jane's limb.

'Well,' Miss Brown said, after a pause, 'I am pleased to tell you that she has not given me cause. At least, I have not felt the need to go that far.' She stuttered to a halt and I saw Jane flash her a meaningful glance. I was quite certain that the young hoyden had strayed beyond the bounds of decorum but had taken full advantage of her aunt's soft and gentle nature to talk her out of due retribution. I was not, however, tempted to pursue the matter and squeezed her knee as I congratulated her.

In due course, Bridget took the girl away, then Miss Brown handed over a tinkling purse stuffed with a pleasing number of golden guineas and took her leave. I ordered another jug of lemonade and awaited Sarah.

She was twenty minutes late, which meant that I was not in the best of humours when she and her mother were ushered in by Vera. My mood was considerably worse ten minutes after that, although my temper was certainly not directed at the young girl. She was entrancing and my desire to see her bottom and exercise all my skills on it was overpowering. It was her mother who had irritated me beyond measure.

My first impressions had been quite favourable. Sarah's lovely fair hair and womanly figure had pleased me immediately and when I noted her soft, wide mouth, her wide blue eyes, her perfect teeth and pure complexion, there was a whole flock of butterflies in my middle. Then she smiled at me, sweetly and shyly, winning me over completely.

Her mother was also strikingly attractive – on the surface. She refused any refreshment and dismissed her daughter as 'a useless, clumsy and utterly stupid child, for whom there is no hope whatsoever'. Then she told me that she had no time for smalltalk as she was taking tea with a Lady Brown. At this point, she had stared at me imperiously.

'I do not suppose that you have made her acquaintance, Mrs Milford. Her husband is Sir John Brown, of Browns Brickworks.

'I do not believe that she has had the pleasure!' I murmured.

She was so enveloped in her own importance that she missed my sarcasm and departed without another word.

I turned to her daughter with considerable relief, then quietly made her welcome and assigned the gentle Connie to be her personal maid.

I rejoined them at supper that evening and by the end felt even more confident that I could develop their abilities and mould their characters for the better.

As Mavis and Bertha were returning to Petworth the following day, I summoned them to my bedroom for a final night together and we spent a quiet time disguising our sadness with detailed discussions on the management of the house and garden. I said farewell with real tears in my eyes, then turned my thoughts to my pupils.

However, before I had time to get to know them, an unexpected and, as it turned out, most satisfying event took place. I had discovered that Aunt Grace's smart carriage was being kept in some stables near Richmond Park and that her two horses were in livery at the same establishment. I wanted to get them back into commission and took a Hansom to the stables, where I interviewed the owner, a man called Mr Jones. He proved to be a rather rough man but rose in my esteem when I saw that all the horses were in prime condition and that the carriage and trappings had been properly maintained. There were stables at Redhand House and it was only the lack of someone to take care of everything which prevented me from ordering the carriage and horses to be sent round immediately. As I was pondering this problem, a scruffy, very dirty youth came scuttling out of one of the loose boxes, with one of the hands in hot pursuit. The man was a deal faster than the lad, and he had soon caught him, tucked him under his left arm and begun to apply a crop with more enthusiasm than skill to the seat of his trousers.

What made me intervene, I cannot think. Urchins were often thrashed in public and the clumsy blows were not hard enough to elicit more than a passing wave of sympathy. Perhaps, on reflection, there was something about the stoical way he accepted his punishment which held my gaze. Maybe I noticed a maturity in his demeanour, suggesting that he was older than I had first thought.

Whatever the reason, I turned to Mr Jones and quietly suggested that enough was enough.

His surprised expression did not deter me and, shrugging his shoulders in obvious wonderment at the softness of the female of the species, he signalled his employee to desist.

'Who is the lad?' I asked, watching as he glared defiantly at the retreating groom, his hands hovering about his injured posterior.

'Oh, he's of no account, ma'am. Just some hobbledehoy who keeps hanging round the stables, getting in our way. He has a way with horses, mind.' He raised his voice. 'Go on, Tom, or whatever your name is. Be off with you. And if I catch you round here again, I'll take a crop to your arse. With your trousers down, and all.'

Tom, red-faced with embarrassment at the humiliation of being so threatened in front of a female, shuffled off, looking around with touching sadness as he went.

I sensed in an instant what made him risk such treatment. His glance at the busy scene which obviously meant so much to him was poignantly eloquent. On impulse, I called out.

'Tom! Wait for me outside. I wish to speak to you.'

He nodded at me, smiled wanly and hobbled out of sight.

Turning to Jones, I questioned him about the lad and he confirmed his ability with horses. Then he took off his cap, scratched his rather greasy head and continued. 'But I wouldn't have anything to do with him, ma'am. Charity is all very well, but it's wasted on the likes of him.'

'I am sure that you are right,' I replied sweetly, 'but then I intend to offer him employment, not charity. And if he errs in his ways, I shall follow your admirable example and apply some suitable implement to his bottom. Thank you for your help, Mr Jones. I shall contact you when I am ready for the horses and the carriage, so if you could continue to take good care of them until then, I would be most grateful. In the meantime, I believe that this will settle the account.' I handed him the money, walked through the gates, and found Tom waiting for me, twisting his shabby cap in his hands.

'Not too sore, I hope, Tom?' I asked breezily.

'Nah, miss,' he said scornfully.

'Madam,' I corrected him. 'How old are you?'

'Eighteen, I think . . . madam.'

'And you like horses. Can you drive a carriage?' As I asked that question, I chided myself on my tactlessness. How could somebody of his station possibly have been allowed near a proper carriage?

'No, madam. But I've often driven my grandpa's cart. He's a removal man and has two horses. I managed fine, honest I did.'

I looked hard and long into his eyes, searching for clues to the real person behind the dirty face and ragged clothes. He held my blue eyes with his. Earnestly. Pride trying to disguise the desperate plea for help. My head told me to send him on his way, but my heart convinced me that there was an honest young man behind the rags.

'Come with me, Tom. If I learn to trust you, I may be tempted to appoint you my coachman. But I should warn you that there is one thing in which Mr Jones and I are in full agreement. Naughty young men should be chastised. Frequently. So, whenever you displease me, I shall wallop your bottom. With your trousers down!'

He held my gaze and I think he blushed – it was hard to see through the grime – but I was certain that I saw a flicker of interest. This did not surprise me. He was not the first to relish the thought of my hand on his bare bottom!

We travelled home in silence and I smiled inwardly at his attempts not to be overawed by his first ride in a cab. I warmed to his gasp of delight when we walked up the short drive and he set eyes on the house's elegant and mellow façade for the first time.

I handed him over to Cook. 'This is Tom, who I hope will be capable of looking after my carriage and horses. Bathe him and find him some temporary clothing – if I remember correctly, we had some male apparel in the entertainment wardrobe. Oh, and can you get a message to Mrs Savage and ask her to measure him up for some suitable uniform? Nothing fancy, mind. Not yet, anyway.'

I left him in her hands and retired to my study to prepare for the afternoon lesson. There was, in fact, little need for much in the way of preparation, for at that early stage I was devoting most of my energies to an assessment of their varied capabilities, so I was able to sit back and reflect on the previous days' events.

Their introduction to The Academy had been a rather mixed blessing for the new pupils. When they had all unpacked and had an early dinner, I had summoned them all to be measured for their uniforms and they had reacted exactly as I had expected, with all three showing signs of excitement at the prospect of new clothes. They had stripped down to their chemises and drawers without demur.

Mrs Savage had been the model of propriety throughout, to the extent that if I had not known that she was as fond of naked female flesh as I, it would not have occurred to me that she was anything but a completely professional dressmaker. While her stubby hands moved briskly about the three firm young bodies, I watched with apparent disinterest, my eyes flicking casually over their charms while my mind idly tried to visualise how they would appear when stripped naked. I had, of course, been treated to a prolonged look at Jane's bottom and the discernible quivering inside her drawers as she swung round to have her back measured made me as keen to see it again as I was to see her friends' derrières for the first time.

For a moment, I regretted my decision to spare them the ordeal of being fully naked but knew that the anticipation would make the eventual revelations all the sweeter.

With her customary speed, Mrs Savage completed the work in just over a day and I summoned the girls again for the final fitting. Their dismay when they saw how much of their nether limbs were exposed by the tunics was most amusing!

'We cannot wear these!' wailed Jane. 'We look like schoolgirls.'

'Of course you do,' I replied with deceptive calm, 'because that is exactly what you are. Although I am sure that you will admit that they are far better made – and of much nicer material – than the normal schoolwear. In fact, you all look most pleasing, I assure you.'

I decided not to point out that the major advantage of the tunic was that it would be easy to raise the skirt, as I was convinced that the subject of spanking was best introduced gradually.

I then made them remove their drawers and try on the new ones, glad to see that they modestly turned their backs on me while they reached under their skirts and rummaged busily for the tapes. I confess to feeling a little disappointment that not one of them was careless enough to reveal even the merest glimpse of buttock in her contortions but was soon mollified by their evident satisfaction with the tightness of their new undergarments.

What I did find most interesting was the effect that the new and strange apparel had on their demeanour. Three young ladies were soon transformed into impish little hoydens! Merry, tinkling laughs changed to mischievous giggles: stately walks became less dignified skips. If I had yearned to smack their naked bottoms before, my desires to raise their youthful skirts and expose their mature posteriors had all but overwhelmed me.

I recalled the first lesson. Strangely, perhaps, assuming the mantle of teacher had had a calming effect on me. I was more keen to further their education than to indulge myself, with the result that the first two lessons had passed uneventfully. None of the girls had given me immediate cause to punish them and, having recovered from their initial nervousness, their individual characters were beginning to emerge. Quite instinctively, I had used praise far more than admonishment, and with Miss Parfitt's example fresh in my memory did all within my power to make my instruction as varied and interesting as possible. They had responded avidly, and as I readied myself for the third period I knew that all of us were settling down well.

As the hands of the clock crept slowly round the dial, I could scarce contain myself, knowing that I would soon be steering them towards that sensual path which was the source of so much pleasure.

As I entered the conservatory, they stood up respectfully to greet me. Three pretty girls, looking deceptively young in their smart yet practical tunics. Mary eager to learn; Sarah beginning to blossom under my gentle encouragement; Jane still wary of me, the memory of her ordeal in the train still fresh.

I sat down, glowing inside at the certainty of naked bottom-flesh soon to be revealed to my eager eyes, and opened their exercise books.

This was the second essay I had given them and so my comments were based on a reasonably solid foundation. I began with the fair Sarah, whose effort was deplorable, but better than the first. I praised the improvements, criticised the failings constructively then, to her evident relief, turned to Jane.

'I very much regret, Jane, that far from showing signs of improvement, your grammar is more slipshod than it was the first time. I have marked the mistakes in your book and you will stay behind after class and write the corrections out. Neatly. In the meantime, I think you need a reminder that I am not to be taken lightly, that your parents are spending a considerable sum on your education and that you owe it to us all to try your hardest. Come here!'

Scarlet faced, she slowly stood and moved to stand before me, her hands twisting with fear and her brown eyes wide and moist. 'Please, Mrs Milford . . . I am sorry . . . What are you going to do to me?'

'I am going to put you across my knee and smack your bare bottom.'

Fat, oily tears trickled down her cheeks. Then her natural ill temper resurfaced. 'You *cannot*! Not in front of the others. I *refuse* to let you.'

Smiling grimly, I rose to my feet, lifted my chair and placed it in front of her open-mouthed companions, its right side towards them. I then strode to the trembling girl and seized her wrists.

'I would have thought that you would know better than to argue with me, Jane. Had you not done so, I would have stayed where I was and my desk would have screened you from your classmates. In view of your impertinent tirade, I shall sit there and they will have a perfect view of the proceedings. And you have no one to blame but yourself.'

I dragged her to the chair, sat down, pulled her over my lap and began to adjust her clothing, a task which normally gives nothing but pleasure but she struggled so violently that nearly a minute passed before my superior strength told and her plump buttocks loomed nakedly up in the air, quivering violently as she writhed in shame and fear.

Blessing my foresight in designing clothing which made baring her relatively easy, I administered the first spank. Hard. Far harder than any she had suffered in the coach. The effect was dramatic. Her feet flew upward as she clenched the muscles of her bottom as tightly as she could and the twin globes rounded and dimpled as the imprint of my hand flared up on her white skin; her howl of pain rose as the sound of flesh on flesh faded.

I tore my eyes away from her bottom and stole a glance at the other two. Both had their hands over their mouths and were staring wide-eyed and pale with shock at Jane's nudity. But neither looked away! I looked down again as the effort of keeping her buttocks clenched became too much for their owner and they softened, then I traced the outline of the pink patch with the tip of my forefinger. 'Now, Jane,' I said quietly. 'That was possibly the hardest spank I have ever delivered. I imagine that it was quite painful.'

'Oh yes, Mrs Milford!' she cried. 'It was! No more, please. I have learned my lesson, I promise.'

I sighed audibly. 'I seem to recall hearing similar promises from you before.' I stroked away and her bottom softened under my hand as she relaxed. It was an exceedingly nice bottom and I revelled in the softness of her flesh and the silky smoothness of her skin as I kept her waiting. 'I do believe that you have learned one lesson at least, Jane,' I continued eventually, 'and that is not to indulge in futile protest when you have been sentenced to a well-deserved punishment. So, if you will get up and lay yourself across my knee properly – and by that I mean humbly and with some semblance of grace – I shall not punish you further for your rebelliousness but simply give you the ordinary spanking your poor work has earned you.'

'Yes, Mrs Milford. I understand. And ... I apologise.'

'Your apology is accepted, Jane. Up you get.'

She struggled up, carefully pushing her skirts down but sensibly letting her loosened drawers flutter to her ankles. She bent forward, placed her hands on my right thigh and then hesitated.

'Er, Mrs Milford,' she whispered. 'Could we not move your chair back behind your desk?'

'Certainly not!' I said loudly. 'If you do not like the thought of your friends watching your bare bottom wobble and redden under punishment, then that is too bad. Besides, I am quite sure that you will have ample opportunity to watch them when it is their turn.'

'Oh!' she said. And with a small smile at the thought, she completed the process of positioning herself and, to my surprise, reached back and pulled up her tunic.

'That is *much* better, Jane,' I told her. 'Just a little further forward, if you please ... good. And your feet perhaps six inches apart. Excellent.' I stroked and pinched each cheek before rolling up my sleeves, resting my left arm firmly across her naked loins and recommencing the spanking. This time each smack was as it should be – firm and crisp but only enough to cause slight pain when judged individually. It is the cumulative effect of a spanking which is important. The girl is in an undignified pose, very aware of the nakedness of a part of her body which she would far prefer not to expose and, in this case, very conscious of her audience. Those emotions are a vital element of a corrective chastisement and if the smacks are too painful, the pain reduces the effect of the shame.

So, with about a second's interval between each visitation, my hand danced methodically over the entire surface until she was gasping audibly and her bottom was a healthy pink. I paused.

'Well, that should have warmed you up, Jane.' I ignored the gasp of dismay from my left and continued. 'I shall now give you six harder smacks. Three on each cheek. All on the part you sit on, so please lift your bottom up a little. That is perfect.' It was indeed a delicious sight – the soft, tight cleft and wide folds more open; the fleshy cheeks trembling in her agitation – and I momentarily regretted my decision to limit her to a mere half-dozen. I could not resist stroking her and the interval was long enough to put a further idea into my head. 'And just in case I forget where we are, I want you to count out each spank, Jane. Before I deliver it. So, when you are ready – and I quite understand if you wish to waggle your bottom about in between smacks – hold still and count aloud. Understand?'

'Y-Yes, Mrs Milford. One.'

I placed my hand on the base of her left buttock, the little finger resting in the fold at the top of her thigh. I pressed down into her yielding flesh, which bulged out delightfully, and I caught a glimpse of exciting pinky-brown in the depths of the distorted cleft. With my heart beating wildly, I raised my hand and sent it flashing down on to the chosen spot. Her entire bottom wobbled; her breath hissed through her clenched teeth; a darker patch came into view where my hand had landed. She bounced on my lap, then her hips rose again.

'Two,' she said in a small voice, and my hand pressed into the base of her other cheek.

She behaved in an exemplary manner. The growing smart meant that the intervals between smacks lengthened appreciably but the shaking and bouncing of her ample curves was so attractive that I minded not one bit.

But all good things must come to an end and as soon as the ringing echoes of the sixth had faded I helped her to her feet, stood up and folded her to my bosom, handing her a handkerchief for her tears as I did so. She dried her eyes, returned the damp silk, smiled at me in rueful confusion and asked if she could replace her drawers.

'Let me just have a quick look at the damage,' I replied, smiling at her. I resumed my seat, turned her so that her back was towards me, held up her skirt and looked long and hard. In an upright position, her bottom looked even more lovely than when she was bent over. The cheeks had a ripeness and the dividing cleft was a great deal longer and deeper. I patted the pink upper part of each side, then the red lower curves, then I bent to take hold of her drawers and hauled them up.

She sat down, still breathing heavily, but quite composed otherwise. I turned to Mary, who was staring at me with the wide-eyed stillness of a rabbit before a fox.

'Your essay was good, Mary. A few spelling mistakes and I do not feel that you summarised your arguments as thoroughly as you should have done. Too rushed, I think. Nevertheless, I am pleased. Right, let us move on. Jane, what can you tell us about the War of Jenkins' Ear?'

At the end of the hour, I dismissed them.

'Thank you, Mrs Milford,' they chorused, and trotted thoughtfully out. Letting out a long, very satisfied sigh, I sat back and relived the sights, sounds and feelings I had just enjoyed.

* * *

As if I had not enjoyed sufficient excitement for one day, I was ambling to the kitchen some time later to pass the time of day with Cook when I heard a maid's voice raised in anger, then the sound of a sharp slap. I hurried onward and came across an enraged Elspeth and a strange youth, who was clutching his cheek and staring at his assailant most indignantly.

'What on earth –' I began, and then my jaw dropped as I recognised the boy. Tom! Scrubbed clean and no longer in rags, he had changed beyond measure. '– is going on?' I managed to ask.

'He pinched my bum . . . er, my bottom, ma'am,' said Elspeth, with typical asperity.

'I didn't mean no harm,' replied Tom defensively.

I could see that one of those futile 'No I didn't' 'Yes you did' arguments was on the brink of developing, so I told Elspeth to go about her business and that I would deal with Tom. I grasped him firmly by one ear and led him into Cook's parlour, which was fortunately unoccupied. I changed my grip from his ear to his chin and addressed him sternly, just managing to keep the inner bubble of laughter from my voice.

'Now listen to me, you young scamp. I know that Elspeth's bottom is well worth a pinch but stablehands treat maids with due respect. In this establishment, anyway. What did I say that I would do to you if you stepped out of line?'

'Wallop me, ma'am,' he said, with admirable promptness.

'Indeed I did. I shall treat you in the way that all naughty little boys should be treated and spank you.' I let go of his chin, moved a suitable chair into the centre of the room, seated myself and beckoned him over. Tight-faced, he stood before me. I unbuttoned his trousers, pulled them down and patted my lap. Swivelling to his left, he set himself down.

'You have been spanked before, I imagine,' I enquired, as I tugged the tail of his shirt clear of a surprisingly chubby little bottom.

'Yes, ma'am. Often.'

'Good!' I responded, and set about him with a will.

With my preference for the female posterior, I had not expected any special sensual pleasure in spanking him, but as I settled into my stride, I was surprised at the degree of enjoyment I was experiencing. He was young and immature, so that his cheeks were smooth and hairless and sufficiently plump to quiver noticeably under the impacts. I was also aware that a male member was squashed against my thighs and felt that in some small way, I was avenging all the slights which his sex had visited upon mine since time immemorial.

With mounting glee, I smacked away until he was bobbing up and down and hissing with pain, then helped him to his feet and made him face me while I pulled up his trousers. Affecting surprise at the sight of his impressively large pego thrusting indecently through the front of his shirt, I uncovered it completely.

'My, oh my, Tom. You *are* a big boy.' I furled my hand around the velvet-covered hardness and he groaned and shuddered. Too excited to show sensible restraint, I could not let him go, and of its own accord my hand smoothed up and down the straining shaft. Before I had time for second thoughts, he began to jerk up and down, his muscles went rigid and a torrent of creamy spend spurted out from the red protruding tip.

'I am so sorry, ma'am.' He stammered, near to tears in his embarrassment.

'Never mind, Tom,' I interrupted. 'You could not help it. Come and let me clean you up . . . There we are. Now button up and on your way. Oh, tell Cook that I think it would be best if you slept in the stables. There is a suitable room there, but it will need cleaning up. And there must be some spare beds somewhere. You can help in the morning. And leave the maids' bottoms alone!'

His grin really was engaging and I could foresee trouble with one or two of the maids. I was about to warn him more forcefully but then remembered that I had an appointment to interview a possible new pupil, so I went back to my study, pondering on how best to keep him out of trouble – and fondly recalling the feel of his manhood.

As I entered my sanctum, Sophie rose respectfully to her feet and all thoughts of Tom vanished.

Six

If the fair Sarah had attracted me from the outset, my initial impression of Sophie was less vivid, despite her prettiness. Her dress, bonnet and gloves all suggested genteel poverty and I assumed that she came from a respectable family which had fallen on relatively hard times. The recommendation had come from a bachelor friend of Aunt Grace's, who knew the family and was happy to offer some help to them. His letter to me had been short on detail, merely telling me that he was sure that the nineteen-year-old Sophie showed every sign of being a bright and pleasant young woman, who would benefit more than most from the opportunity to achieve some learning – especially in the social graces.

As I poured her a glass of lemonade, I blessed the inspiration which had led me to write to all those friends of Aunt Grace whose names and addresses I had found among her effects.

I sipped slowly at my drink and studied the girl over the top of my glass. Her hair was essentially a dark brown, but with a reddish tint to it which lifted her colouring from the ordinary. As far as I could tell, her complexion was as fair and flawless as one could wish. She was blessed with a wide forehead and cheekbones; brown eyes, pleasingly round and set wide apart; a snub nose and a small but full-lipped mouth. Her chin was narrow, almost pointed, and with a sweet little dimple in its centre.

She told me, with a moving steadiness in her voice,

that her father had left his family for another woman and that, as the oldest child, she had to try and find a way of supporting the others. With evident gratitude, she mentioned my friend's kindness and said that she would apply herself to the utmost to whatever tasks I set.

'I know that this is a heaven-sent opportunity to better myself, Mrs Milford,' she said. 'I owe it to Mr Craxton to take full advantage of it. I beg you to pull me up short if I show the slightest sign of being a slacker.'

I smiled at her. 'I certainly shall, Sophie, have no fear.' For a moment I was tempted to raise the subject of physical discipline but some instinct held me back and I confined the discussion to a survey of those subjects which she most desired to learn. I then handed her to the duty maid, telling her to run a bath in time for supper.

I then walked into the kitchen and asked Cook to join me for dinner and, after agreeing on the food and wine, repaired to my own quarters for a lengthy, contemplative bath.

As I lay in the scented and steaming tub, my confidence in the path I had just begun to follow grew tenfold. My first pupils were already showing promise in a variety of directions. Jane had already given me cause to spank her; Mary was proving an adept and challenging scholar and, although I guessed that her posterior was a little on the meagre side for my tastes, I had no doubts that I would find spanking her quite satisfactory. Nor that it would do her good, for she was already showing signs of intellectual arrogance. Sarah, in contrast, was convinced that she had no talents at all. So far, I had not found the lever which would start the process of drawing her out of her shell but had every confidence that I would do so before too long. In the meantime, for all my desires to have her across my knee, it would be bad for her development to make undue haste. As far as Sophie was concerned, her attitude at her interview did her nothing but credit but time alone would tell if she lived up to that early promise. My mind dwelt on that soft, sweet face and then recalled a promising sway in the seat of her skirt.

I stood up and soaped my thighs and bottom, an action which somehow reminded me of Jane's spanking! I recalled the hollowness in my stomach when I had faced them in the classroom and had known with absolute certainty that I would be punishing her very shortly. The intensity of the feeling had almost surprised me. I lay down again, turned the tap to add a little more hot water (blessing Mr Percival's cleverness as I did so) and relived the experience, concentrating more on the emotions than the physical pleasures, significant though they had been.

I decided that the key element was that it was a sublimely satisfying exercise in power. To be able to summon a young woman whose strength probably matched mine and make her lie across my lap in a childish and humiliating position, and to then bare a private part of her anatomy in the full view of her classmates and cause her some degree of pain, was indeed a testimonial to the extent of my control.

I did not feel the slightest pang of guilt. Her bottom would have recovered quickly but the memory of her spanking would last for days. She needed punishment. Correction of her waywardness was the major reason for her presence at The Academy, so I was doing my duty.

And if carrying out my duty in the way I had gave me great pleasure, then all to the good.

Lastly, if by spanking her I could induce sensual feelings within her, then she would benefit by finding another source of pleasure in her life!

My thoughts turned to Sarah. I knew that my desire

to spank her was inspired more by my own lusts than her needs, so I vowed to proceed with due caution. '*Celui qui chastise le plus, aime le plus,*' was one of Phillip's favourite sayings. 'Whoever chastises the most, loves the most.' Sarah would have to know that, when my hand landed on her bare bottom, it was loving her as much as it was correcting. She was such a tempting little morsel! The womanly breadth of her hips was plain to see and there was sufficient movement beneath her loose tunic to suggest a proper plumpness about her youthful hemispheres.

Her skin was delightful to look at. Well, the immediately visible areas were. I had deliberately brushed my hand against her forearm and the smoothness had thrilled me, so my expectations that her posterior would delight both eye and hand were realistic.

I stood up to dry myself and looked forward to the morrow. All my tomorrows. If I could combine the two pleasures of putting Sarah across my knee and mending some of the harm her awful mother had done to her, then I would have achieved much.

My chance came the next day. Luckily, I had not been too sated after my lustful evening but the opportunity had nearly escaped. I had set them an essay and was sitting supervising their work, shifting my weight on a bottom which still throbbed gently after Cook's expert ministrations. The pause refreshed me so I then led a discussion on poetry with my usual energy.

Mary treated Sarah's stumbling reading of a Wordsworth poem with sneering contempt, and thus gave me ample cause to spank her. I found her surprisingly appealing. Firstly, her manner was admirably contrite from start to end and, more importantly, she presented a far more attractive derrière than I had expected. The two cheeks were chubby – they had quivered delightfully under my steady barrage – and her bottom as a whole had a nice pertness to it. The flawlessly white skin had reddened nicely and she had apologised prettily to both myself and Sarah before restoring her clothing and resuming her seat.

It was the combination of my own sore bottom and the memory of Mary's which almost led me to overlook the clue. I set them another essay and, in an attempt to ease the stiffness in my haunches, walked around the room, casting a casual eye over my pupils' bent heads and busy arms. As I passed behind them, I saw that Sarah had a blank page before her, even though she had given every sign of working industriously. A prickling twinge in my right buttock distracted me and I thought no more of it until much later, when I was marking their efforts.

Some instinct made me turn through the pages of her exercise book and her secret was revealed towards the end – a drawing of a girl bent across an anonymous lap, her bare bottom looming into the air and a blurred arm, hand stiffly extended, caught in mid-air. It was crudely drawn but, allowing for the difficult circumstances, had a startling vividness to it. My first reaction was to tear out the page and lock it in my desk with those similar pictures from my husband's far more experienced hand. Then I hesitated. A moment later I rang the bell and asked Vera to find Sarah and bring her to see me. With a pounding heart, I addressed myself to her legitimate work and had just finished appending my comments when there was a knock on the door.

An impassive Vera shooed a clearly frightened girl up to my desk and disappeared, firmly shutting the door behind her.

'Do sit down, Sarah,' I said loudly and then, motioning her to silence, walked slowly to the door and flung it open. As I suspected, Vera was crouched with her ear to the keyhole. Perfect! I upbraided her loudly and told her that I would be summoning her later for a sound spanking. I then returned to my desk, successfully keeping my features properly stern and fierce. I then turned to the ashen-faced girl and smiled reassuringly.

'I am sorry about that, Sarah. She was clearly hoping to listen to you being spanked.'

She stared at me, wide-eyed. 'Are you going to spank me, Mrs Milford?' she asked nervously.

I widened my own eyes in response. 'Have you done anything to deserve a spanking, Sarah?'

'No . . . I don't think so,' she stuttered. 'But you have my essay in front of you and . . .' She gazed at me and a blush spread over her pretty face.

'Ah, your essay,' I said thoughtfully. 'But why should I wish to discuss that in private? Both Jane and Mary have been punished in the classroom – in public – so, if I were planning to punish you, why should you be spared the added penalty of having witnesses?'

She looked down, the red blush intensifying and her intertwined fingers writhing on her lap. 'I – I don't know, Mrs Milford,' she admitted.

'Well, there you are then,' I said brightly. 'So it must be something else, then. But before I raise the subject, I do wish to make something clear to you. I shall never punish you simply for the sake of it. If your conscience is clear, then you must not be afraid of me. I do believe in discipline, as you know. I am sure that you will have noticed that both of the others showed a marked improvement in their behaviour after they had been corrected. And if – or perhaps when – I feel that you need to be corrected, I shall not hesitate to punish you accordingly. Is that clear?'

I picked up her book, found the page containing the drawing and placed it before her. The blush returned.

'Oh,' she said, then fell silent.

'I have one question and one observation, Sarah,' I continued, my voice low and gentle. 'The question is simply this. What made you want to draw a picture of Mary being spanked?'

She shifted in her chair, looked quickly up at me, then down again. 'I don't know. It just stayed in my mind. The sight of her –'

'Her bare bottom,' I prompted.

'Yes, Mrs Milford. It was so pretty. And I was struggling with my essay and kept on thinking about it. And her. So I found myself drawing it. That's all.'

'Fine,' I said. 'Now for my observation. Oh, I have another question. Have you ever been spanked? Or witnessed a spanking?

'No, Mrs Milford.'

'I see. Well, my observation is quite straightforward. Your effort is artistically very promising. It is an excellent piece of work. Let me explain.' I rose to my feet, moved behind her, rested my hand on her shoulder and carefully pointed out all the praiseworthy aspects. Then I resumed my seat and looked steadily at her. Her face was still pink but her expression was subtly different. The fear had left her and I could see the first signs of her blossoming under the gentle and unaccustomed rain of my compliments.

'I *am* going to spank you, Sarah,' I said quietly. 'Firstly for wasting paper and secondly for not informing me that you have artistic leanings. Do you object?'

'No, Mrs Milford,' she mumbled, looking down at her lap. 'But does it have to be on my bare ... with my drawers down?'

I did not reply immediately, but walked round to her, raised her upright and rested my hands on her upper arms, looking straight into her eyes. 'Yes it does, Sarah,' I whispered. 'For a number of reasons. It smarts more on the naked skin; the feeling that such an intimate part of your person is so openly exposed is good for the soul; by submitting gracefully to the embarrassment as well as the pain, you show me that you accept that you have erred. Lastly, my dear, you are a very pretty girl and I sincerely wish to see your bottom, which I wager is as pretty as the rest of you.' At that, I reached forward and kissed her, briefly, softly and full on those delicious lips.

To my surprise, after a moment's staring at me like a startled fawn, she flung her arms around my waist, buried her head in my shoulder and burst into tears. I held her close, making soothing noises and patting her back until she composed herself. When her shoulders had stopped shaking, I led her over to the *chaise-longue* and helped her into position, before eagerly addressing myself to the task of baring her. My hands trembled as they tugged the hem of her tunic upward and folded it neatly above her waist. My heart thudded in my ears as my fingers fumbled with the tape securing her drawers. There was a vast emptiness in my belly as I nervously eased them down over the twin mounds of creamy flesh, separated by a perfect cleft and delineated by two long, curving folds.

I left her last item of protection in tangled disarray halfway down her plump thighs and gazed down, spellbound.

In retrospect, both Arabella and Bertha had prettier posteriors but Sarah's did not fall far short of their remarkably high standards. It lay quivering before me, filling my vision, thrilling me.

I took a long breath in an attempt to regain some sort of composure and then reached out and rested my hand on the crown of the nearer cheek. My cunny opened moistly as I touched her intimate skin and I could hardly restrain myself from burying my face in that amplitude of tightly divided flesh.

'Oh, Sarah!' I whispered. 'It is as lovely as I had imagined.' My hand roved with increasing passion, pressing into the firmly yielding mounds and trailing down the cleft. I could not resist prising the twin globes apart and gazing in rapture at the wrinkled, pinky-brown anus which tightened in surprise. I let her go and the red mists evaporated as I once again donned the mantle of headmistress. Patting both buttocks hard enough to make them shimmer deliciously, I collected myself.

'I must spank you now, Sarah,' I said, with something approaching due authority.

'Yes, Mrs Milford,' she replied, bravely lifting her hips.

It was a memorable spanking. Both of us were in a highly emotional state, of course, so that all my senses were fully alert and all the pleasurable aspects of chastising a pretty girl were especially vivid. The outstanding one was the sight of her shapely bottom, filling my vision as my hand flashed down and sank into the yielding flesh, setting it wobbling like a blancmange and leaving its pink visiting card at every blow.

After a short time, I was quite out of breath and leant back to survey the effects of my initial onslaught. I had been too carried away to direct the spanks with my usual accuracy, so that the red stain was not as evenly spread as I would have wished. None the less, her bottom presented an arresting sight as she rhythmically clenched and relaxed it in a vain attempt to reduce the sting. I watched, enthralled at the changes in the shape of her buttocks and the texture of her skin as they tightened and softened. Delicious dimples came and went. Her soft cleft closed up then opened. The folds lengthened and shortened. I composed myself and prepared for the second round.

'Well, young Sarah, that has evidently warmed you up nicely. It is time for the next phase. Could you move forward a trifle, please? I would like your bottom in the centre of my lap. Your feet further apart, perhaps. Excellent.'

The minor alteration in her position made a noticeable difference to the presentation of her derrière. The lower portions of the cheeks were now more easily accessible and the separation between them more marked.

She shuddered a little as my hand roved freely and she pressed the centre of her body into my thighs. This was an enjoyable sensation, but I felt a flare of disappointment that she had apparently shrunk from my hand, rather than pressed her bottom against it. I then recommenced her spanking, in a much more considered and methodical fashion, slowing the tempo down and aiming with care to spread the colour more evenly.

Each smack was accompanied by a small cry of pain, a shuddering wobble, a clenching of her buttocks and jerk of her legs. Each time I waited patiently for her to present her bottom properly and, when it was still and nicely rounded, patted the area I intended to smack next and let fly.

Her cries, wriggles and jerks grew more pronounced at each visitation and before long she was showing clear signs of genuine distress. As I had never intended to do more than provide a reasonably testing introduction to the arts of corporal punishment, I finished with a flurry of sharp pats to the base of her bottom, straddling the cleft and hoping that the resulting shifting of her flesh would give some pleasurable feelings.

I then raised her to her feet and watched with a little smile as she hopped from foot to foot, rubbing frantically at her smarting behind, with her face screwed up most prettily. After a while her movements became less desperate and it was time to take her a step further.

Helping her down to sit comfortably on my lap, still with her tunic tucked up and her drawers around her ankles, I held her head to my bosom and stroked her hot buttocks with my left hand.

The healthy tears of release flowed steadily into my blouse and I could feel the tenseness leaving her. I kissed the top of her head, breathing in the sweet scent of her hair.

'That was not too painful, was it, Sarah?' I asked.

'Oh, Mrs Milford, I have never known such pain,' she replied, a tremor in her voice.

'Oh, come now, you must have done,' I laughed, stroking busily away. 'But is my hand not soothing you?'

'Oh yes,' she sighed, and wriggled on my lap. 'It is very nice.'

I smiled broadly and tingled all over. 'So is your bottom, my dear. Nice, I mean. Very nice.'

'Do you really mean that, Mrs Milford? As nice as the other girls?'

'Certainly,' I replied briskly. 'In fact, so pretty that I would like to see it again. Lie across my lap and I shall rub it for you. Hold on, let me move up a little so that you can stretch out comfortably.'

With a shy smile, she turned and placed herself across my thighs, sighing contentedly as I stroked and soothed her pinkened skin. With her body far less curved, her bottom was noticeably more solid. Even nicer to look at, if not quite as satisfactory to spank. I could not resist another peep at her anus and felt another surge of disappointment when her first reaction was to try and resist the pressure of my fingers.

Nevertheless, I had thoroughly enjoyed spanking her and let her up with some reluctance. The prospect of administering similar – and considerably more vigorous – treatment to Vera's fat buttocks was, however, very adequate compensation and I dismissed her with another affectionate kiss.

Before I slipped into a contented sleep that night, I realised I had been disappointed with the standard of her essay and would therefore have the pleasure of turning her up in front of her classmates in the morning. A happy thought!

In the event, it was Sophie rather than Sarah who brought new joy into my life.

I had spent some little time re-reading their essays and, incredible though it may seem, trying to find reasons to let Mary and Jane off with no more than a lecture. I wanted to concentrate fully on Sarah. In the event, I concluded that nothing would be served by sparing the other two and decided that they had both presented work that was sufficiently slipshod to merit a taste of the birch. The more I considered my plan the more it appealed.

Both Jane and Mary would benefit from the more strenuous punishment and, at the same time, I had every reason to hope that Sarah would be so relieved at having to suffer no more than a spanking that she would lose most of the nervousness she had exhibited the first time. In addition, witnessing the three chastisements would certainly show Sophie what she would have to face in the future.

On the hour, I strode into the classroom, returned the girls' respectful greeting, placed my papers on my desk and addressed them.

'I am displeased with your essays. I told you quite clearly that you must go to the library to write them, for the simple reason that there are several atlases there. Had you obeyed my instructions, none of you would have been reduced to the degree of guesswork you have all displayed. I shall now punish you.' I paused and studied their expressions.

Jane and Mary grimaced a little, but otherwise seemed quite resigned to their fate. Sarah blushed furiously and stared down into her lap. Sophie stared back, wide-eyed. Then the pink tip of her tongue slipped out and ran slowly over her lips. I felt a tiny flicker of emotion deep within me. Then I continued.

'Sarah.' She looked up at me and I almost smiled at the woebegone look on her dear little face. 'One thing in your favour is that you have obviously taken more care this time. Your handwriting shows a distinct improvement and your maps are beautifully drawn. If inaccurate? You will be spanked.'

'Yes, Mrs Milford,' she mumbled.

I turned to the other miscreants. 'You two need a sharper lesson. You will feel the birch!'

In perfect unison, their eyes widened and their jaws dropped. Naturally, the only spoken protest came from Jane.

'Oh, Mrs Milford!' she exclaimed. 'Surely we do not deserve to be flogged?'

I smiled. 'I do not have the slightest intention of flogging you, my dear.' I reached under the desk, withdrew one of the rods from the bucket which I had secreted there before breakfast and showed it to them. 'See how light the twigs are, and how nice and bushy it is. It will be more painful than my hand, but that is the point.' I placed the implement on the desk, walked up to her and cupped her cheek. 'I could never do you – or your pretty bottom – lasting harm, Jane,' I continued softly. 'I am far too fond of you. And of your nice posterior. Her relief was manifest from her answering smile and the way she pressed her cheek against my hand. I returned to the desk and moved my chair round to its front, sideways on to the girls, unmistakably placed to offer them a full view.

'Come here, Sarah. I shall start with you.'

Scarlet with shame and humiliation, she rose slowly to her feet, cast an anguished glance at her companions and then stumbled to my side, flinging herself over my thighs with a moan of dismay.

There was no hurry. Hers was far too delicious a rump to treat in a cavalier manner, so I bared her with tantalising deliberation, then made her adjust her position until I was satisfied. Needless to say, both her naked buttocks had to be thoroughly felt before another adjustment was ordered! I felt some of the tenseness leave her when I again praised the qualities of her bottom, although she stiffened once more when she felt my left hand press her down.

I spanked her in a far more formal manner this time,

allowing five seconds between smacks. Each one was markedly crisper than any I had administered the previous day, sending a rippling quiver through both reddening mounds so that she was crying aloud by the time I deemed that she had suffered enough. I helped her up, dried her tears and pulled up her drawers. She returned to her desk with obvious relief.

It was then that I noticed Sophie. I had intended to cast an eye over the watchers in the hope of gleaning some idea of their reaction to the public spanking but had been so absorbed by the sight of Sarah's bare bottom that I had quite forgotten. In the event, it mattered not. Although she had looked away the second she felt my gaze upon her, I had seen enough of her expression to send a surge of joy through me. Her brown eyes were wide and moist with emotion and her lips were parted sufficiently to give me a glimpse of her perfect teeth. On their own, those signs could have signified little more than sympathy with her companion's shame and pain. I knew better. There was a tightness about her face which suggested keen interest. Intrigued, I pointed at my second victim of the day.

'You next please, Mary.'

Holding her shoulders back and with little more than a trembling lower lip betraying her fear, she approached me. 'How would you like me, Mrs Milford?' she asked in a voice distinctly more high-pitched than usual.

I had already determined to follow the example set by Miss Parfitt, both in the positioning and the arrangement of the clothing.

'Just lean forward with your hands on the top of the desk, please, Mary.'

'Shall I bare my bottom for you?'

'No, my dear,' I replied warmly. 'I will deal with that. But thank you.'

Without further ado, she was in place, the seat of her tunic jutting out promisingly. Leaning over her and standing well clear so that everybody had a fair view, I bared her bottom, refastening the tape of her drawers midway down her slender thighs. Then I carefully examined my target.

'Down on to your elbows, I think, Mary. Good. And your feet further apart. Yes, that is fine.' I moved to stand in front of her and, holding her gaze as I stroked her cheek, gave her a little lecture.

'As I said to Jane, this will not resemble a flogging in any respect. I am going to make your nice little bottom sting and it will be quite red by the time I am done. But the effects will have worn off by the end of the day and there will be no lasting marks. I do hope, however, that the memory will remain in your mind for a great deal longer than the marks will stay on your bottom. You are an exceptionally gifted girl and I am punishing you first and foremost for making light of your abilities. Do I make myself clear, Mary?'

'Yes, Mrs Milford,' she gulped.

I nodded and straightened up, casting a swift glance at the other girls as I did so. Jane was looking very tense and her eyes flickered away from Mary's derrière and then back, reluctantly fascinated. Sarah was staring at it thoughtfully and I hoped that she was memorising the contours for another drawing! Sophie was riveted. She was leaning forward to get the closest possible view, her lips parted and her eyes shining with excitement.

With growing hope that I had found another enthusiast, I raised my pretty little rod and whisked it against the centre of Mary's pretty little bottom.

She gasped as the flexible twigs bit into her rounded curves, then jerked upright and shook her hips in an instinctive attempt to alleviate the smart. I was watching her face rather than her bottom and was not unamused at the contrasting emotions which flickered across her features. Dismay at the initial sting; surprise that it was not as bad as she had feared; relief as the pain ebbed away and was replaced by the pleasing warmth which characterises a sympathetically delivered first stroke from that mistress of all punishment implements. Lastly, a slight embarrassment at her fallibility. She turned her head towards me, gave me a rueful smile, and stuck her bottom out in readiness for the second.

Better prepared, her reaction was restricted to a hissing intake of breath and slight wriggle.

I stepped back to distribute the special sting of the tips more evenly and gave her the third.

'Ow!' she cried softly, and her efforts to maintain her pose were clearly more demanding.

As I crossed to her right side for the next three, I examined her carefully, pleased at my handiwork. The spreading of the rod as it landed had resulted in her right cheek apparently suffering more than its sister, which had three red bands across it compared with a broader tracery of individual weals and dots. I smoothed my hand briefly over the warm surface, took aim again, and let fly.

Her fortitude was admirable, considering that this was her first taste of the rod. After the fifth, I looked at her face again. Although her eyes were screwed tightly shut and she was biting her lower lip, there were no visible tears. To me, it would have been little more than an exciting tingling but I already sensed that she found no pleasure in the pain. I was witnessing strength of character more than anything else.

I completed her due dozen, told her to stay in position, then bent down behind her. Her bottom glowed very prettily in the bright morning light and was obviously quite sore. She was trembling all over and panting rapidly. Quivering ripples were an eloquent testimony to the softness of her flesh but the condition of her bottom and her demeanour proved that I had gauged the severity correctly.

'I think that will do, Mary,' I announced, as I walked

round to face her. 'You may rub your bottom now, if you wish.'

She did so. Tentatively to start with but with increasing vigour. Before I moved to watch the exciting agitation of her fleshy mounds, I stole a quick glance at the audience. Sarah was looking on fairly impassively and Jane was even more nervous as her time was obviously nigh, but Sophie brought another surge of eager anticipation to my heart. She was rocking to and fro on the fulcrum of her own bottom, the yearning plain to see.

In something of a daze, I pulled up Mary's drawers and lowered her tunic, and I am sorry to admit that I did not do Jane's far more generous behind full justice, whipping her more perfunctorily than it deserved. Not that I sensed any complaint on her part! It was more that the uneven redness offended my sense of aesthetics!

The remainder of the lesson passed quickly. None of the girls was in the mood to devote her full attention to the work and, for my part, I was plotting how to get Sophie across my knee in the most advantageous circumstances.

Fortunately for my peace of mind, I had already arranged to give them a half-day holiday, as a friend of Jane's Aunt Maud wished to take them into London to see the sights. I waved them goodbye, suggested that Sarah would especially enjoy a visit to an art gallery, and sought distraction in the many tasks and decisions which demanded my time and attention.

One of the most pleasurable was to accompany Tom to the livery stables. Our own facilities were ready and I could hardly contain my impatience. Nothing provided a more definite symbol of my elevated status than my own carriage. I watched anxiously as he guided the horses (two elegant greys) between the shafts but his confident manner eased my worries. I also took great delight in informing the groom who had beaten Tom during my earlier visit that the urchin whom he had treated in such a cavalier manner was the same smart and capable coachman he was now watching with respect.

We travelled back the long way. After a very few minutes, I sat back and revelled in the luxurious interior, acknowledging the respectful salutations of the crowds enjoying the early summer air. Tom was proving conclusively that he had a natural affinity with horses as they were responding quickly to his commands and he used his whip sparingly.

My happiness enveloped me like a warm eiderdown on a cold night. I had not realised it at the time but the prospect of applying the rod had rather unnerved me. I had still felt a lingering concern that my penchant for spanking would encourage me to punish where such a course would not be fair or just and I would therefore lose the respect of my charges.

The manner in which Jane, Sarah and Mary had accepted their punishments was immensely reassuring. And if Sarah did not seem to be the natural disciple I had hoped for, then Sophie was showing promise.

And, here I was, a lady of property trotting rhythmically through a lovely park, the object of many an envious stare, in my own conveyance pulled by a pair of thoroughbred horses under the direction of a smart and handsome coachman. I smiled in my contentment and wriggled in my seat. True to form, lascivious thoughts began to rescue me from the sins of pride and complacency! I dwelt on the pleasing prospect of giving the lad another spanking and stayed on the alert for the slightest fault in his driving.

When we eventually clattered up to the front door, I adjusted my bonnet, stood as he opened the door, smoothed my skirts and alighted with an appropriately nonchalant air. Tom and I stood face to face and I could see that he was bursting with pride at his new status. With due cause, for he had made the most of the sudden stroke of fortune and I was already impressed with him. That was not, however, going to spare his bottom.

'Well done, Tom,' I said, beaming. 'You fill me with confidence. But I do seem to remember that you allowed the left rear wheel to ride up over the kerb as we passed through Sheen Gate. Naughty boy! Settle the horses down – and make sure that they have plenty to eat – and then come up to my study. Let me see. It should take you an hour, so at four o'clock. I think that your bottom is due for a course of my special treatment.'

The impudent little monkey had the gall to grin cheekily at the sentence. 'Yes, Mrs Milford,' he replied, not the least abashed at the thought of having to present his naked posterior to a member of the opposite sex. Grinning back at him conspiratorially, I swept indoors, up to my bedroom, ran a quick bath and enjoyed a long, scented soak. As the water cooled, I felt in the mood for some intimate pampering and rang the bell. I was pleased when the duty maid turned out to be Connie, of whom I had seen little since I moved in.

Bidding her to strip to the buff, I stroked and caressed her while she dried me, lay over her lap while she powdered my bottom, and then gazed peacefully at her exposed charms in the looking-glass while she dressed me.

I arrived in my study just before the hour and was apparently engrossed in some papers when he knocked firmly.

He provided a perfect ending to a memorable day. Handling male flesh made a welcome change from female, despite my preference for the latter, and his willingness to submit quietly while I bared, bent and spanked him made me glow with pleasure. There could be no doubting from his expression throughout that he already worshipped me, and his wonderment that I should condescend to fondle his pego until the seed spurted out was touching.

I summoned Connie to my bed that night and the memory of his steely manhood demanded full use of the dildoes to quench the inner fires.

The very next day, after two excellent lessons, Sophie relit them with a vengeance. After my hopes for Sarah had been so far fruitless, I had not built up any great expectations over my latest recruit. She had given me no cause to spank her during the day and I was sitting in my drawing room with a pot of tea, some cake and *The Times* when Elspeth knocked on the door.

'Miss Sophie would like a word, madam,' she said nervously, knowing that I liked to take tea in peace.

I frowned, more in puzzlement than anger. 'Well, send her in. Oh, and bring another cup and a fresh pot, if you please, Elspeth.'

Sophie crept in, looking extremely nervous and ill at ease. I sat her down and we made small talk until Elspeth returned with the refreshment. The tea calmed her somewhat and my general praise of her comportment to date furthered the soothing process. When she had tidied up the cups and plates, I led her over to the sofa, sat her down, took her trembling hand and simply asked her what was ailing her.

She took a deep breath, looked me straight in the eye, and said firmly, 'Please, Mrs Milford, will you give me a good spanking? I just cannot wait any longer.'

I am certain that my astonishment – and delight – caused me to blink but other than that, I believe I kept a reasonably straight face.

'Why?' I asked.

She blushed most prettily and looked down at the floor. 'I just want to feel what it is like.' She raised her head and stared imploringly into my eyes. 'I watched you dealing with the others ... and their posteriors looked so pretty. I have never seen a girl in that state before. And you looked so lovely ... staring at their nakedness. You whipped them so gracefully. And the way you stroked them ... I want to feel those beautiful hands on my bare bottom. Your eyes looking at it. I could see that you found pleasure in their charms and I hope with all my heart that mine will also please you.' She stammered to a halt and looked down again, her confusion making her more desirable than ever.

My heart was so full that for several minutes I could only respond by squeezing her hand, which trembled in mine like a captive bird. Then, after a tremulous sigh, I broke the silence.

'My dearest Sophie. Your entreaty would, I am sure, soften the hardest heart. And mine is far from hard.' She looked up again and her smile excited me yet further. 'I shall certainly smack your bare bottom for you; but first you must kiss me.'

With a moan which illustrated the depths of her pent-up passion more clearly than any words, she flung an arm around my shoulders and glued the full softness of her lips to mine.

All of a sudden, my emotions were equally aroused. I had found Sophie attractive from the outset but, probably because I had still been carrying a torch for Sarah, I had taken less note of her than otherwise would have been the case. As my hands closed round the firmness of her back, as I felt her plump bosom crushed against mine, as her panting echoed through my head and as my lips ached under her desperate kisses, the red mists blurred both vision and discretion.

Gasping for breath, we parted and I stared at her with a new perspective. Her brown eyes were moist and shining and her parted lips were wet. Loose strands of dark hair clung to her damp temples. She was beautiful by any standards and the combination of lust and love in her expression made her into the most desirable creature on earth. I kissed her again. My tongue forced its way between her teeth into her mouth. Her gasps and moans at the novel sensation matched my own. Her mouth was sweet. And wet. And hot. Her cunny would be sweeter, wetter and hotter. I longed to thrust my tongue into the slippery coral at the core of her femininity. I yearned for the silken softness of her intimate skin. Her thighs, breasts, belly. Her buttocks. Especially her buttocks.

Gradually I regained my senses and withdrew my bruised lips, resting my hand against her cheek and stroking her mouth with the ball of my extended thumb.

'Well, well, Sophie,' I said, smiling at her. 'Am I correct in assuming that my kisses do not displease you?'

'Oh, Mrs Milford,' she sighed, pressing against my hand and making my desire to see and feel her nether cheeks even more urgent. 'I have never known such physical pleasure!'

I leaned forward and kissed her again, softly. 'I shall ensure that you will experience a great deal more pleasure while you are here, my sweet. But you have been most forward, child. I cannot imagine what possessed you.

Her expression matched mine for false solemnity. 'It is just that I am a wicked girl, Mrs Milford.'

Another little kiss and I kept my mouth close to hers so that she breathed in my words. 'A very wicked girl, Sophie. I shall have to punish you. Do you not agree?'

Her eyes closed for a moment. 'Oh yes, Mrs Milford, most severely,' she whispered. 'I think I should be spanked. On my wicked, naughty bottom.'

My response was delayed while I forced a hand underneath her. 'I agree, Sophie. And it is such a naughty little bottom that I think that I should lay it quite bare before smacking it.'

'Yes please,' was all she could say. She stretched her neck, emphasising its slender, graceful length. I kissed it, running my mouth up and down, inhaling her scent and revelling in the smooth skin.

I pulled my hand from under her posterior, took hold of hers and helped her to her feet. 'Come, Sophie, we shall retire to my study. We can be more private there.'

My excitement was nearly unbearable. Her hot little hand trembled in my grasp and her footsteps were unrhythmical as her nervousness disturbed the usual grace of her walk. My own limbs felt detached. It was like a dream, when one cannot feel the ground. There was a hollowness in my middle – not an empty void but a cavern filled with pulsating tingles.

Still in a daze, I floated into my elegant room and then my bottom settled into the cushioned seat of the *chaise-longue*. Sophie flung herself on to my lap with a little cry. Softly heavy and warm. Her tunic tightened over her hips and I had my first inkling of the shape of her buttocks. They were like Elizabeth's maid's, whom I had spanked at the meeting of The Society – narrow but with a pronounced jut.

My shaking hands reached down to grip the hem and begin the upward journey. Her calves were slim, her thighs properly round, her drawers like a second skin. I fumbled for the tape, loosened it and, holding my breath, slipped her last garment down until her bottom swam nakedly before me. I was too enthralled to study it in detail. I just had an impression of jutting hillocks, pure white skin and a long, deep cleft. Then my right hand rose and fell and the room echoed to the sounds of Sophie's bare bottom receiving a good spanking.

My smacks were restrained. Some instinct moderated my enthusiasm so that I did not exhaust her before time and, as I regained my senses, I was able to take better note of her qualities. The first impression was of the delectable springiness of her flesh. If Sarah's was softer and wobbled rather than quivered, there was an elasticity in Sophie which would have tempted a plaster saint.

Then there was her obvious delight in being spanked

by me. She could not contain herself and was bobbing and weaving in time with my flailing palm, so that her glowing bottom always seemed to raise itself to meet me. Her skin reddened far more slowly than either Bertha's or Arabella's, but by the time I needed to pause was glorious red.

I rested my throbbing palm on the coolness of her left thigh and caught my breath, gazing avidly down at her. She continued her blatantly sensual movements, despite the pause, rhythmically moving up and down.

'Oh, Mrs Milford, please don't stop!' she gasped. 'I have never known such feelings.' She thrust her hips right into the air, so that her bottom was but inches from my face. I kissed the crown of the nearer side and it felt even more satiny to my lips than it had done to my palm. And hotter.

My pursed lips followed the exciting contours and as they dipped into the tight cleft, she moaned audibly. I found myself torn between a number of conflicting desires. I wanted to spank her again: to kiss every inch of smooth skin: explore every nook and cranny of her lissom body: to feel her hands and eyes on my more opulent curves. I wanted it all, and as soon as possible.

For the moment, a fulfilling spanking would suffice. I pressed her back down against my lap and resumed the assault, this time with my mind clearer. The beauty of her bottom struck me most forcibly and as the smarting approached her levels of tolerance, I alternated between lighter smacks and lingering caresses.

I soon sensed that she was approaching that blissful state where pain and pleasure combine. Her whole bottom was red and hot; she was moaning continuously and writhing helplessly; her hips churned, her legs kicked and my nostrils were assailed by the unmistakable scent of her arousal. Forcing my left hand underneath her, I wriggled it into the fork of her body. The hair there was fine, soft and damp, especially as I pressed a finger into the top of her tight slit and found her pleasure-spot. Her breath whooped in and out of her lungs as the waves built up.

My right hand found its way unerringly into the cleft between her cheeks until I felt the tip of my fingers pressing against her warm anus. She drew her feet up and apart. Her rear end loomed up towards me and the twin halves parted. She began to scream out in her ecstasy and I could feel the spasmodic jerks of her bottom-hole. Her body went rigid as the waves crashed through her, trapping my hands in softness. Then the breath whistled out of her lungs and she slumped loosely across my thighs.

I stroked her quivering bottom and whispered little words of affection until she had recovered sufficiently to sit on my lap, with her tear-stained face buried against my shoulder.

Another disciple had joined my select band.

From that day onward, I went about with a song in my heart. Hardly a lesson passed without Sophie willingly presenting her delicious rump for my best attentions, and somehow her attitude encouraged the others to lose their fear of my punishment. Even Sarah bestowed an occasional smile at me as I guided her into position, and admitted during a private spanking in my study that she derived no little pleasure from my caresses to her derrière. Her shy comment inspired me to reward her good work by placing her over my knee, baring her plump bottom and stroking it until she was sighing with delight. And, after an initial reluctance, she began to enjoy having her dear little anus exposed and tickled.

All four responded most gratifyingly to my teaching and the sound of laughter was as much a characteristic of our lessons as the sounds of a bare bottom being smacked!

For variety, there was always Tom, who never failed

to expose a rigid pego whenever I took down his trousers.

The next development came perhaps two weeks after Sophie's first spanking. I received an intriguing little note from a Mr Fortescue, asking permission to call on me the following morning. Judging from the address and the quality of the notepaper, he was a man of some substance and I awaited his arrival with anticipation. At the appointed time, Elspeth ushered him into my study and we talked in a desultory manner until we were both supplied with coffee and cake. He was a tall, distinguished man, with a fine set of whiskers and an overall air of quiet authority. After we had exhausted the normal social pleasantries, he cleared his throat.

'Mrs Milford, if I may come straight to the point. I am a magistrate on the local bench and, as such, have a general interest in correction.' He stared out of the window and then turned his steady gaze to me. My pulse quickened. He continued. 'I feel a certain sympathy for some of the poor wretches who appear before me. In many cases, life has dealt them a losing hand and I know that prison is going to do little to correct their errant ways.'

I leant forward, hanging on to every word. 'Forgive me for interrupting, Mr Fortescue, but I could not agree more fervently . . .' I went on to describe the transformation I had made to Tom, mentioning simply that I had chastised him whenever he required it. He nodded solemnly, pondered my words and then continued, his relief at the meeting of our minds clear in his voice.

'That is exactly the type of case which concerns me, Mrs Milford. Not an evil person, more an unfortunate one. In days of yore, it would have been within my powers to order a reasonable whipping and then the miscreant could have walked free to rue his – or her – crime, and hopefully to stick to the straight and narrow.

Now, I am acquainted with Miss Brown, whose niece is currently in your charge. I understand that Miss Brown is delighted with her progress. Jane's letters are full of enthusiastic references to the excellence of your methods. In brief, Mrs Milford, my proposition is this. When a miscreant whom I consider would benefit from corporal punishment comes to my notice, I would like you to administer the punishment. I trust you to be firm but fair and all I ask is that you send me a written report of the whipping and the miscreant's reactions to it. To my home, if you please. The local superintendent of police and I are, by the by, in full accord and so there will be no record of the offence.'

I agreed with alacrity, only suggsting that it should be made perfectly clear to the sinner that further offences would be dealt with officially – and mercilessly.

We parted on the most cordial of terms and I awaited my first victim impatiently. Two days later, Vera brought in a note from the magistrate and said that the girl who had brought it was waiting by the back door. With trembling hands, I broke the seal and opened the missive.

Dear Mrs Milford,
Daisy Higgins was apprehended for stealing apples. She claims that she wanted them to feed horses and I am inclined to believe her. She is rather an appealing girl and I hope that a sharp lesson from you will convince her that theft is wrong.
Your obedient servant, etc. etc.

I rang the bell, told Vera to bring the girl to me, sat back and waited somewhat nervously, as I knew that I had to act responsibly.

She turned out to be quite a pretty girl, with clean if shabby clothes and an old cap pulled down over her face. I told her to remove it and her tangled fair hair tumbled loosely over her shoulders. She was plainly terrified and my first reaction was to sit her down and order some lemonade. Then I thought that this approach was hardly right considering the judicial nature of our interview. I then realised that my role was to complement the formality of court proceedings, not to try and copy them. So I rang the bell and asked Vera to bring in a jug of cordial and two glasses. Turning back to the bewildered girl, I smiled at her.

'Now, Daisy, what is this all about?'

With many a pause, she admitted to stealing the apples, hotly denied breaking into the stables as the gates were open and the door to the storage area unlocked, then repeated her assertion that all she wanted to do was to make friends with the horses.

I looked at her studiously and felt certain that she was telling the truth. 'I know that it was only a few apples, Daisy, but theft is theft, as you well know. You could go to prison. If you are charged and found guilty, of course. What would your family think about that? I should imagine that the shame would be too much to bear.'

'Oh, I don't want to go to gaol, ma'am!' she cried. 'The man said I wouldn't have to if you agree to beat me. Oh, madam, please whip me! Please!

I smiled again, genuinely warming to her. 'All right, Daisy, I shall whip you. Quite hard, mind, but you will be spared prison. Now, when did you last eat?'

She stared at me, bewilderment overcoming her relief. 'Pardon, ma'am?'

'When did you last have a decent meal?' I repeated patiently.

'Dunno, ma'am. Yesterday dinner weren't bad. Turnips and gravy.'

'I see. Well, I only have one firm rule and that is never to beat a girl on an empty stomach. Vera will take you to the kitchen and cook will give you some bread and dripping. Then come back here.'

'Yes ma'am. Thank you, ma'am.'

In her absence, I considered the best method of punishing her and felt a flare of sensual excitement at the prospect of seeing her bare bottom. Then I did all I could to quash the feelings, sensing that I should not gain enjoyment from punishing a nice, basically good girl.

Her shapeless dress had given me few clues as to her form but there were no signs of real poverty about her so that it was a reasonable assumption that she would be well covered. There was no reason for undue haste and therefore I could whip her at leaisure, with unhurried preparations. The cane? Or the birch? I decided on the latter and had just selected a nice bushy rod when there was a knock on the door and she was led in again.

I immediately noticed that her face was much cleaner and realised that cook had given her a quick scrub. Something to eat and the wash had done much to calm her nerves and she looked at the implement of her correction with no more than a wince. She then stood upright and met my gaze, waiting for instructions.

I warmed to her. With her nice round face and fair hair, she was pretty enough, and her courage in the face of what must have been a frightening ordeal was exemplary. A little intrigued, I told her to sit down and asked her to tell me something about herself, discovering that she was just eighteen, had just moved in with her older sister and her husband, and was hoping to find employment locally. As she spoke, her eyes kept darting to the waiting rod and I felt a surge of guilt at prolonging her ordeal unnecessarily. I speedily made the one point which had occurred to me when I spotted the coincidence in the fact that both she and Tom had found themselves in trouble because of their love of horses.

'You like horses, I imagine, Daisy?'

'Oh yes, ma'am,' she said animatedly.

'Well,' I replied, 'I may need some help in our stables

here. We shall discuss it later after you have recovered from your whipping. Please remove your clothes.'

'All of them?' she enquired nervously.

'Yes please.'

I sat and watched as she obeyed. Now that I had been able to make some positive contribution to her future, my conscience was clear and I felt quite free to enjoy her naked charms. She whisked her dress off with little delay but her natural modesty made her fingers less sure when she started on her underclothing. Her blush returned when she was down to her shift, which was sufficiently thin to reveal the dark spots of her nipples and an exciting triangle at the base of her belly. Typically, she was not wearing any drawers. With a final, anguished look, she slipped her last garment off her shoulders, slithered it down to her feet and stepped free of it. I studied her with frank enjoyment.

'Turn around please, Daisy,' I ordered, once I had had my fill of her buxom breasts and broad thighs. 'I want to see your bottom.'

She shuffled round and a lovely broad, white bottom quivered into my view. I gazed happily for a minute or two, then told her to turn about again and passed sentence.

'Daisy, your crime was not a serious one and the fact that you did not steal for your own gains is in your favour. None the less, you deserve to be punished and I intend to give you a sharp dose of the birch. On your bottom. Have you been beaten before?'

'Oh yes, ma'am, lots of times, but never with one of them,' she replied.

'In which case you will find it a different experience, which is all to the good. But do not worry unduly. It smarts well enough but will do no lasting harm. Will you please lay yourself across the arm of the sofa, with your head on the seat and your legs straight out behind you.'

The few steps that she had to take to reach the sofa were enough to demonstrate an unusually mobile posterior, and when she had assumed the position, a quick pass of my hand proved that it was also delightfully firm.

It was a most satisfying ten minutes. As it was a punishment, I did not have to consider her enjoyment and so concentrated fully on the reactions of her bottom. I wanted to make it sufficiently sore to remind her of the consequences if she was ever tempted to steal in the future, so had selected one of my weightier rods. I also wielded it with a little more force than was my custom.

I administered the first half-dozen quite rapidly, not allowing her to become accustomed to the unique bite in a leisurely manner. It was effective!

'Oh, ma'am ... Oohh ... *Ow* ... *Oww* ... Oh lumme ... *Ahhhh!*'

I paused, looking down on a trembling, bright pink bottom with its tracery of red weals. She squeezed and relaxed her broad cheeks, rocking from side to side as she tried to absorb the pain.

I then reverted to my normal approach, whisking the worthy implement down across the full width of her buttocks, snapping my wrist to impart an extra bite to each stroke but waiting for the effect to wax, then wane, before administering the next.

She made no efforts to avoid her punishment but neither did she show the fortitude which was typical of my pupils. At each blow, she heaved her middle around, shaking the fleshy masses in an instinctive attempt to rid them of the burning. She howled and wailed. Tears flowed as she sobbed. But not once did she beg for mercy! Instead, her pleas were for forgiveness for her crime and my heart warmed to her.

Her big bottom was the colour of a ripe cherry by the time I decided to apply the last dozen. Only the closest examination revealed the individual lines left by the twigs on her once-smooth skin. Her cries were no longer coherent and her strength had left her, so that she slumped immodestly over the supporting arm, her thighs splayed casually apart.

Moving to stand by her left side, I administered the finale vertically, starting on the nearer flank, visiting the softness of her long bottom-cleft, and ending on the further reaches of her right cheek.

I then comforted her with as much dedication as I had whipped her. Gentle caresses; damp cloths; soothing words of praise and forgiveness. All combined to restore her, mentally and physically.

She walked out of the room eventually, with her head held high and the promise of a proper role in life to give her real hope.

Seven

My face screwed up in ecstasy as I lowered my throbbing and naked bottom into the cool water of the fountain around my statue. Soft skin and yielding flesh met hard and unyielding stone. Roughness against living satin. Bliss! I sighed happily and lay back until my head was resting comfortably on the low wall. My feet floated apart, opening my tingling love-nest so that cool wetness and the warm moisture of excitement mingled.

I was utterly content. I adjusted my straw hat to shade my face and savoured the peacefulness. My pupils were on a nature ramble organised by an enthusiastic friend, the maids were variously enjoying a half-day, and Cook had taken full advantage of the situation by taking me to the basement, stripping me naked, tying me tightly to the ladder and spanking me until I could take no more. Then she had carried me to the whipping bench, laid me on my back, and bound my hands and feet above my head so that I was completely exposed and helpless, with her gloating face hovering over my blatantly displayed charms. Her glittering eyes had fixed themselves on my two open orifices, while her full lips had described with relish what her eyes could see. She had stroked and poked; prodded and patted. She had smacked the backs of my thighs from knee to buttock and then had thrust one forefinger firmly up my bottom-hole and the other into my cunny. Then she had applied tawse and martinet to devastating effect.

Lastly, she had stripped naked, refastened my feet to

the end of the bench, straddled me with her back to my face and lowered her big bottom on to my breasts. She carefully arranged her position so that my aching nipples were in turn guided into the depths of her cleft, rubbing her anus and cunny against them.

Then she had moved back so that my vision was filled with her white, splayed bottom. Soft flesh had enveloped my face, blinding me, and my tongue had eagerly sought out her intimacies.

The submission had been exactly what I had needed and I sighed deeply, truly content.

My academy was succeeding beyond my wildest dreams. In the month since I had opened, my first four pupils had blossomed: Sophie's enthusiasm for spanking was proving as great as my own and she would very shortly join the select number who could claim to be my lovers; Daisy had become a member of my staff, spending most of her time helping Tom in the stables; the maids seemed as happy in the new regime as they had been under the old; and last week, three of the members of The Society had spent a fruitful few days as prefects and all had returned home with contented faces and sore bottoms. Their last night, when I had taken all three into the basement and used the full range of equipment on them, eagerly watched by the maids, had been especially satisfying.

If I felt a touch of sadness that Mary and Jane were due to return to their families on the morrow, this was ameliorated by the happy news that word had spread and a further six pupils were due to replace them.

I turned over to warm my back and experienced an unexpected thrill. The water was too shallow to support me properly, so my toes, knees and elbows rested on the rough stone, while my naked bottom bobbed gently up and down on the surface. The contrast between the sun on my buttocks and the water running in and out of the cleft was quite enough to take my mind off all else for several minutes! Then I pressed myself down below the surface so that I was less exposed to the damaging rays, and took stock.

I was surrounded by lovely girls and women who enjoyed all the sensual elements of spanking, and therefore had a handsome range of bottoms at my disposal. I never failed to find tingling pleasure in kissing a pretty female and ordering her to bend over. Whether it was slender Elspeth or plump Vera, I would approach the poised derrière eagerly. However familiar the contours beneath the tautened apparel, there was still great pleasure to be had in seeing them bare, fondling them, then reddening the satiny skin.

If I yearned to receive rather than give, there was always Arabella or Cook, who were happy to oblige me and understood me well enough to satisfy me completely.

On top of all that, there was the inner glow from teaching. I felt that I had genuinely achieved a great deal with my first four pupils, although the amount of improvement varied. Mary was now far more disciplined intellectually. She knew that she could no longer rely on her exceptional mind to see her through life's exercises and hard work had become second nature. Although this had meant fewer opportunities to bare her pretty little bottom, the gain had outweighed the loss.

Jane was no longer a vain, rebellious child. She fully acknowledged her failings and twice had come to my study on her own account, bared her fat buttocks and bent over, asking me to give her a sharp little spanking – 'To keep me up to the mark, Mrs Milford.' I had grown very fond of her and for all the pleasure I found in the feel of my hand sinking into her softness, her new character pleased me far more.

Sarah represented my greatest triumph. As I had suspected from the outset, she had seldom been given cause to feel confident in any of her abilities. If luck had led me to spot her drawing of Mary being spanked, my desire to see her develop had made me praise her talent rather than chide her for the choice of subject. In the four weeks that she had been in my care, I had nurtured her with all the devotion of an ardent gardener with a favourite shrub. She was also the only one of the four whom I had seen completely naked by this point, and my only frustration was that I had not felt it right to seduce her. On the other hand, Sophie's imminent invitation to my boudoir was compensation enough!

I turned over again, settling down so that only the tips of my breasts peeped above the water. My mind drifted comfortably to the first sight of Sarah's nudity.

She had obviously enjoyed reproducing the female form and I had encouraged this without demur. We had spent many an hour poring over the several volumes on the great Masters and I had had little compunction in lingering over those paintings which featured the nude. My own enthusiasm for the subject had allowed me to instruct her without silly coyness and my own talent had sufficed to educate her on at least some of the finer points of technique. I had then suggested that she should use my goddess as a model and had been effusive in my praise for her efforts. She, by contast, had been so self-effacing that she was close to showing an annoying false modesty. I had assumed my sternest expression.

'Are you suggesting that I am too ignorant to be able to judge your work honestly, Sarah?' I had asked.

'Oh no, Mrs Milford,' she had cried, her distress at my insinuation quite plain. 'It is just that I cannot believe that they are worthy of your praise!'

I rested a hand on her knee. 'If I say that you have talent, then you may confidently assume that it is so. My husband is a successful artist and he has taught me a great deal.'

She blushed and looked down at her lap. 'I am sorry,

Mrs Milford. It is just that . . .' She shifted in her seat and fell silent.

'It is just what, Sarah?' I asked in the friendliest of tones.

'That nobody has ever said that I am any good. At anything, really.'

Placing an arm about her shoulders, I drew her head close to mine, breathing in the sweet scent of her golden hair. 'Well, I say that you have great potential as an artist. I can also say that you are a very pretty girl, a singularly sweet and gentle person and I am very fond of you.'

She jerked away and turned to look me in the eye. 'Am I really? Pretty, I mean.'

'Of course you are! Have I not made that clear?'

She suddenly blushed again and giggled mischievously. 'I know that you like my bottom!'

'Quite correct,' I replied, unabashed. 'It is lovely.'

She stared for a moment, anxiously searching my face for signs that I was teasing her. 'Nicer than Sophie's?' she asked shyly.

'That is very hard to say, Sarah. Truthfully. Your bottoms are so different that it is rather like trying to choose between say, beef or pork. Both are splendid meats and one would be happy with either. But be honest, have you never studied your rear aspects in a looking-glass?'

'Never!' she cried. Her initial sense of shock soon changed to a realisation that it was a tempting thought.

If I were to adopt a motto, it would be *'Carpe Diem'* – 'Seize the Day'. I smiled at her. 'Well, that is something we shall correct immediately. But I think that I shall also spank you. For not believing my compliments.'

Her face fell. 'Oh, do you have to, Mrs Milford? It hurts!'

'You silly goose!' I laughed. 'I shall not do it in anger

but merely for the pleasure of putting you across my knee.'

'Oh,' she replied, blushing furiously and with a shy smile curving her mouth. She was adorable and the thought of holding her nakedness tightly to mine while I tasted those soft lips sent a shudder through me.

I took her hand, led her to the *chaise-longue*, seated myself, and guided her gently into position. This, I realised, was my best – and probably last – chance to test her. If she only felt the pain of a spank and none of the pleasure, then my fading hopes for her elevation to the rank of full disciple could be finally laid to rest.

I made the relevant preparations as sensual as I could, all the while concentrating on her reactions. I listened to her. Was that little gasp when I rested my hand on the seat of her skirt pleasure or dismay? Was the tenseness as I rolled up her tunic caused by shame or excitement? As I tugged her drawers down, was the slight tremble caused by a tingle or affronted modesty? As soon as I had bared her, I forgot these considerations while I looked at her naked buttocks, which tightened convulsively as though shrinking from my gaze. The soft cleft grew longer and tighter and the smooth mounds bunched and dimpled.

As I carefully rolled up my sleeves, she relaxed again. Then she felt my bare forearm press down on the small of her back. She clenched and I just heard a little moan of apprehension. I rested my right hand on the base of her left cheek, curving it to match the contours and pushing my little finger in the crease where it joined her thigh. She sighed and the flesh softened.

I spanked her twelve times, my hand dancing rapidly over her bottom, making it quiver but hardly marking her skin. She squeaked and waggled her hips. Then I desisted and stroked again until she was once more at ease, her body moulding itself to my thighs. I tickled the deep division and she squirmed a little. Holding my breath, I prised her buttocks open, just catching a glimpse of the pinky-brown hole before she stiffened and closed the gap.

'Do you not like that part of you being seen, Sarah?' I asked softly.

'Oh dear,' she stammered. 'Not really. It is surely not very nice. And private. I am sorry.'

Her confusion was total and I had no desire to press her further, so gave her a more leisurely dozen – which she took with reasonable fortitude – and then helped her to her feet. She rearranged her clothing, and her relief at the ending of what she clearly saw as an ordeal was plain.

I smiled up at her, rose to my feet, and kissed her with affection rather than passion. Her lips were so warm and soft that I again felt a pang of disappointment, but this soon left me and we went upstairs to my chamber, chattering like old friends.

When we arrived there, I was all brisk efficiency. I told her to remove all her clothes while I arranged the glasses, and by the time I had completed my task, she was standing naked with her hands modestly covering bosom and cunny. I moved her into position and stood beside her as we both gazed at her frontal aspects. Maintaining the pretence of artistic rather than personal interest, I praised all before me and then we both transferred our attentions to her rear. Once again, my comments were restricted to anatomical proportions, seasoned with advice on how best to capture flesh tones. Then, with my hand passing eagerly over the rounded masses, I made her focus on her bottom, telling her how best to portray the cleft.

She was soon completely at ease and the artist in me glowed at the way she absorbed all that I was telling her. Putting all lustful thoughts aside, I told her to wait, then scampered back to my study, found some pencils and a sketching pad, and returned quite breathless to encourage her to use the mirrors to draw a series of self-portraits. With a lingering backward look at her palely gleaming form, I left her and prepared for an interview with the parent of a prospective pupil.

When I had the chance to study her efforts, they were generally excellent. I could easily see which were her first and which her last. Her strong sense of modesty made her earlier drawings very tentative but, as I had hoped, her desire to create overcame her diffidence. It was then no more than a mild inspiration to suggest that she should ask one of the maids to pose for her.

'Oh, thank you, Mrs Milford. That would indeed be challenging. But ... er ... I hardly know them. Do you think I could approach Sophie? I have seen her bottom — when you have spanked her – and we are on quite amicable terms.'

'An excellent idea, Sarah. And if she does demur – which I doubt – do come back to me and we shall select one of the maids to act as your model. Do not concern yourself about making the request. I shall deal with it.'

'Thank you, Mrs Milford. Very much.' She had skipped out like a little girl.

Chilled, I rose from the fountain's wide pool and perched on the top of the low wall, enjoying the warmth of the sun on my body and the roughness of the stone under my buttocks.

It was a heavenly day. The sun was bright and hot and yet there was a lovely breeze to lessen its effects. Birds fluttered around the garden, there was the occasional distant clatter of horses' hooves on the road, and then a butterfly hovered around me before settling on my left breast to sip at a drop of water clinging to the upper surface. I could feel the tiny imprint of its feet as it gripped the silken surface and watched the nipple grow taut as the aching tingle spread. My thoughts strayed to Sophie and I ground my bottom against the stone in my frustration.

I cast off my sun hat as soon as the pretty insect had flown away, and loosened my hair until it flowed over my shoulders. I was again too hot and the rippling water beckoned me. It would cool my ardour as well as refresh my body. I slipped back in and forced my mind towards less sensual, albeit equally fascinating, memories.

Mr Fortescue had sent four more women to be whipped and each had proved interesting and challenging, though none had induced any desire for further contact.

The most memorable had been a Mrs Gordy. She had been the leader of a small group who had rounded on some poor child whom they accused of sticking her tongue out at them. A confrontation with the child's mother had rapidly degenerated into an unseemly brawl and she had been taken in by the police. Mr Fortescue had been reluctant to have her brought before him, since she had three young children of her own and her husband was at sea. Had she been tried, he would have found it all but impossible to avoid sending her to prison, leaving her children parentless for several months.

She appeared in my study, full of defiance and refusing all offers of refreshment. I tried to reason with her but to no avail. She just sat there, glowering at me as though challenging me to do my worst. I ended up doing my very best – and it was far too good for the likes of her!

'This is your last chance, Mrs Gordy,' I said quietly. 'I am going to punish you in the old-fashioned way – by whipping you quite hard on your bare bottom. I hope that you will remember the shame and pain for the rest of your life and that next time you imagine that you are being insulted, you will pause for thought before assaulting anybody. Have you anything to say before I inflict the punishment?'

She glared at me. 'So it's all right for you to use violence on me but not all right for me to stick up for my rights?'

It was a fair point. 'To use violence in défence of your family or possessions is one thing; to use it as you did is another,' I replied, not unsympathetically. 'You are being whipped after full consideration of the facts and circumstances. And may I remind you that the alternative is prison. You will undoubtedly have a very sore bottom by the time I have finished with it but at least you will be home to look after your little ones in an hour or so. It will all be over. And in a day or two, your posterior will have recovered completely and only the memories will remain.'

'I suppose so,' she said, looking more subdued. 'What will you use on me? A horse whip?'

'Oh no, nothing as vicious as that. Stand up, turn around and strip naked so that I can have a good look at your bottom. Then I shall decide.'

She just stared at me. I stared back, rather relishing the battle of wills. She was a handsome woman, nearing 30 I assumed. Stoutish, but by no means obese, and I found that I was quite looking forward to seeing her bare posterior. Eventually she lowered her eyes and shuffled round until her broad back was towards me. Her hands began to unbutton her dress.

'It's not right that I should be naked for the whipping,' she mumbled, as the shabby clothing fell to the floor.

'If I say that it will be on your bare bottom, then there is no further discussion. Come on, Mrs Gordy, everything off, please.'

As I watched a most satisfying bottom come into view, I felt a notable lift in my spirits. My steady and implacable approach had already eroded the woman's defiance and I was able to study her rear view at my leisure. As I have said, she was of buxom build, with a well-muscled back. Her bottom was a trifle disappointing, perhaps – her hips lacked that pleasing outward curve as her waist was almost non-existent, and so her buttocks seemed a little small in proportion to the rest of her body. On the other hand, they were nicely white and tightly divided, with a pronounced overhang at their base.

They were also rather fat and dimpled. Whichever implement I eventually selected would sink into her flesh most effectively and I knew that she would wobble delightfully under punishment.

My lengthy scrutiny began to disturb her, for suddenly her derrière twitched as nervousness overcame shame. I was inwardly debating the relative merits of strap and cane, when I decided that I could find no good reason for not applying both.

'I have made up my mind, Mrs Gordy. A strapping to warm you up, followed by a crisp dozen with the cane. Then we shall see.'

The quick clenching of her buttocks was an eloquent statement that she had not dismissed my sentence lightly!

I led her down the back staircase to the cellar, ignoring her horrified protests at the display of her nudity, and then into the small room containing the rail. She stood meekly against it, spasmodic shudders rippling through her fleshier parts, but did not struggle as I fastened her wrists to the topmost rail, so that the upper part of her body formed an angle of about 45 degrees from the vertical. This projected her hindquarters nicely, spreading her buttocks slightly and opening up the deep folds at their base, but ensuring a nice wobbly target. After a quick feel all over, I picked up my latest implement and prepared to christen it.

I had given Tom the task of making it from the leather of a discarded saddle, claiming that I needed something wider and longer than my trusty tawse to cope with Daisy's big, womanly bottom. He had grinned broadly at my order and the startled look on his face when I told him that it would have to serve with equal efficiency on him made me laugh aloud. He had completed it the day before and if Mrs Gordy's bare bottom was to feel it before Daisy's, that did not seem to matter in the least. It was about a foot and a half long, three inches wide, nicely stiff and well polished, with a wooden handle.

I took careful aim, ignoring the victim's wide eyes staring at me from over her shoulder, and brought it whistling down. It made a lovely 'CRACK' on impact and she flung her head back and cried out with the shock of the smart. Her buttocks shuddered dramatically as the strap bit into her flesh, and then quivered delightfully as she shook her hips.

The second landed a little above the first and I immediately moved behind her to study the results properly. It was evidently a more punishing tool than I expected, for there were two bright red swathes right across her bottom, slightly overlapping and standing noticeably pround on the unmarked flesh. I resolved to use less force and when I next inspected her the swelling caused by the first two had diminished and the rest of her bottom was a lighter red.

I moved round and studied her face. There were no tears but she was breathing heavily. 'It is painful, is it not?'

'Yes, ma'am. My arse feels like you've lit a fire on it.'

'I fear that there is more to come. But you have borne up bravely and I shall take that into account. I think that another six will see you well prepared for the cane. Brace yourself.'

I allowed time for the burning from each stroke to reach a peak before delivering the next, and by the time the fifth had landed, she was swerving her hips from side to side, wailing with dismay.

'The last one, Mrs Gordy, then we shall have a pause. Now keep still and stick your bottom out properly, please.'

She planted her feet firmly on the floor and I could see the tension in her muscles as she strove to obey. After a quick look at her dramatically red derrière, I swept the strap against the base of the target, bringing it in an upward sweep which made the fleshy masses wobble like a big blancmange. She tossed her head to and fro and stamped her feet with the pain before slumping forward and panting with relief.

I stood to her side, gently stroking her warm bottom. 'Now, Mrs Gordy,' I said, my voice low but firm, 'I do hope that you are beginning to learn your lesson. As I said to you, your bottom will be very sore by the time I have done. Worse than it is now. But the pain will soon pass. The woman you attacked lost several handfuls of hair, thanks to your assault, and it will be a long time before that grows back. We cannot accept behaviour of that nature, which is why you are in this position. As naked as the day you were born, with your fat bare bottom sticking out and as red as a cherry. Do you think that you will remember this moment next time you feel like bullying someone weaker and smaller than yourself?'

'Oh yes, ma'am, I promise. I'll never do it again ... Do I have to be caned, ma'am? My bum's really sore. I don't think it can take any more.'

'Of course it can. But I do believe that you are indeed sorry, so I shall give you no more than a dozen, with a light cane. It will sting, but will not leave you badly bruised. Now let me alter your position. I am going to have you bent right down. This will spread your bottom and make it tighter. And will make the lower portions more accessible.'

She whimpered as I reached up for her wrists but said no more while I refastened them to the rail on the floor and then tied her ankles to her wrists, forcing her lower limbs to bend at the knee. I tied the last knot then squatted down behind her, close enough for her posterior to fill my vision entirely. It was a splendid sight. Both cheeks were bright red and were now sufficiently parted to reveal a white strip of unmarked skin between them, with her hairy cunny providing an exciting contrast to the smooth flesh all around.

I stared and stared, thoroughly enjoying the broad vista of vulnerable femininity until I noticed that she was beginning to pull against her bonds. I then appreciated that the key to breaking her rebellious spirit lay as much in humiliation as in pain so, to emphasise her complete helplessness, I gripped hold of a cheek in each hand and moved them vigorously about, up and down, from side to side. She cried out in her distress and I slapped her quite hard.

'Keep still, Mrs Gordy,' I snapped. 'I am enjoying having your bare bottom completely at my mercy!'

'But it's not decent!' she cried.

'Neither was your behaviour!' I retorted, slapping her thigh.

As a final gesture, I took hold of her cheeks again and drew them remorselessly apart until a neat brown anus was staring at me. Her struggles grew desperate, but to no avail. I forced her bottom as wide open as I could and ignored her spluttering wails.

Then I let go, stood up, selected a nice whippy rattan cane from the rack and measured it across her jutting bottom.

'Now, Mrs Gordy, an extra three for protesting. That makes fifteen all told and after every three, I shall move behind you and closely examine your bare bottom, including the middle. Before I administer a stroke, I shall tap your bottom – like this – to warn you that I am ready. When you feel the cane, I want you to stay perfectly still and silent. The first so that I can aim properly and the second so that I can hear the sound of the impact. Afterwards you may howl and wriggle. Do I make myself clear?'

'Yes, ma'am,' she sobbed. 'But I'll be good, honest. Please can we get it over as quick as possible?'

'There are some things which are better not rushed,' I said, rather pompously. 'And whipping your fat bare bottom is one of them.'

I tapped, she moaned through gritted teeth; I smacked, she jerked and gasped. I had not hit hard, knowing that fifteen such strokes would cause ample suffering for what was a relatively minor offence. The humiliation of a long period on display, coupled with the sense of utter helplessness as I helped myself to her private parts, would make the punishment no less effective than a harder thrashing and probably more so.

My first inspection proved that I had judged the force of the strokes correctly. The three pink weals were clearly visible but had not formed the double ridges typical of a full-blooded swipe. I had been careful to place the cane so that the tip was well clear of her right buttock, with the gratifying result that the stripes were reasonably evenly spread across both cheeks. I massaged her and prised her open, ignoring her moaned protests, then pressed the cane in.

A quarter of an hour later, the last stroke bounced off and I replaced the cane before examining her again. Her bottom was a fair bit redder and certainly looked quite sore but I could see that it was hardly bruised and that she would recover quickly. I untied her and helped her to stand up, looking closely into her face as I did so. There were a few signs of tears and she was certainly breathing very heavily, but otherwise she was quite composed. I cupped her cheek and smiled at her.

'Well, Mrs Gordy, it is all over. You behaved well at the end and have earned a liberal application of soothing cream for your poor bottom. Is it fearfully sore?'

'Not too bad, ma'am,' she mumbled.

'Do you think that you have learned your lesson?' I persisted.

'Oh yes, ma'am,' she stated animatedly. 'I never want to go through anything like that ever again. Not never!'

'I am delighted to hear it. Now let us return to my study and I shall find some nice ointment for you.'

I followed her along, enjoying the way the red stripes seemed to dance as her buttocks bunched and rounded, and then soothed her as promised. Her demeanour as she left was in complete contrast to that at the outset and I was confident that I had again struck the right note. I had certainly enjoyed myself. If her bottom had not attracted me much, the power to bend her to my will had proved a very effective aphrodisiac! As Connie was to discover soon afterwards!

My period of solitude had refreshed my mind as much as my bathe had cooled my body, so I rose, stretched and, careless of my nudity, walked around the garden until I was dry. Then it was back to work.

I wanted to bid farewell to my departing pupils with something of a flourish and had invited all four to supper in my private quarters. I had been most gratified at the alacrity with which they had accepted my invitation and we had chosen the menu with care. I had refused to allow them to wear their own clothes but had lent them all some of my jewellery to honour the occasion. On time, four shining-faced young girls stepped a little shyly into my room.

I opened the first of the bottles of champagne, filled the glasses and proposed a toast.

'To Jane and Mary. May what they have learned here help them in the future – and may their pretty bottoms never want for proper attention!'

'Hear, hear!' responded Sophie, with her most engaging grin, and the mood was set for a lively evening. The wine soon relaxed them and the conversation over dinner ranged freely over a variety of subjects. I took but a small part, quite happy to sit back and observe.

As I watched, I could not help but feel a glow of satisfaction. All four were now far more vivacious than they had been but – and to me even more important – they had learned the basic social graces. For example, Sarah made some rather naïve comment about the royal family and Mary corrected her in the nicest manner possible. Not long before, she would not have been able to keep the scorn from her voice.

Elspeth poured out the Burgundy which cook had recommended as the ideal accompaniment to the beefsteaks, and while we waited for them, Sophie raised her glass and called for silence. I looked at her warmly. Her hair gleamed in the candlelight and her eyes glistened. The contents of her glass glowed like molten rubies and she smiled at each of us in turn. The distant clatter of serving dishes did nothing to distract her.

'Ladies,' she began, her voice soft and mellow. 'Let us drink to Mrs Milford; thank her not only for educating us all so well but also for this splendid dinner.' I smiled and nodded with proper modesty, trying hard not to show how moved I was. 'And may you have a constant procession of lovely bottoms on which you can exercise your skills.'

I laughed aloud. 'I shall join you in that toast,' I declared happily, and the rich, heady wine lifted my spirits even further.

As soon as we had been served and the maids had left us, Jane looked up at me. 'Do you enjoy spanking, Mrs Milford?'

Had the occasion been less friendly and informal, I would probably have answered evasively, but somehow only the complete truth seemed appropriate. While I collected my thoughts, I studied their faces, searching for signs of insubordination. All I saw was eager curiosity and genuine enthusiasm. Even from Sarah.

'That is not, in fact, a simple question to answer,' I said slowly. 'So much depends on the circumstances. If I am angry with the culprit, then my anger predominates and the desire to punish is paramount. I hasten to add that none of you have reduced me to that state! Basically, as far as you four are concerned, I firmly believe in discipline and equally, that corporal punishment is far and away the best method of instilling learning. In girls and boys. But I do confess that I derive no little pleasure from the sight and feel of a girl's naked derrière. Does that answer your question?'

They looked at me with solemn concentration. Then Sophie broke the silence. 'I quite understand that, Mrs Milford. I know that whenever I have had a spanking, I always feel much better afterwards. I mean, I work much better.' She blushed furiously and I grinned conspiratorially at her.

'How about you, Jane?' I asked.

'Well, I hated the first spanking you gave me but after a while, I realised that I had deserved it and then when I came here, I knew what to expect. I still do not like it much. You really know how to hurt a girl's bottom, Mrs Milford, but like Sophie, I know that I have benefited from it. And yes, it is fun watching another girl getting it.'

'And you, Sarah?' before she could reply, the main course arrived and the next quarter of an hour was devoted to appreciative chewing. It was not until we had demolished cook's trifle, had toyed with the cheese and retired to the drawing room for coffee and Madeira that I prompted Sarah and thus brought the conversation back to my favourite theme. Time, excellent food and a sufficiency of fine wines had clearly rid her of all inhibitions.

'I find no pleasure in the pain. Although the warm glow afterwards is something to which I look forward throughout the punishment – and enjoy when it comes.'

They all nodded in agreement. 'But to me,' she continued, 'a girl's bottom is one of the most beautiful things I have ever seen. I cannot explain why –'

'Do not bother to try, Sarah,' I interrupted. 'Simply appreciate your good fortune in being able to see what most people would be blind to.'

The conversation continued in similar vein and I sipped my Madeira and enjoyed every word. I was reminded of similar dinners at meetings of The Society, when we had sat in elegant surroundings, digesting an excellent repast and talking about carnal delights in an open and frank manner. What the present gathering lacked in sophistication was countered by their enthusiasm. I was pondering how to lead them from discussion to more physical demonstrations of their thoughts when Mary gave me a perfect opportunity.

'It seems such a shame,' she said thoughtfully, 'to be leaving in such a state of ignorance.' We stared at her, puzzled. 'I always imagined that when I was watching the others being chastised that they were suffering the torments of the damned. Yet all three of you have openly confessed almost to enjoying yourselves. How did you express it just now, Sophie? Oh yes, "A nice crisp spanking makes me glow all over." Oh well, I shall often think of your fat little bottom turned up over Mrs Milford's nice soft lap and regret that I did not enjoy the sight to the full when I did have the opportunity.' She sighed theatrically and the look of desolation on her face was most convincing.

I seized the chance. 'My dear Mary. Your departure grieves me enough as it is, without the added sadness of such frustration. I am sure that you agree with me, ladies, when I say that Sophie's table manners have not been of the standard expected of my academy and therefore a spanking would be wholly justified?'

'I could not agree more, Mrs Milford,' Mary said primly. 'And may I stand close? In order to get the best view possible?'

'Of course you may,' I replied.

'How will you place her?' asked Jane.

I pretended to give the question earnest consideration. 'Across my knee, I think. Or perhaps bending over the back of a chair. Or even kneeling on that ottoman. Let me think.'

'What about all three?' chimed in Sarah.

'An excellent idea,' I enthused. 'And to make our decision easier, let us bare her bottom now and study it carefully before deciding finally.'

We turned to Sophie, who was trying to look terrified but failing dismally. 'Well, if I have to suffer such indignities, at least it is providing pleasure to others,' she responded. 'My martyrdom is therefore tolerable. Will you all sit together on the sofa with me standing before you, or shall I parade before each of you in turn?'

'The latter, I think. Beginning with Mary.'

With all the natural fervour of the new convert, Mary examined the naked posterior thoroughly and with evident glee. Jane was more inhibited and Sarah's devotion to duty almost matched Mary's.

The eager victim was then made to assume a variety of poses, starting with the traditional one over my knee. With pleasure for all the one and only criterion, I was able to concentrate fully on the exceptional beauty of her bottom, smacking only hard enough to send a small ripple through the plump globes and pausing at frequent intervals to stroke and knead them, letting what smart I had induced die away before recommencing.

If I had harboured any lingering doubts that she shared my taste for a smacked bottom, her behaviour soon rid me of them. Her sighs were of ecstasy and nothing else: her little wriggles and heaves on my lap could only be caused by a desire to elevate her bottom and not to evade my hand.

Her audience was far from silent. They felt free to move around, so that they could observe the action from differing viewpoints, and felt no embarrassment at expressing their thoughts aloud. Happily, they were all positive and I could sense Sophie's pleasure at the praise which was heaped on her.

We moved to the back of the armchair and she bent gracefully over the back, parting her feet and bending her knees so that her buttocks protruded quite beautifully. I let the girls squat behind her for a detailed assessment and their attentions had Sophie mewing softly with pleasure. I then took my place behind her and made all of them gasp when I completed my examination by prising her jutting cheeks apart and gazing at her delectable little bottom-hole.

I let her friends smack her and they all began coyly but were soon seduced by the novel sensations and set about her with a will.

By the time we had finished with the chair, her bottom was bright red and I decreed that we should let her recover and have another glass of Madeira.

'Oh thank you, Mrs Milford!' Sophie gasped. 'Please may I keep my bottom bare and let the air cool it?'

'Of course you may,' I said, and moved over to help her remove her drawers, then tucked her skirts firmly into the white sash round her waist. We stood looking deeply into the other's eyes for a moment and the passion I saw in her expression made me tingle all over.

Needless to say, Sophie refused to sit down and shamelessly paraded her nudity in front of us all while we openly admired her. I was, however, surprised and delighted when she claimed to be too hot and stripped down to her shoes and stockings, without so much as a by-your-leave. From that moment on, any chances of finishing the dinner with some semblance of decorum were ruined.

Sophie announced that it was grossly unjust that hers should be the only red bottom in the room and soon coerced her friends into baring and bending.

They also deemed the temperature too high for clothing and all four little minxes stood before me, pleading with me to judge which one had the reddest bottom. It was, of course, a most difficult decision, which demanded a lengthy examination before I could declare Sophie the winner.

She then told the other three to kneel side by side on the seat of the sofa, so that she could render them all equal.

When she had done that, her bottom had paled sufficiently to need further attention.

By this time, my mind was in a whirl. The four delicious naked bodies had quite intoxicated me and I became desperate to join them. For an instant, I thought that I should not forsake my dignity but the temptation soon overcame any reservations.

'Ladies,' I said, with only the slightest tremble in my voice. 'While I have been watching your delightful romps, I have been mulling over the various punishments I have meted out and recollect that I have given each one of you at least one spanking which was not fully merited. My conscience troubles me. Perhaps one of you can think of a way I can make amends.'

I looked sorrowfully at each in turn and they studied me in some confusion until the import of my statement dawned and expressions of unholy glee spread over their features. Then, as one, they advanced on me with evil intent. My eyes flickered over bobbing bosoms, neat triangles of variously coloured hair and round, bare thighs. My cunny ached and my buttocks flared into tingling life. Hands grasped my upper arms and pulled me to my feet. A smiling Jane found a sash and blindfolded me. The skirts of my gown were folded up, then my petticoats and chemise. My drawers were untied and fluttered down to my feet. Hardly able to stay upright in my excitement, I stumbled as I tried to kick them clear and the unseen hands propped me up while others disentangled me.

I was walked up and down the room, briskly and unrhythmically, so that my bare bottom jostled and wobbled.

I was laid across four naked laps and spanked to a frazzle.

My clothes were removed entirely and I was forced on to my knees.

'She looked at my bottom-hole. I want to see hers.' Sophie's voice was low and heavy with lust. I moaned and knew that my throbbing cunny was weeping. I could feel the cooling love-honey on the inside of my thighs. Warm hands gripped my cheeks and pulled them apart. Fingers probed the open cleft. My dangling breasts were squeezed.

A finger slipped ruthlessly up my bottom and at least one more up my cunny. Soft lips pressed against my open mouth and a tongue slithered in. I spent and all but collapsed.

They released me and I rolled around the floor as the waves ebbed and died away and my breathing returned to normal. Then I removed the sash, stood up and glared around me. Four white faces looked guiltily at me.

'Well, girls,' I said in icy tones. 'I had not expected to be ravished as well as spanked.' They exchanged shifty glances and the fear of retribution was clearly foremost in their minds. 'However,' I continued after a pregnant pause, 'I enjoyed the experience enormously!' Four very relieved grins greeted my pronouncement.

I had the upper hand again and took full advantage. Sophie was told to go to my study and fetch the tawse and martinet from the cupboard and I set to work. One by one, they had to kneel up on the ottoman with their splayed buttocks stuck up in the air and their bottom-holes in full view while they received six crisp smacks from each implement.

Then I made them lie on the floor with their feet

towards me and their knees parted and raised so that I could see their cunnies, and made them play with their own pleasure spots until the room echoed with their cries of bliss.

At last, utterly exhausted, we retired to our separate beds.

I would have preferred it if the following day had been quiet and free of incident but my wish was not granted. Mary's people sent a Hansom to collect her and her departure was emotional but not taxing otherwise. Miss Brown, by contrast, asked for an hour of my time before driving away with her niece and it was only my affection for the woman which prevented me from proffering some excuse.

In the event, I was very pleased that I agreed to see her. We talked inconsequentially over a cup of chocolate and she asked the expected questions about Jane's progress, appearing most satisfied with my replies. Then she had taken me by surprise.

'The thing is, Mrs Milford, I have been so impressed with the improvement in my niece's demeanour since we met in the coach that I have resolved to continue in the same vein while she is in my care.'

I nodded my approval. 'I believe that you will notice even greater changes in her now, Miss Brown. She is not only accustomed to chastisement but welcomes it. I do warn you, however, that you must always be fair and never punish her without good reason.'

'I quite understand, Mrs Milford. But I have a request. One that you will probably consider quite strange but please try and understand. I realise that her behaviour was largely due to my ineffectiveness as a guardian and therefore I must shoulder a great deal of the blame. Secondly, if I am to spank her properly, I should know what it is like to receive a spanking and hope that you will oblige me. Now, I am a plain woman and my posterior is large and I should imagine not especially attractive, so I have put on a fine chemise and left off my drawers. I shall feel the smacks but you will be spared the sight of my naked flesh.'

I blinked at her and I am certain that my open mouth emphasised my astonishment. Then the prospect of spanking a nice mature woman made me gather my wits in an instant. 'I shall certainly oblige you, Miss Brown, and I applaud the seriousness of your intent. I shall, however, refuse your request to keep your derrière covered. Whether it is pretty or not is quite immaterial. It is important that you feel the shame of having a very personal part of your anatomy not only completely bare but prominently displayed right before my eyes. And this nakedness is further reinforced when you feel my hand in contact with your skin.'

I looked at her pale and determined face with new eyes and saw that she may have been a little dowdy, but to call her plain was an exaggeration. She had a very nice face and I felt reasonably optimistic that her bottom would not disappoint me.

It did not. Not surprisingly, it no longer had the firmness of youth but both skin and flesh were admirably soft and the cleft, although short, was quite charming. I saw no cause not to voice my opinions and emphasised my words with both hands, soon having her squirming over my lap as the strange sensations flooded through her. I also explained the finer points of spanking as I administered hers.

'It is best, I think, to warm up the surface of the buttocks with a series of light spanks delivered very quickly. Like this. My, how your bottom quivers and wobbles. Quite charming, I assure you. As soon as all is a nice pink, pause, stroke both cheeks and then give six crisp ones to each side. If there is plenty of time, I recommend making some adjustment to the position – move up a trifle. Raise your hips and part your feet.

That is ideal. Tell the erring girl what you are about to do and make her count the smacks aloud. This does wonders for the concentration. And her bottom must be in position before you smack it ... And now, another brief rest before another series of lighter ones.

Her fortitude was impressive, helped perhaps by her willingness to learn, but her whole bottom was a bright scarlet before I deemed that she had had sufficient for the day. But then, as she stood in front of me, facing away and massaging her burning flesh with exciting vigour, I decided that one more little lesson would not come amiss. Reminding her that the shame of exposure was an important element of the procedure, I made her kneel up on the footstool with her nice brown anus in full view while I smacked gently away at the inrolling of her bounteous cheeks.

I eventually waved them goodbye, feeling considerably better.

Two days later, I had my full complement of six pupils and I was kept extremely busy. The household affairs were managed by Cook and I was able to devote my full attention to the academic side of my life. After our post-dinner orgy, I was far less inhibited about administering punishments to the new girls, all of whom soon lost any unreasonable fears in presenting their bare bottoms. Admittedly, Sophie's evident enthusiasm helped to reassure them!

Their happy attitude was made quite apparent one night when I was disturbed by sounds of horseplay from upstairs. Pausing only to throw on my peignoir, I strode up to their floor and interrupted a full-blown pillow fight. My sudden arrival made them call an instant halt to the festivities and six red-faced, panting girls, all in just nightgowns, faced me. Miranda, one of the new girls, whose ample bosom was heaving most attractively, took control.

'Oh dear! We are sorry, Mrs Milford, it all got out of hand. Smacked bottoms all round?'

'Yes,' I replied firmly.

Without further ado, they trooped into the nearest room, whisked up their gowns and knelt up on the bed, all in a row, so that I was faced with the splendid sight of six perfectly presented bare bottoms, with the lower parts of six cunnies peeping out below. I smacked away with a will and all were a lovely bright pink in no time. To show that there was no ill-feeling, I took each one in my arms and kissed her affectionately before urging them back to bed.

In complete contrast, Mr Fortescue's miscreants turned up on a regular basis and the more severe implements of correction which decorated the walls of the cellar rooms were put to good use.

Two significant events occurred during the following few weeks. The first was that Sophie and I became lovers in the full sense of the word. She had come to see me after supper one evening and, once again, asked me to spank her soundly but had been surprisingly vague when I pressed her for details of her misdemeanour. She had looked at me so plaintively that I could not resist her plea and put her across my lap with mixed emotions. Naturally I wanted to spank her but was still a little reserved about giving my sensuality a free rein with a pupil. After I had reddened her plump little tail and was holding her in my arms to comfort her, she burst into a flood of tears and confessed that she loved me more than anything else in the whole world.

With a full heart I had pressed her tightly to my bosom and then, without another word, taken her up to my bedroom, undressed her and laid her on my bed. Having spent a good quarter of an hour studying her bare bottom, I had devoted all my energies to her front, moving slowly from her mouth to her breasts, lingering awhile on her deep belly-button, then skirting around her furry mound on to her thighs, legs and toes before launching myself on her weeping cunny.

With the enthusiasm of a small puppy, she had then stripped me naked and explored every inch. If her touch had been inexpert at first, she proved to be a fast learner and her whispered comments on the pleasure she derived from the sight and feel of all my intimate parts were delightful.

Much later, she fell asleep in my arms and as I lay, sated and blissfully happy, I had one of my better inspirations. She would be The Academy's first proper prefect.

I told her of my decision when we both awoke the following morning and her joy was most moving. Her family's finances had improved more than a little, so she could stay for as long as I needed her.

While she was bathing me, I told her that she would have to maintain even higher standards now that she was in a position of authority and therefore any punishments she earned would be more extreme.

'Good!' she replied simply. 'And could you please kneel up so that I can wash your bottom properly?' I complied without a murmur.

After breakfast, I sent a note round to Mrs Savage, the dressmaker, and all three of us enjoyed a prolonged session planning a suitable uniform for her, eventually settling on a slightly less severe version of my own white blouse and tight, dark skirt, with more elegant shoes and fine stockings.

She settled into her new role as though to the manner born, and three days later I allowed her to take a class, with the one proviso that she was not to administer any punishments on her own account, but to report to me afterwards. Her face had fallen as I had made this point and I had smiled at her.

'Do not worry, Sophie. You will be able to spank them, but in my presence only. After all, if you derive so much pleasure from watching, is it not reasonable that I feel the same?'

With a broad grin she had scampered off.

Taking full advantage of the unexpected freedom, I decided to enjoy a drive in Richmond Park, so ambled over to the stables. As I approached, I heard the sounds of a furious squabble and stormed in to find Tom and Daisy fighting like a pair of alley cats. Very angry at having my plans disturbed, I sentenced both to a sound strapping.

'You first, Daisy. Get your skirts up and bend over that rail. Tom, fetch the strap, please.'

As he handed it to me, I caught sight of his face and the red mists of anger disappeared in a trice. He was staring at the waiting Daisy, open-mouthed and wide-eyed. I also looked and realised that for a lad who had probably never seen a bare female bottom, it was a sight well worthy of his undivided attention.

I knew that Daisy had a nice bottom, and seeing it through Tom's eyes it was beautiful. Very white, and well parted by her position, the two buttocks gleamed temptingly in the subdued light. I noticed her face peering back at us, watching us watching her. Had she seen the protrusion in the front of Tom's trousers?

Inwardly smiling, I took the strap from his trembling hand and walked over to the waiting girl.

I palmed her bottom thoughtfully, admiring the fleshiness of the cheeks, despite her tightly bent position. A glance over to the boy confirmed that his excitement was no less rampant. The devil in me took over.

'Come over here, Tom!' I ordered. 'I want you to watch closely. I know, drag the bale across, put it right there and sit down. But do not get too excited, for Daisy will have the same viewpoint when it is your turn!'

Eventually we had all settled. I raised the stiff strip of leather and brought it down firmly. The loud 'THWACK' echoed through the stable: one of the horses stamped and whinnied; Daisy gasped and waggled her bottom; a red stripe appeared like magic. Tom gave a little moan. Sympathy with her torment? Or lust at her nakedness?

I beat her methodically, giving her ample time to absorb the sting from each stroke and then for the glow to take over. I worked up and down her curves, from the top of her cleft to the tops of her thighs. She turned from bright red to scarlet and the stripes mingled and overlapped. She cried out and stamped her feet. Her fat bottom quivered and shook. But she did not plead for mercy and always stuck out her hips in readiness, taking eighteen strokes before the quality of her cries indicated that she was reaching the limit of her endurance. I stopped, and a quick inspection confirmed that I had beaten her well, but not cruelly.

They changed places as soon as Daisy had recovered sufficiently to appreciate the alternative point of view. I stood to the side as Tom let down his trousers, watching her expression with amusement when his bare bottom came into view. He bent over and thrust his bottom out before I could order him to do so. She blushed as she saw his balls but did not look away!

I gave him eighteen as well, slightly more forcefully as befitted a member of the stronger sex, and his much smaller bottom was a great deal redder than hers by the end. But he had not uttered a murmur, and as I tossed the strap aside I realised that I had suddenly become very fond of them both. Their evident enjoyment of the other's nudity promised well for their future relationship. I bade them to soothe each other's bottoms before preparing my carriage. Then I went to change into a more elegant gown and bonnet in readiness for the drive, and on my return noticed that they were exchanging most promising glances!

Very satisfied, I sank into the comfort of my seat and we clopped briskly down the drive.

Eight

As the girls clattered out of the classroom, I slumped back in my chair and massaged my aching temples. I felt distinctly out of sorts and could not for the life of me imagine why. As evidence of my confusion, I had just had perfectly reasonable excuses to punish Sarah, Miranda and Charlotte, another of the new girls, and yet had let them all off. Had I not been so afflicted, I would have turned them up with pleasure, especially as they had such nicely contrasting bottoms. Sarah's broad and so delightfully soft; Miranda's big, round and firm; Charlotte's small and neat; and all them accepted a spanking with grace. Sighing despondently, I gathered up my papers and retired to my quarters. I rang the bell to order a cold luncheon and a bottle of hock, hoping that the wine would lift my spirits.

It helped but I was still feeling untypically lackadaisical when I wandered into the garden, stripped naked and sat in the fountain pool, hoping that the cool water would refresh my soul as well as my skin. As always, I found complete nudity both relaxing and invigorating.

I lay back, adjusted my sun hat so that my face was completely shaded, closed my eyes and dozed off, lulled by the combination of warmth and coolness. My mind nibbled lazily at my problem. Why had I lost my enthusiasm? What was lacking in my life?

I was, without doubt, tired. With so many pretty girls available to pander to my various desires, it was proving difficult to resist just one more excursion into the realms of heady pleasure.

As I turned over to warm my back and cool off my front, it occurred to me that what I needed above all was a rest. My thoughts turned to the peacefulness of my Sussex home and, with a surge of relief, determined that I would slip down there for a few days.

Three days later, Tom guided my carriage towards the Dorking road and my spirits lifted with every turn of the wheels.

The preparations for my holiday had been hectic, to say the least. I sent a silent prayer winging up to heaven that Sophie would manage as capably as she promised and smiled at the memory of her expressions when I had broken the news that she would be in charge. At first a look of unholy glee as the prospect of unlimited access to the girls' bottoms, then a furrowed brow as it occurred to her that she would have to take the lessons and reinforce her authority with superior knowledge. She had chewed the inside of her lower lip in her anxiety, but when I had promised to rearrange the curriculum to suit her abilities, the relief had been plain. She had reverted to the unholy glee!

We had summoned Cook and between us agreed to devote more time than usual on domestic subjects. The good woman not only had the confidence of long practice but had also learned to communicate her skills to the pupils, who had always found her lessons enjoyable and beneficial. As had I, for I had often sat in the background listening avidly, and had added considerably to my own store of knowledge.

With these matters of lesser importance settled, I had then devoted the remainder of the available time in instructing Sophie on the most vital element of her new position. Spanking. This had proved to be enormously entertaining. I had begun by lecturing her on the basic principles, beginning with how to pronounce sentence.

'A great deal depends on the circumstances, Sophie. And, of course, the girl. Sarah, for example, was painfully shy when she first came and had no faith in her prettiness. It would have been cruel to have lectured her at length. I simply used to tell her that I was about to smack her pretty bottom and then order her into position. Note that I inevitably used the word "pretty" when referring to her derrière. She eventually appreciated that hers *is* pretty and blossomed accordingly.'

Sophie nodded her understanding. 'It is much the same for me, Mrs Milford. Knowing that you are at least fond of my bottom makes a spanking much more exciting.'

I patted her thigh. 'Fond is *far* too mild a word, Sophie. I adore it. And by the by, when we are alone, please call me Annie.'

She smiled shyly at me and I could not resist leaning forward to kiss her.

The following hour passed most agreeably. With my love of teaching, a subject very dear to my heart, a willing pupil and a genuine reason for imparting my knowledge as effectively as possible, how could it have failed to thrill me?

We covered the importance of the introductory lecture – and I emphasised the importance of using the phrase 'bare bottom' – before dealing with preparation and positioning.

At that stage, it seemed logical to include practical demonstration and Sophie proffered her bottom with an earnestness which only just failed to hide her glee. I showed her how to alter the effects of one's spanks and the basic variations in rhythm. We altered the position of her bottom, from relaxed and wobbly to tight and spread. Obviously, I used only moderate force, but by the time I had dealt with the basic principles in sufficient detail, she was bright-eyed and both sets of cheeks glowed a healthy red.

It was then time for her to exercise her newfound expertise. I summoned Elspeth and Vera for her to practise on, calculating that they offered very contrasting bottoms, they liked being spanked, they were both mischievous little minxes who needed regular discipline, and lastly, both would be in full sympathy with Sophie's requirements.

It all proved most satisfying and the pleased expression on Sophie's flushed face when they kissed her farewell was a picture.

We summarised our discussions over supper and retired early to bed.

I was therefore able to anticipate my little holiday with the certain knowledge that my academy affairs were in good hands, and the journey passed quickly with the result that I arrived in good order. Mavis and Bertha greeted me effusively and Tom cautiously, and I spent the next hour or so in a whirl of gossip and chatter. Having made sure that Tom was settled in Bertha's old room in the main outbuilding and that he had cared for the horses, I ran upstairs, changed into a riding habit and took Matilda out for a long ride. It took me a little while to feel completely at one with her – I had not set my bottom in a saddle for several months – but I soon felt my confidence flowing back.

Oh, the joy of it! The air was as sparkling as the best champagne after London and the sense of freedom just as intoxicating. Sadly, my muscles had grown slack with the relative inactivity of my other life and I was blowing and exhausted far too soon. I was not greatly concerned, however, for as we trotted homeward, I was able to enjoy the open countryside and the rolling sweep of the Downs to greater effect than would have been possible normally.

I had ordered an early supper, which we ate in the kitchen while Tom had his in his room, and then I was very ready for a long, hot bath and a solitary bed. As I announced my plans, both Mavis and Bertha expressed their disappointment.

'If that's what you wish, madam,' said the former.

'And I was really looking forward to seeing you all naked again,' sighed the latter soulfully.

I laughed aloud. 'How sweetly you both compliment me!' I exclaimed. 'But I really am most weary, so would only fall asleep before we had enjoyed the first kiss. But you may still see my naked charms when you bathe me and put me to bed. And you will also feel my eyes upon yours as you do so, for I order you both to undress completely. Before you fill the bath, Bertha!'

The hot, scented water eased all my aches and pains and I awoke the next morning fully refreshed. I put on an old dress – and nothing else – ready for a spell working in my garden.

Tom had asked if he could exercise the greys, so was bound to be away for several hours, and the two women were busy about their usual tasks, so I could slip away in peace, quiet and glorious solitude.

It was a lovely summer day and although the garden had been well maintained in my absence, there was still a plethora of little tasks to keep me happily occupied.

Whenever I was busy in a shady part, I slipped off my dress and revelled in the simple, childlike joy of unfettered freedom. My mind shed its many burdens one by one until I was at last at peace with myself.

I was weeding one of the beds in the kitchen garden, stark naked and on my knees with my bare bottom cocked up in the air, idly thinking of Elizabeth and hoping that she would reply to my letter before too long, when I heard a sound behind me and froze. There was silence and I realised that it had probably been a bird in one of the trees, so relaxed and leaned forward to attack a dandelion. Another sound. A small twig breaking? With my heart in my mouth, I whirled around. There was nothing. Smiling at my nervousness, I settled back to my labours and had just uprooted the stubborn weed when my heart leapt back into my mouth. A soft voice greeted me.

'Hello, Annie. What a pretty bottom-hole!'

It was Elizabeth! Squeaking with pleasure, I threw myself into her arms, kissed her, and let her hands rove freely over my nudity before common sense prevailed and I made myself decent.

We spent the rest of the morning chattering like a couple of magpies, right up to the time of her departure after luncheon. I was so keen to inform her of all the exciting events which were making my life so rewarding – and she listened so avidly to each little detail – that apart from our first caress, we hardly laid a hand on the other. It mattered not. Our friendship encompassed far more than sensual thrills, however much we enjoyed those when the circumstances were right.

It was much the same with Mavis and Bertha. Admittedly, Tom's presence inhibited us during the day and it was only when we knew that he was making full use of the space and freedom of the countryside to hone his burgeoning riding skills that we felt able to be ourselves. We wandered freely around the garden in Eve's costume, fondling and caressing each other with easy familiarity.

Otherwise, we were content to behave with unusual decorum until he had retired to his quarters. We could then take ourselves to my bedroom and give free rein to our desires.

In contrast to the pleasures of the bed chamber, I derived growing satisfaction in accompanying Tom on his rides. He had changed out of all recognition from the scruffy little urchin I had first encountered and was now a smart, confident young man. He never treated me with anything but complete respect but neither did he feel constrained in voicing his opinions, even if these ran contrary to mine.

I did not deem it wise to spank him in front of my servants, although the temptation to watch Bertha's face at the sight of his nudity was most tempting! I felt that to do so would hurt his pride more than was desirable. So, if he annoyed me – or if I felt like seeing his bottom and fondling his pego – I took advantage of the rural solitude and dealt with him in the open.

In the space of three days, I had regained all my zest for life. The weariness had disappeared, there was a glow in my cheeks, and I was sleeping like a baby.

I worked in the garden with renewed energy and devoted the last days to making sure that both Mavis and Bertha knew that I loved them as much as ever, deriving special pleasure in insisting on a good increase in their wages, overcoming their objections by pointing out that their responsibilities were now much more onerous.

All too soon it was time to return, and without a backward glance I looked forward to resuming the role of educator.

I arrived in the middle of the morning, and knowing that Sophie would be taking a class I decided to impose on Cook for some refreshment before bathing and changing. As I approached the kitchen, my ears were assaulted with the loudest caterwauling I had heard for ages and knew immediately that Elspeth was being chastised. Although she enjoyed a warm posterior as much as any, she felt no inhibitions about letting her feelings be known and began her anguished wails from the first touch of a hand on her flesh. Smiling happily, I made haste and was duly greeted by the sight of the dear girl sprawled across Cook's ample lap. Her bare bottom bore two pink patches, one on each cheek, so I had arrived in good time.

Cook looked up at me, her brawny arm poised over her head, and beamed her pleasure at seeing me.

'Oh, Annie!' she exclaimed. 'You are nice and early.

May I just finish with Elspeth? If I smack her harder than usual, it won't take long.'

I gave the matter serious consideration. 'I am not sure, Cook,' I replied thoughtfully. 'It seems a shame to hurry unduly and I am very thirsty. Why do we not make her stand in the corner so that she can contemplate her sins at leisure. Then we can enjoy a glass or two of your lemonade and, when we are ready, she can pay for her sins at leisure.'

Elspeth treated me to her most impish grin before clambering up and shuffling over to the corner, muttering something about how cruel it was to keep a poor, innocent girl waiting for a spanking. 'Specially with her bottom all bare!' she added, hauling her skirts up to her waist as her drawers slithered down to her feet.

While Cook and I drank and gossiped, we both gazed fondly at the little bottom so willingly displayed. I was as fond of Elspeth's rear as of her elfin little face. It was possibly the smallest of all the maids', but with a delightful pertness to the apple-round cheeks, and her cleft was so lovely and tight that from a fair distance her bottom almost seemed like a solid globe. Our conversation was, therefore, a little distracted, especially when she slowly clenched and eased her posterior muscles to tempt us to hurry.

Eventually, my throat was no longer dry and dusty and I suggested that the chastisement could continue. With another grin, Elspeth approached the broad lap and bent herself over it, making quite sure that her contortions were as revealing as possible. Then she parted her feet, dug her toes into the floor and announced that she was ready for her torture to begin.

A broadly smiling Cook decided to keep her waiting and enjoyed a prolonged manual inspection before getting to work. I cannot deny that I enjoyed the spectator's role immensely. I was able to move around, surveying both participants from a variety of angles, and felt quite free to offer advice, whether necessary or not.

'A few more on her left buttock, Cook.' Or, 'Stick your bottom up a little, Elspeth, so that Cook can smack the lower parts more easily.

In between my helpful comments, Elspeth added her own commentary. 'Oh, Cookie, I felt that one!' And, 'Please can I have some more on the other cheek, please? Even me up a bit.'

I also noted that Cook had taught herself to alter the rhythm and strength of the spanking. After a barrage of light, rapid smacks which kept even Elspeth's little bottom quivering constantly, she would administer a dozen or so proper spanks with a full sweep of her mighty arm and a minute's interval between each.

Both approaches were most exciting to observe. The former had the dear girl on the receiving end keening and wailing in mock dismay and bobbing her bottom up and down, while the latter made her cry out in earnest, and at each one the stiff hand sank into her flesh in the most dramatic manner. I loved moving my gaze from her bottom to her face: I would see the tight orb shudder and quake, then look at her expression as the burn spread through her middle.

When her punishment was eventually at an end, I enjoyed the comforting of her hot derrière almost as much as the spanking!

A most entertaining homecoming!

Then I was back in the fray. Sophie had been delighted to see me and reported that all had gone well in my absence. The girls had made no attempt to take advantage of her and had presented themselves for chastisement without demur. She promised with utmost solemnity that she had administered very few spankings – but freely admitted that she had thoroughly enjoyed each and every one!

* * *

The following weeks flew by. I had an increasing number of applications for places and was soon having to purchase some more beds to accommodate the extra bodies. If there was a disadvantage in this success, it was that it became harder for me to get to know the girls. Sophie proved to be a most capable deputy in all respects and so I did not have any concerns that their education would suffer. What did worry me was that I was less sure of the best ways of improving their characters, as opposed to their learning.

I therefore began to invite them to tea or supper: one at a time and without formality, so that we could talk freely and discuss their progress openly. I could, for example, ask them in which subjects they felt confident and vice versa, so that we could arrange the curriculum accordingly. All were a trifle shy to begin with but when I made every effort to put them at ease and soon convinced them that I would not spank them, even if I were displeased with some aspect of their progress, they relaxed and we were able to be friends.

The shy ones began to blossom. Over-confidence was gently pricked. I flirted gently with the plainer girls and ensured that the beautiful appreciated that beauty was only skin deep.

Spanking them sensitively was the best method of achieving all this. For example, Sarah was now one of the leading lights. Her merry laughter rang through the halls and corridors and the way she helped the less able in the art lessons was a revelation.

A new girl, Betty, was so lovely that she took my breath away. From her glorious, shining, raven-black hair to her dainty little feet, she was a picture. For her first few punishments, I made no reference to the glories of her derrière but simply laid it bare and smacked it without comment. On the other hand, the rather dowdy and plump Dorothy was always summoned to my lap with a phrase which indicated that seeing her bare bottom was something of a treat.

I noticed that my approach soon caused them all to lose their shyness at being turned up. Invariably, on the first occasion they felt their drawers sliding downward, their bottoms would contract in embarrassment at their outraged modesty, but usually by the second time they would be reacting quite normally. Rather than a huddled, nervous pair of buttocks, I would be facing a smoothly rounded posterior, even if the thought of the impending soreness would result in the occasional twitch.

They also soon became accustomed to the role of spectator. I was never aware of any unpleasant gloating at a colleague's discomfiture, but if at first a new girl would blush and apparently have to force herself to look, in no time I noted an honest interest if nothing more.

Only twice did I feel the need for more extreme punishments. One was a case of petty theft and the other an incidence of minor bullying. In both instances, I judged that increased formality would be more effective than just greater pain.

The thief, Dorothy, was birched. All the pupils were told to report to the cellar. I had previously arranged to have the bench moved from its little room on to the stage and, when the audience arrived, there was a gasp of surprise at the ominous sight of the long, broad piece of furniture with the dangling straps at each end and in the centre. Then they saw the bucket, with two birch rods, soaking to ensure their proper flexibility. Their wide eyes settled on the trembling culprit in her loose gown and their eyes widened in sympathy.

As soon as I had placed them in a semicircle around the end of the bench. I summoned Dorothy from the corner and removed her gown. The girls gasped again at the sight of her dressed only in a black corset, shoes and stockings, with bright red garters adding a threatening splash of colour.

I made her stand with her back to them while I lectured her briefly and then told her to lie down on the bench. Swift glances while I was strapping her wrists, ankles and waist revealed pale faces and wide-open eyes staring candidly at the enticingly posed bottom. I was pleased that I had insisted on the stays. I knew that they would emphasise the slenderness of her waist and also add both prominence and sensitivity to her bare bottom.

Without further ado, I took the first rod from the bucket and laid it across her cringing posterior, making minor alterations to my stance until I was satisfied. Then I raised my arm and whisked the bushy little rod down in a sweeping stroke across the full and generous width before me.

Dorothy had clearly never felt the unique kiss of the birch and her reaction was typical. It is undoubtedly a threatening implement and quite capable of striking fear in the stoutest heart but, provided that the rod is light and the stroke moderate, the initial sting is easily tolerable. I once heard a girl describe the effect as 'watery – like having stinging liquid poured over your bottom'. This is an admirable summary of the sensation but on the first occasion it takes several moments to appreciate it, such is one's state of nervousness.

She howled and her fat buttocks clamped together. Then she was suddenly silent and lay still for a moment, as though unable to credit the fact that she was not in agony. Finally, the burning feeling bit in and spread. She gasped and shook her hips about, bouncing her belly on the wooden surface below her.

The silent spectators gazed in awe at the wobbling mounds with the tracery of fine, pink lines spreading as they watched.

I waited for well over a minute before raising the rod for the second. By then, she was completely calm and recieved the next five with the equanimity I expected from a pupil at my academy. Then the pain waxed to the level where she could stay neither still nor silent.

She moaned, gasped and whimpered, and her hips slowly churned, up and down and from side to side. Her fleshy parts quivered and wobbled ceaselessly as I quickened the tempo until her bare bottom and my rod were dancing in harmony.

At the first sign of tears, I paused. When she was again perfectly still, I bent by her head and told her that I would give her only six more and enjoined her to be brave. She was, and after I had freed her, could clamber to her feet without assistance. Her bottom still burned, though. She could not stand still, but hopped about panting like a steam engine and with her hands clutching the afflicted parts.

All went back upstairs in a most thoughtful mood and I was confident that not one was tempted to transgress to the same degree.

Betty's caning was less dramatic. It was again in public but I decided that my study was an adequate arena and her contrition when I accused her was so genuine that I restricted her sentence to six strokes. On her bare bottom, naturally, and each cut etched a red line across her beautiful cheeks.

Never again did she raise her hand to another girl.

In both cases, I made it clear to them that I was punishing the sin more than the sinner, and made sure that they were welcomed back into the fold as soon as the echo of the last stroke had died away.

We were all fortunate in having Richmond Park nearby. I had been raised on a farm in Leicestershire and was therefore far more closely attuned with the countryside than the city. I began to derive great pleasure in accompanying the girls on long walks through the park. It was clearly not the same as having rolling acres of wild country to explore and I missed the fruitfulness of an agricultural community: the green shoots and blossoms of spring; those shoots growing in early summer, then the first ears appearing; tiny buds growing into apples, pears, cherries; ripening wheat denoting the fullness of summer and then the growing excitement as the harvest drew near.

The herds of deer in the park were glorious to behold and never ceased to fascinate but there were times when I longed to lean on a gate, surveying a healthy herd of cows or a flock of contented sheep.

Nevertheless, we all revelled in the open space, the fresh air and the variety of trees and wild shrubs. The walk there and back alone was sufficient to exercise young limbs, so we inevitably arrived back footsore and dusty. It was on such occasions that I blessed Mr Percival's foresight in suggesting the new range, because it was now so simple for all of us to enjoy a hot bath.

Until an alternative refreshment occurred to me one particularly hot day. As we plodded back home, my thoughts turned to my goddess and her cool fountain, fondly remembering that delicious feeling as one slowly dipped one's bare bottom into the water. I cast my eyes about my handsome group and the thought of seeing them all stark naked appealed more and more with every step.

My eventual suggestion was greeted with initial enthusiasm, only slightly modified when the implications struck home. Then Miranda, a bold and impudent girl whom I liked very much, looked at me with wide-eyed innocence.

'Will you be joining us, Mrs Milford?'

'Yes, of course!' I replied, as though it was the most natural thing in the world. Her eyes flickered up and down, obviously assessing my body and the prospect of seeing it naked. To my relief, the thought did not displease her – she blushed most prettily and was silent for at least five minutes!

Needless to say, I enjoyed our naughty romp immensely. I suggested that we undressed in the conservatory so that our clothes were not strewn about on the dusty lawn and had deliberately hastened so that I was the first one naked. With my charms to distract them, I could more easily enjoy the revelation of theirs.

Then I led them out into the garden and to the statue, exaggerating the natural sway of my hips and very conscious of eight pairs of eyes behind me.

Not surprisingly, they were all a little shy to begin with but the blissful immersion in the cool water soon overcame the strongest sense of modesty and before long, the conversation was flowing as freely as the fountain's waters.

'My bottom needs warming up,' I announced, and rolled over, pressing my toes into the stone so that the relevant part bobbed gently above the surface. There was a sudden silence as all gazed at me and I could have sworn that their intensity was as effective as the sun in eliminating the chill in my flesh.

From that moment, it was easy to guide the conversation to more personal and exciting themes. I rolled back and saw that Dorothy had copied my pose, and the sight of her smooth, glistening bottom caught my eye immediately.

'May I examine your derrière to see if there are any traces of your birching?' I asked in a matter-of-fact tone.

'Of course,' she replied easily.

There were none. 'Such a lovely plump bottom!' I sighed, as I patted it affectionately. 'Betty, come here and let me see yours.'

With a happy smile, she waded across to me and bent over, gripping her ankles and treating me to a delectable view of the back of her hairy cunny.

'Is mine still red after this morning's spanking?' asked the fair-haired Fiona.

'I doubt it,' I said lazily. Then I grinned and told her to bring it to me for a proper examination. The relieved look on her pretty face made me smile. I enjoyed a long hard look at her chubby little cheeks, pronounced them free of all redness, and gave each one a quick kiss.

It seemed a perfect time to fetch some wine. The sun had lost most of its heat and so I felt it safe to wander about the garden. I suggested that we should retrieve our bonnets and move to the summerhouse. I then felt sorry for the maids, who had been stuck indoors all day, and thought that the fresh air would do them good.

Still naked, I marched into the kitchen, requested an armful of champagne and sufficient buckets of ice to chill them, and then told all the maids and Cook to strip off and join us.

Half an hour later, during which naked pupils had eyed bare maids with growing curiosity – and vice versa – a memorable evening got underway.

Tradition demanded a croquet tournament. I insisted that maids and pupils should play together rather than against one another, not wishing to encourage factions.

Winning pairs spanked the losers.

The champagne flowed and inhibitions vanished. Fiona held Vera's hand and Connie pinched Miranda's bottom. When Beatrice and Elspeth beat Janet and Bridget, they hugged and kissed each other in their delight.

Cook and I lost to Sophie and Maria, and the excitement when we had to present our bottoms to be smacked was so infectious that we had to stay bent so that everyone could help themselves to a few spanks.

Eventually, it was time for bed and we trooped back inside. It had been not only a very joyful evening but I knew that I had done something to awaken the pupils' latent sensuality. I was happy and made love to Sophie with special energy that night.

I had already grown extremely fond of her, and for all the pleasure I derived from her jutting bottom, plump little bosoms, soft skin and sweet cunny, her companionship did so much to ease the burdens of responsibility. Her loving nature made it easy for her to make friends with the girls and not one ever resented the spankings she gave them.

She was quick-witted and eager to learn. On her own initiative, she took lessons in Greek so that we had yet another subject on the curriculum. She was also a natural teacher, with a patient and understanding nature.

Above all, her sensuality matched mine. Our loving was intensely satisfying. She had a sweet, soft voice and used it to excellent effect to set my cunny weeping before laying a hand on me.

'Annie,' she would announce as we undressed. 'I sense that you are in the right mood for some loving attention to your bottom. I shall kiss every inch of both cheeks, then pull them apart and gaze longingly upon your little bottom-hole. Then I shall kiss that until you are in sixth heaven. My tongue will then take you to seventh heaven.'

When she had done as promised, she would roll me on to my back and lie on top of me, grinding her mound against mine while we kissed. I would drum my heels against her firm bottom and then, if I had not declared my own intentions for her pleasure, she would politely ask me to do whatever she desired. It was always a thrill to obey.

Luckily, she and Arabella fell in lust with each other at first sight and our bedtime threesomes were as thrilling as our duets. She took particular pleasure in commencing our activities by making Arabella and me lie over the side of the bed, so close together that our flanks touched. She would roll up our nightdresses with tantalising deliberation, toying with our bared bottoms then spanking us at length.

We would lie there, holding hands and gazing into each other's eyes. I would know when her bottom had been bared from her dreamy expression and could then devote all my awareness to my own exposure.

Then I would hear the 'SPLAT' of the stiffened palm. I would feel the quivering of her buttock against mine, her breath would hiss through her clenched teeth, and she would grip my hand tightly as her big blue eyes gazed into the distance.

After six crisp spanks, I would tighten my grip on her hand, and my eyes would gaze unseeing at the far wall as the skin on my bottom crawled in happy expectation.

Soon the smart was all and our mouths joined to share our little moans and gasps.

Then it was Sophie's turn for delicious suffering!

One evening, we were sitting after supper and I looked at Sophie with such love in my heart that I could no longer resist putting to her a proposition which had been exercising me for some days. She was looking so lovely in her low-cut gown (revealing an enticing *décolletage*), a pearl necklace and her hair flowing freely over her white shoulders, that I decided to abandon our planned game of whist.

'Sophie,' I said quietly, 'I love you dearly.' She smiled at me, her brown eyes gleaming in the candlelight. 'I am going to ask you to give me something. Something very precious. Please give my request proper consideration, because it is an important sacrifice on your part and I shall not be offended if you say no.'

She looked curious rather than puzzled. 'Ask away, Annie,' she replied warmly. 'Whatever I have is yours.'

I stared intently into her eyes. 'Your maidenhead,' I said softly.

Her mouth opened. She licked her lips slowly. 'It is yours!'

There was no more to be said. I led her slowly up to our bedroom, undressed her lasciviously and laid her on the bed before removing my clothes.

I lay on top of her and kissed her with increasing passion. My mouth slithered down her slender neck and

I laved her breasts, sucking her nipples until they were like unripe mulberries against my tongue. Pausing only on her belly-button, I set about her hot, wet cunny until she was crying out in ecstasy.

Then I reached for the little wooden dildo which I had hidden under the bedclothes and moved on top of her, with her left thigh clamped between mine. I kissed her again and fingered her prominent 'spot' until she was squirming uninhibitedly and the entrance to her virgin orifice was wet and slippery.

I nuzzled the knob against the portals. She closed her eyes and stiffened. I pressed in until I felt the resistance of her maidenhead. Phillip had been very gentle with me, and I remembered, paused, kissed her passionately and kneaded her breasts with my free hand while I pressed steadily. To the accompaniment of a little cry, my implement slipped slowly into her.

Her pent-up breath whistled from her lungs and she grimaced at the strange pain. I left the dildo inside her and stroked her thighs and bottom, then pushed a finger into the tight division, finding her puckered rosebud and slipping inside so that the more familiar penetration of her smaller passage relaxed the larger.

Taking hold of the protruding end, I began to work the dildo in and out, slowly, gently and lovingly, Soon she grew accustomed to the invasions and her bottom started to buck and heave as the waves of pleasure grew in strength. She spent with a glad cry and her tearful thanks gladdened my heart.

Any lingering soreness had vanished by the next night and her shy little request for another ravishing was granted. I used a bigger dildo that time, with the smallest slipped up her bottom-hole, and her bliss knew no bounds.

She showed no less enthusiasm for delving between my parted thighs and treating me in like manner, cooing happily at the sight of the glistening shaft disappearing into my depths.

I realised that I was missing my husband less and less.

For similar reasons, any temptations which I had felt to seduce the pupils faded to nothingness.

Spanking them satisfied most of my desires for their naked flesh and when we repeated our naked romp in the garden I could enjoy their complete nudity with a clear conscience.

I was truly happy.

Then, towards the end of August, it was time for everyone to have a summer holiday. I certainly was looking forward to several weeks in Sussex, especially as I already had a full complement of new pupils for the winter semester.

Sophie and I decided to plan a proper (or to be strictly accurate, a most *improper*) prize-giving ceremony. All past pupils were invited, as were those parents and guardians whose enthusiasm for corporal punishment had matched ours – Miss Brown, Jane's aunt, for example.

Arabella joined in several of our discussions and, not surprisingly, she entered into the spirit with bright-eyed enthusiasm, making a number of excellent recommendations and volunteering to look after several complex details.

My growing excitement communicated itself to the rest of the establishment, for our activities were conducted with even greater energy and enthusiasm, to the extent that I began to regret the need for sleep.

There was, however, one event which tested me to the full and which, to my undying relief, I handled successfully.

Mr Fortescue had sent me a note requesting a private audience and duly appeared with an expression so grave and earnest that my interest quickened immediately, sensing that he was about to discuss something quite out of the ordinary.

'Mrs Milford,' he began, clearing his throat nervously. 'I must confess that I am a little reluctant to involve you in this case and, should you feel that it would not be judicious for you to assist me, then I shall quite understand.'

'Of course, Mr Fortescue,' I said impatiently, my curiosity growing by the second.

'Basically,' he continued, 'I have been notified that a lady flogged one of her servants so cruelly that she is in hospital.'

I frowned. 'Well, surely that is a straightforward case of assault and she deserves to be prosecuted in the normal manner.'

'Yes indeed,' he replied, still nervous. 'The problem is that she is of high rank. Very high rank. A duchess, no less. The scandal . . .'

His voice died away and he looked unhappily out of the window.

'And you know her?' I said sympathetically, after a pause.

'Yes.'

'I see.' I sat back in furious thought. Obviously there were dangers for me. If I overstepped the mark in dealing with a woman with such powerful connections, the consequences could be dire. And yet . . . the thought of making a duchess bare her bottom and bend it to my will was, to say the least, tempting! And Elizabeth was the daughter of a marquess and I had spanked her often enough! I realised that I would always rue my cowardice if I turned down such a rare opportunity. Taking a deep breath, I told Mr Fortescue that I would see the duchess and would, of course, exercise great discretion.

He thanked me with evident relief and, when we had agreed a suitable time, departed.

As I awaited Her Grace, I found that I was surprisingly calm, presumably as my natural anger at her senseless cruelty counterbalanced my nervousness. With two hours at my disposal, I had ample time to ring the changes in my approach and therefore felt confident that I would find the best way of inducing true repentance.

I had decided that it was important that I display perfect manners, initially at least, so that when she was ushered in, I rose, walked to her, curtsied and, in a tone of voice which was both deferential and firm, made her welcome.

'May I offer you refreshment, Your Grace?' I asked.

'No thank you,' she replied coldly.

Smiling inwardly, I resumed my seat and stared at her steadily. She was a striking woman, perhaps in her mid-40s, with golden hair, lovely blue eyes and a full, shapely figure. Only a disagreeable set to her mouth spoiled her beauty.

I broke the silence. 'You have a simple choice, Your Grace. Your offence was too grave to be ignored and you must be punished.' Her eyes glittered threateningly. I continued blithely. 'The choice concerns your punishment. Either you suffer the full process of the law, or you submit to corporal punishment at my hands ... Please be silent and hear me out, Your Grace ... In the former case, the scandal will be such that I doubt if you will be welcome at court for some years. In the latter, all those who are anxious to see you damned will be advised that you have paid for your crime and that they should forget the whole thing. Your public reputation will be safe.'

There was a long pause and her expression softened a little. The pink tip of her tongue passed quickly over her mouth and I saw that her hands were trembling.

'I see,' she said eventually. 'You can guarantee that my whipping will be a secret?'

'Yes,' I replied simply.

'In that case, do your worst.'

My relief showed itself in a long sigh. 'I assure you, Your Grace, that I shall do my very best!'

I had considered several alternative methods of dealing with her, and while she sat grimly awaiting my next move I pondered them, then decided. 'I shall first teach you a lesson, then punish you,' I announced, my voice suddenly hard and full of authority. 'Stand up, please, and remove your bonnet.' I had purposely placed her in my favourite spanking chair, so it was easy to replace her bottom with mine and be ready for the opening salvo. Without further ado, I pulled her down across my lap, taking her by surprise. She grunted, wriggled briefly, and then lay still.

'What is your given name?' I asked.

'Deborah,' she replied, her puzzlement evident.

'Thank you, Deborah. Have you ever been spanked?'

'Yes. In the nursery. Who has not?'

'You would be surprised!' I retorted, and began to pull her skirts and petticoats. She gasped in dismay but wisely kept silent and even helped by raising her hips, so that I soon had her bottom all bare and was gazing in silent admiration.

I suppose that aristocrats do have some advantages when it comes to maintaining their figures. They tend to live in enormous houses with miles of corridors, so that simply moving from one part to another involves a great deal of healthy exercise. At the same time, they eat well and often. Deborah's bottom certainly added credence to my theory. It was big. But the swelling mounds were obviously firm, the division between them long and tight and her gluteal folds wide and clear-cut. Her skin was absolutely flawless to the eye and my hands soon confirmed that it was as soft to the touch.

Her nervousness was apparent. She was pressing her front hard into my thighs in an attempt to reduce the size and prominence of her fleshy masses and her efforts were rewarded by a nice dimpling of the lower portions.

With another deep sigh, I raised my right hand and brought it down with full force on to the centre of her left buttock. She gasped and clenched her cheeks even more tightly, and I rested my hand on her naked thigh while I watched the pink patch flare up. Her bottom relaxed as the effort of holding the muscles so taut became too much. My hand flashed down on to the right cheek, this time sinking into the flesh rather than rebounding upward. She jumped but did not gasp.

Smiling happily, I settled down into a good rhythm, beating her slowly and crisply, covering every inch of her delicious bare bottom with unusual relish. She showed all the fortitude one would expect from a woman of her breeding and did all within her power to hide her pain and humiliation. Each ringing spank was greeted by a hiss of sharply indrawn breath and for at least the first two dozen she strove to keep her buttocks as firmly clenched as she could.

Then, inevitably, the burning smart overcame her best intentions. I sensed a gradual lightening of her weight on my lap; her bottom began to wobble rather than quiver; her hisses became loud gasps, interspersed with the occasional whimper.

Her fine skin reddened quickly and beautifully. I concentrated my smacks on the wide base of her bottom and made the entire globe shudder delightfully.

Her resistance cracked and she began to cry out, rocking and bouncing on my lap, her legs kicking. I sensed tears and stopped.

I did not keep her on my lap but ordered her to stand in the corner with her skirts up. Her startlingly red bottom glowed in the soft light, a warning beacon to all transgressors. Quivering and twitching. Magnificent.

When she had gathered her wits, I broke the silence. 'Well, Deborah, I trust that you appreciate that a sound spanking administered to the bare bottom is more than a nursery punishment. You are very red indeed and I imagine that it is hot and sore. Remember the pain – and the shame – next time a maid displeases you and resist all temptation to reach for your whip.'

'Yes,' she replied softly.

'Good. Now I shall conclude your lesson. Step back, move your feet apart, bend down and take hold of your ankles.'

I walked across to her then squatted down and squeezed each rounded buttock, thrilling to their yielding fleshiness, even when quite tightly bent. I longed to prise them apart but stayed my hand and stood up.

'Should you feel that a sterner punishment is required, then I recommend a hairbrush. Like this one,' I added, thrusting it in front of her face. 'I shall give you six on each buttock. You will count them aloud.'

She did not enjoy the ensuing few minutes. As I knew full well, the shiny wooden surface was capable of imparting a unique smart, especially on bare, well-spanked skin. She was crying by the end and I was having to wait several minutes between spanks.

I tossed the brush on to the floor and told her to stand up.

'You may rub your bottom if you wish,' I told her coldly, and returned to my desk, idly watching her frantic hands at work and noticing that the brush had left clearly defined patches of even darker red.

I rang the bell, told her to sit down – which she did with understandable caution – and ordered a pot of my best coffee.

It came and we drank in complete silence. When Vera had taken away the tray, I stood and looked my victim straight in the eye.

'You have had your lesson, Deborah. Now for your punishment.' She paled and licked her lips nervously. I paused for several minutes while she stared at me, her blinking eyes and fluttering hands clear indications that I was beginning to win.

I can clearly remember my feelings. My underlying anger at her cruelty was as sharp as ever. She of all people should have known better than to injure a devoted servant so seriously and her tangible fear gave me both pleasure and satisfaction. I knew exactly how to break her now. To punish her with the same severity which she had shown would be wrong – what she needed was abasement, coupled with a slow and steady increase in her pain. I would make her beg for mercy.

She did. Eventually. I had noticed the first signs of returning arrogance in her as her bottom cooled down and so made her remove every stitch of clothing and all her jewellery, and unfasten her hair so that it flowed over her shoulders.

I made her walk up and down the room, criticising her deportment. I made her run around the room and gloated loudly over the way her naked bosoms and buttocks bounced and wobbled. I found a marble and made her go down on all fours to push it along the floor, making quite certain that she was aware that both her cunny and anus were in full view.

Fat tears trickled down her cheeks.

I took her down to the cellar and to the room with the bench and she prostrated herself with an air of relief, lying still while I fastened her feet to one end and her outstretched arms to the other. Only when I was tightening the broad strap round her waist did the first little moan escape.

I birched her and her great buttocks quivered gently under my moderate strokes. I moved down to her thighs and she called out in distress. 'Oh, please not there, Mrs Milford!'

I paused. 'Oh I see, Deborah. You prefer me to whip you on your fat bare bottom, do you?'

'Yes.'

'Well ask me nicely.'

She groaned and took a deep breath. 'Please, Mrs

Milford, will you whip my bottom, not my thighs?' she asked through gritted teeth.

'Your what bottom?' I asked sweetly.

She collected her scattered wits. 'Oh! Please whip me on my fat bare bottom?'

'That is better,' I stated – and continued on the broad backs of her thighs!

A close inspection confirmed that I had judged both the quality and quantity of the strokes to perfection. She was clearly very sore – her buttocks were scarlet and very hot, and were opening and closing in that sensual rhythm the French call '*la danse du croup*'. Her thighs were pink and the tracery of fine weals and little dots clearly visible. It was time for the finale.

I unstrapped her and helped her into the room containing the whipping stool. Her teeth chattered with fear when she set eyes on it but I guided her into position with implacable determination, tucking her widely parted knees well forward and fastening her wrists tightly to the front.

The vulnerability of her exposed position made her moan but I took no notice, selected one of my whippiest canes, and laid it on the floor before her eyes.

The thought of its bite on her sore flesh was the straw which broke the camel's back, and she burst into a flood of apologies mixed with firm promises of reformation and, at last, pleas for mercy.

Silently I crouched behind her, close enough for her bottom to fill my vision entirely. I stroked it gently enough to soothe her and her lamentations died away. Then I took a hot cheek in each hand and drew them ruthelessly – and clearly painfully – apart. She shrieked in her outrage and writhed desperately. To no avail. With calm deliberation, I wet my right forefinger in my mouth, then pressed it firmly against the pinky-brown rosebud and thrust it right into her fundament. She burst into floods of tears and my task was all but done.

I slowly removed the offending digit, then picked up the cane and gave her a dozen sharp strokes full across the generous width of her widely divided moon. In truth, they were little more than flicks, but her bottom was so sore that they stung as much as full-blooded swipes.

Replacing the cane in the rack, I moved in front of her and gazed into her ravaged face, noting the wet, red eyes, her tear-stained cheeks and her twisted mouth with satisfaction. Then I kissed her, stroked her cheeks, and told her quietly that her ordeal was over. She almost swooned in her relief and was so weakened that I had to help her up the stairs. Back in my study, I laid wet cloths on her bottom, applied a soothing ointment and then made her drink several glasses of wine. When she at last showed signs of recovery, I helped her to her feet, folded her in my arms and rested my hands gently on the twin swells of her bottom.

'You have been very well punished, my dear, and yet there is no need for medical assistance. Your bottom will soon be back to its usual, exceptional beauty.'

'I understand, Mrs Milford,' she replied in a low, soft voice. 'I shall never do such a thing again. And ... thank you.'

'Not at all ... Your Grace.'

She smiled shyly and, with some help from me, dressed and left.

Prize-giving day dawned brightly and by eleven o'clock the happily chattering throng, suitably refreshed with champagne, crowded into the theatre.

I raised my hand for silence and summoned Jane to join me on the stage, reminding everyone that she had been my first pupil. I placed my arm affectionately around her waist and, in ringing tones, described her accomplishments during her time in The Academy. My fulsome praise made her wriggle with pleasure and a quick sideways glance showed a modest blush suffusing her pretty face. I came to an end and the round of applause embarrassed her even further.

'However,' I continued, 'I feel that it is my duty to remind her – and to inform you – that she was not always perfect. I had to spank her on several occasions!'

While she grinned sheepishly, her friends applauded loudly. 'It is true,' she admitted. 'And I know that I benefited from every spank!'

There was another burst of clapping and I continued. 'I am delighted that she admits to gaining from her various ordeals. Jane is the proud possessor of a delightfully plump and shapely bottom and the sight of it spread across my lap never failed to please –' I held up a hand to still the cheering '– and I see no reason why I should not see it again. Nor why all gathered should not be treated to a view of it, whether for the first time or not.'

Very red-faced but still grinning, Jane turned her back and slowly raised her skirts and petticoats, eventually displaying the delightful sight of her rear end poking cheekily out from the wide slit in her drawers. My heart pounded as I looked at it and then thudded when she loosened the tape and her last garment slithered down to the floor. Turning her head to smile at me radiantly, she slowly bent to clasp her ankles.

I gave her a dozen ringing spanks, which were received and witnessed in complete silence. She stayed bent while I gently stroked her, my eyes prickling in gratitude at her ready compliance. I had had every intention of spanking her but had anticipated some protest!

She trotted happily back to her seat. Mary came up and was treated in the same way, as were all the girls in turn. The varied array of beautiful female flesh delighted one and all.

After that, each girl came up to be presented with a prize. Sarah and I had laboured night and day to complete watercolour portraits of them all. Naturally, these were not traditional portraits but depicted them lying over my knee with a bright red bottom below my raised right hand. They were all drawn from the same viewpoint, from more or less behind, with the buttocks as the predominant feature but with the owner peering backwards so that if the rear end was not immediately recognisable, the face was. They were accurate as well as artistic and were greeted with squeals of pleasure by each recipient.

Before they trotted back with their pictures, I asked them to choose a silver brooch. There were three types on offer – a birch, a cane or a tawse. Each was beautifully modelled by a sympathetic silversmith and again were received with cries of delight, even when I announced that, when the girl had made her selection, the real implement would be applied three times to her bare bottom!

To my surprise, Jane looked at me steadily and loudly asked for an example of each one! I made her rest her hands on the desk for the birch, grip her ankles for the rattan and kneel on the footstool for the tawse. She clambered up, accepted the loud applause with becoming modesty and then walked slowly back to her place, clasping her prizes with justifiable pride.

Fortunately, I had ordered ample supplies, for every one of the girls professed to be unable to decide between the models and bravely qualified for all three.

We then enjoyed a magnificent luncheon with more champagne, before repairing to the cellar once again.

I stood on the stage and addressed the beaming throng. 'Ladies! A famous man once stated that it is more blessed to give than to receive and, if that is indeed true, I am very blessed on this august occasion. However, in some circumstances, I feel that it should be the other way round!' The light laughter which had greeted my opening remark died away and all leaned forward expectantly.

Smiling broadly, I continued. 'I can think of no better way of complementing the girls on the graceful way they all received than to offer them the chance to give. I offer my own bottom to all.' There was a loud gasp, shortly followed by an outburst of clapping and cheering. I curtsied, smiled and then held my hand up for silence. 'Each girl can give me a sharp little spanking and then three strokes with one of the implements available. Including the martinet, which was excluded in the range of brooches, only because it was harder to manufacture.

'I shall obey each girl's orders in terms of presentation and preparation. Jane, as the first of my pupils, I feel that the privilege of having a virginally white bottom to deal with should be yours. Would you like to come up here?'

My ordeal lasted over an hour and took me to the limits of my endurance. It also provided a memory which will last for ever.

As Jane bounded up the steps on to the stage, I felt completely at ease with myself. I had had the idea to offer myself two days before and had been torn between the conflicting interests. On the one hand, the idea of submitting to the pupils had thrilled me to the core but, on the other, I was unsure whether such an action was right and proper. In the end, the knowledge that they were all leaving swayed me and I decided to yield to my bizarre desires. The excitement which had greeted my announcement had laid my doubts to rest.

Jane's evident delight at the prospect of spanking me was the conclusive proof that I had decided correctly. She could scarcely contain herself as she ordered me to bare my bottom and clasp my ankles.

Tingling all over, I turned, hefted up my skirts and petticoats, and tucked them under my elbows while I loosened my drawers. They seemed reluctant to yield to the inevitable and rested on the crowns of my buttocks, so that I had to shake my hips to free them and encourage them to slither all the way down. I bent over, slowly and tantalisingly. Jane stood beside me and, with her left arm resting on my loins, spanked me with more enthusiasm than expertise, while I peered back past my legs at the gleaming eyes fixed on my jiggling flesh.

Her hand fell away, then she told me to bend over the table and grip the further edge for the birch.

Mary took her place while I restored my clothing, and put me across her lap and bared my bottom for me. Then she caned me, while I knelt up on the stool.

One after the other they trooped up, indulged themselves, kissed me in thanks and went happily back to their seats. Some made me adjust my own clothing, others preferred to take the opportunity to fondle my intimacies as they fumbled at my drawers.

Sophie thrilled me beyond reason by stripping me stark naked after a traditional spanking, then making me lie face up on the desk and tuck my knees into my bosom while she trickled the end of the tawse down my open cleft before applying it to my drum-tight cheeks.

Almost too soon, the last girl left the stage and I stood for several moments with my naked bottom towards the audience, letting them gaze freely at the discoloration. By then, my cunny was weeping copiously but my eyes were as dry as they had been at the outset.

I did cry when I bade them all farewell, however. Such sweet, sensual and talented girls, who had left an indelible impression on me. I was gratified beyond measure when nearly all of them declared that they had every intention of returning if at all possible.

Then, two days later, my coach headed for Petworth. Sophie was beside me, while Tom and Daisy drove with smooth skill. I sat back, holding my new lover's soft little hand, and contemplated the immediate future.

I would take my ease for several days. I knew that

Sophie, Mavis and Bertha would entertain each other and Tom and Daisy would have the horses as well as themselves for company.

Then I would begin to indulge my sensual tastes again. Closing my eyes, I imagined how entertaining it would be to watch the slender Sophie spanking the voluptuous Mavis.

Or how deeply satisfying it would be to be under our tree, with Tom away riding, leaving the four girls in my tender care. Would Daisy enjoy our naked feasts? I saw no reason why not and had a delightful vision of them all on knees and elbows, bottoms straining upward to expose the secrets between and below the rounded cheeks. I would contemplate the sight at some length, debating what to do first. And to whom.

Once Daisy had been seduced by us, I would ensure that she and Tom 'made the beast with two backs'. Under my supervision, naturally.

And in Phillip's continued absence, perhaps it would be pleasing to feel Tom's nice shaft in the depths of my bottom.

I did not anticipate that I would recall my summer holiday with anything but fondness!

Stretching luxuriously, I looked across at Sophie. 'Why wait till Petworth?' I asked myself, taking hold of her wrist and easing her across my lap.

NEW BOOKS

Coming up from Nexus and Black Lace

Nexus

Annie's Further Education by Evelyn Culber
August 1996   Price £4.99   ISBN: 0 352 33096 1
Helped by some obliging and enthusiastic friends, servants and fellow members of the Flagellation Society, Annie establishes Redhand House Academy – an institution for women desiring disciplined education. Yet it is soon evident that success has gone to Annie's head, and that she, too, has some harsh lessons to learn before her own education is complete.

The Chaste Legacy by Susanna Hughes
August 1996   Price £4.99   ISBN: 0 352 33097 X
Shipwrecked in a storm, the beautiful Corinda Chaste finds herself the prisoner of Constantine Stephanikis, a Greek pirate. As he teaches her to satisfy even the most bizarre sexual tastes, she proves to be an eager and totally uninhibited pupil. She is, however, unaware that Stephanikis has other – more sinister – plans for her.

Bound to Serve by Amanda Ware
September 1996   Price £4.99   ISBN: 0352 33099 6
When the cruel and manipulative Clive offers Caroline West a means of saving her master, Liam, from bankruptcy, she agrees to become his slave for three weeks. Having undergone all manner of humiliations, she is then handed over to her former mistress – for even harsher training. Unbeknownst to Clive, Lynne is a friend of Liam and, convinced that Caroline is betraying him, she subjects the girl to the most severe punishment. Treatment which Caroline finds is to her liking.

The Governess Abroad by Yolanda Celbridge
September 1996   Price £4.99   ISBN: 0352 33100 3
When Miss Constance de Comynge – the Governess – goes on a luxurious cruise, inhibitions – and clothes – are soon shed, and like-minded friends are made in every port of call. Then the happy band is captured and taken to an island ruled by a strict and cruel matriarchy. Will the Governess's strength of character and expertise in domination be enough to save them all from a life of bondage and punishment?

The Houseshare by Pat O'Brien
August 1996   Price £4.99   ISBN: 0 352 33094 5
When Rupe bares his most intimate desires over the Internet, he does not know that his electronic confidante is Tine, his landlady. With anonymity guaranteed, cybersexual encounters are limited only by the bounds of the imagination, but what will happen when Tine attempts to make the virtual real?

The King's Girl by Sylvie Ouellette
August 1996   Price £4.99   ISBN: 0 352 33095 3
The early 1600s. Under the care of the decadent Monsieur and Madame Lampron, Laure, a lusty, spirited young Frenchwoman, has learned much about darker pleasures. Sent to the newly established colony in North America, she tries – and fails – to behave as a good Catholic girl should, and is soon embarking on a series of wild sexual adventures.

To Take a Queen by Jan Smith
September 1996   Price £4.99   ISBN: 0352 3309 8
The Scottish Highlands, winter 1314. Lady Blanche McNaghten is rediscovering – and broadening – her taste for sexual pleasure with a variety of lovers, when fate throws her into the path of the imposing and hot-blooded Black McGregor, a sworn enemy of her clan. Their mutual lust does not diminish their antagonism and, in the ensuing power struggle, neither hesitates to use sex as their primary strategic weapon.

Dance of Obsession by Olivia Christie
September 1996   Price £4.99   ISBN: 0352 33101 1
When Georgia d'Essange is widowed, her fiery stepson, Dominic, makes it clear that he intends to succeed his father, both as the host of an erotic club for rich Parisiennes and in Georgia's bed. Georgia's attempts to divert his attentions towards Natasha – a beautiful but virginal dancer – only increase his determination to pursue his stepmother. Further complications arise when Georgia's first lover reappears on the scene.